"Put me down! You can't carry me!"

Lacey exclaimed.

"Funny," Tucker teased, grinning down at her as he started up the stairs. "It looks like I already am."

He watched her eyes snap at him, and he couldn't help but remember another time when he had held her close and the light in her eyes had had nothing to do with anger. For a moment it was difficult to maintain the light, mocking tone he knew would take her mind off her trauma. But then he chuckled. "Nice try, kid, but it's not going to work. Looks like you're stuck with me until you're strong enough to throw me out on your own."

Memories hit Lacey in the face. "Don't call me that!" she said sharply. "I'm not a kid."

No, she wasn't. And that was the whole problem.

∧∧∧∧∧∧∧∧∧∧∧∧
❦FAMILY❧

Dear Reader,

Moonlight and Lace has always been one of my favorite books, so I was delighted when I learned Silhouette was going to reissue it. It's a story about extended family, adventure and the unexpected twists and turns life can throw you when you least expect it, which are all the things I love in a romance. Family has always been important to me, and this book has a stronger connection to my family than most. When I went to New Orleans to research the story, my family went with me, and we had a wonderful time in the French Quarter. The heroine's name is Lacey Conrad, and several years after I wrote the book, my twin sister had twin girls and named one of the babies Lacey. I can't think of *Moonlight and Lace* without thinking of her. Enjoy.

Linda Turner

Please address questions and book requests to:
Silhouette Reader Service
U.S.: 3010 Walden Ave., P.O. Box 1325, Buffalo, NY 14269
Canadian: P.O. Box 609, Fort Erie, Ont. L2A 5X3

Prologue

Kurt Donovon pounded on the door to the apartment again, determined to stay there all night if he had to. "Damn it, Tucker, I know you've got to be in there. I've looked everywhere else. Open up!"

Inside, a rough, angry voiced growled, "Go away." Seconds later the television clicked on, the volume turned to maximum to drown out the sounds at the door.

Swearing, Kurt dropped his clenched fist to his side. Two days ago Tucker had returned to Washington, stalked into the office to drop off his report, then stalked right back out. No one had seen him since. Kurt wasn't surprised. The minute the coup had gone down in Costa Oro two weeks before the State Department had expected it, he'd known Tucker would blame himself for that particular mistake. As a troubleshooter who had been sent to Central America by Washington to monitor events and prevent them if at all possible, it was Tucker's job to predict when the fat would hit the fire and get government employees out safely. Despite the miscalculation, his quick thinking had saved an embassy full of Americans. Kurt, as one of his best friends and his supervisor, knew that two staff members who suffered minor injuries were two too many as far as Tucker was concerned. For a man who had a talent for always using the rules to his advantage, he was unexpectedly conscientious about his responsibilities. It was the wedding of those two traits that made him the best at his job. Also, after years in the field, it put him too close to the edge of burnout.

From inside the apartment, the upbeat music of a beer commercial was followed by the greeting of a local news announcer giving a newsbreak. "The two American embassy employees injured during the coup in Costa Oro were released from the hospital today—"

The television clicked off abruptly, leaving a silence that echoed.

Kurt softly rapped on the door. "Cut yourself some slack, Tucker," he said quietly. "All right, so two people were shot. Don't forget, fifty others got out without a scratch!"

There was no response, not even a whisper of sound. Kurt had raised his hand to knock again when the door was suddenly jerked open. Tucker Stevens, dressed in nothing but jeans, scowled at him, his lean, unsmiling face as hard and unyielding as stone. "That was just luck and you know it," he retorted coldly. "They could have just as easily been killed."

"I'm not concerned with what could have been, but what is. And the bottom line is that you pulled a miracle out of your hat getting our people out."

Tucker's eyes narrowed. "Don't you start with the hero crap," he warned. "I've had it up to here," he said, making a quick slash under his chin. "I think every reporter in D.C. has tried to get me on the phone during the last forty-eight hours, and I'm sick of it! I'm not a hero, and I don't want to be treated like one for bungling a job."

"Then you'd better tell the people you rescued to shut

up because they can't seem to stop singing your praises. They have the misguided notion that you're the greatest thing since Superman.'' Without waiting for an invitation he knew might not come, he stepped past Tucker into the apartment. ''I need to talk to you. You got any coffee?''

The smile that curled one side of Tucker's mouth was hard and cynical, reflecting the glint in his dark eyes. ''Anybody ever tell you you've got a skin like an elephant's? No, I don't have any coffee and I don't want to talk. Especially about what happened in Costa Oro.''

Kurt only grinned and dropped down to the couch. ''Good, because I'm not here to talk about the coup. And I'll take a beer instead.''

Without a word, Tucker strode to the kitchen, retrieved two beers from the refrigerator and tossed Kurt one as he stepped back to the breakfast bar that separated the two rooms. Can tabs popped in unison. ''Okay, let's have it. Why are you here? Have you got a new assignment for me?''

Never one to hedge, Kurt shook his head and braced himself for the explosion he knew was sure to come. ''No. What you need right now is a vacation, not work.''

''The hell I do,'' Tucker snapped, slamming his beer down to the counter. ''I've already got too much time to think as it is now. A vacation would be nothing but a waste of time. Give me something to do, Kurt. Anything. Anywhere. I don't care just as long as I'm busy.''

Kurt frowned. He'd known this wasn't going to be easy. ''I can't, Tuck. You're too close to breaking. Don't bother to deny it,'' he continued quickly. ''Five, hell, even two years ago you would have been able to predict when that coup was going to blow within hours of when it happened. You missed this by weeks. And that's not an accusation, it's a fact. If you don't want it to happen again, you better face the truth and do something about it.''

''If you're suggesting what I think you are, you can forget it. I don't want a desk job. I'll never want one.''

"Then you're going to die with your boots on, buddy," his boss retorted coldly. "Every assignment you take has the potential to blow up in your face. A smart man knows to get out while he still can." When Tucker only snorted at that, unconvinced, Kurt pulled a letter from the inside pocket of his suit coat and crossed the room to him. "You might be interested in this."

Tucker eyed it warily. "What is it?"

"Notification of a deputy chief of staff post available in the Caribbean. I have it on good authority that it's yours if you want it. Take it, Tucker," he advised. "Do yourself a favor and get a couple of years' experience behind a desk. With your background and connections, that's all you need to make the world your oyster."

The word was never said, but Tucker knew Kurt was dangling a future ambassadorship under his nose. He refused to be tempted. He knew himself too well. He was a restless man who had never been content staying anywhere too long. Even the walls of his apartment started to close in on him when he was in D.C. between assignments. "Nobody's chaining me to a desk, Kurt," he said flatly. "Give it to somebody else."

Kurt shrugged, not surprised by the rejection. "Don't be so quick to turn it down," he suggested. "Do you realize you're the only one of the old gang still out in the field?"

"That wasn't necessarily by choice," he retorted. "Most of those guys made the mistake of losing their heads over a woman. That's not going to happen to me. I'm not giving up my job for a skirt."

Since he was one of the ones who had chosen a wife over the excitement and danger of working in the field, Kurt could hardly argue with him. Except to point out, "There are advantages to being home every night with the same woman. Think about it on your vacation. After some time off, you may decide it's just what you want."

The tension that had eased from Tucker's chiseled face

immediately snapped back into place. "Damn it, Kurt, I told you I don't need a vacation!"

"Well, you've got one, whether you want it or not. And there's no use bitching at me about it. The order comes from higher up. You've got a month off, courtesy of Uncle Sam."

"A month!"

Kurt grinned at his friend's roar of outrage. "That's right. Thirty-one beautiful days of doing absolutely nothing."

Tucker glowered at him, unamused. "You've got to be kidding. I'll be climbing the walls within a week."

"No, you won't." He chuckled as he finished his beer, then rose to his feet and headed for the door. "You're not going to be here. I've got a friend in Aruba who's offered me a room at his hotel there whenever I want it. You're going to take it instead. I've already called him and set it up."

"Damn it, Kurt, I appreciate the offer, but I don't want a vacation," he said with a scowl as he followed him to the door. "All I want to do is go back to work."

"Sorry, pal, you're out of luck. For the next month the only work you're going to do is lie on the beach and soak up some sun. Have an affair with a blond beach bunny and forget you've even got a job for a while." Slapping him on the back, he grinned. "Send me a postcard." And before Tucker could argue further he was gone, slipping out into the night.

Chapter 1

Lacey Conrad had always thought she was good at reading people's faces, but she hadn't a clue as to what Dr. Hamilton was thinking as he examined her injuries. With sure, knowing hands, he inspected the ugly gash on her forehead he had neatly stitched when she'd been rushed to the emergency room sometime during the middle of the night. His lined face enigmatic, he gave her only a noncommittal "Hmm," before turning his attention to her badly wrenched right shoulder, the purple-and-yellow bruise on her thigh, the various scrapes and cuts that stood out in bold relief on her ivory skin.

Lacey waited expectantly for him to say something, *anything*, but he only reached for the pencil-slim flashlight in the pocket of his lab coat and aimed it into her eyes, watching her pupils carefully. Enduring the silence as long as she could, she pulled back abruptly, her green eyes darkening with impatience. "Well?"

Dr. Pete Hamilton rocked back on his heels, his rotund stomach perched out before him like a swimmer's inner tube. He scowled. "Well?" he repeated in the gruff bedside manner that never failed to delight Lacey. "Hell, no, you're not well. You came damn close to cashing in your chips last night, young lady! If your reflexes had been a fraction slower, you'd be in the morgue right now instead of the hospital. What the devil were you doing taking a stroll through that part of the Quarter by yourself after midnight, anyway? You've lived in New Orleans long enough to know better than that."

"I wasn't exactly out for a walk in the moonlight," she objected dryly. "My car broke down on the way back from dinner with some friends. I was only four blocks from home, so I decided to walk."

He only sniffed at that, unappeased. "Ever heard of a taxi?"

She started to shrug, remembered her shoulder and froze, slowly releasing the painful breath that had caught in her throat. Pride kept her from admitting that last night a cab had seemed like an extravagance she couldn't afford. How could she have known that the fare would have been nothing compared to the hospital bill she now had? "I figured I could be home by the time I found a phone," she said stiffly. But she'd never made it home.

Two blocks from her car and almost within sight of her apartment, she'd turned down a dark, deserted street and stumbled across an armored-car robbery in progress.

She shuddered, trying in vain to push away the memories that crowded into her head like the dark clouds of a gathering storm. It had all happened so quickly! One minute she was alone in the night, the staccato refrain of her footsteps following her down the quiet street, and the next the lights of the robber's getaway car illuminated the holdup as if it was a poorly lit scene from a B-movie. One guard had already been killed and lay dead on the pavement, while the second fell as she watched, shot by a man whose cruel, hard face was indelibly etched in her mind.

Had she made a sound? She frowned, the stitches in her

forehead twinging in pain as she tried to remember. One minute she had stood frozen to the spot, and the next the robber had spied her hovering at the edge of the light, witnessing everything. In the blink of an eye he'd raised his gun and fired at her, missing her by mere inches. Before he could get off another shot, she'd turned and run for her life down a black alley. She could still hear his curses, the angry roar of his car as he'd jumped in it and floored it, still taste the terror on her tongue as the heat from the engine seemed to lick at the back of her neck. He'd quickly caught her, and she'd tried to jump out of the way, but his bumper had caught her on the thigh and thrown her into the air. For the span of a heartbeat, time had stood still. Then she'd crashed into a building and she'd known only blackness as her attacker sped off into the night, leaving her for dead.

A sudden chill swept through her at the thought, turning her blood icy. Shivering, she hugged herself, but the cold was still there, haunting her. "I want to go home," she said huskily.

"Don't they all," the doctor muttered wryly, eyeing her with a frown. Her oval face with its delicate features was etched with the fineness of porcelain. Breakable. It was an adjective that immediately came to mind when he looked at the soft, sensuous lines of her wide mouth, her angled jaw and high cheekbones, the cloud of reddish-brown hair that swirled about her in haphazard disarray. If she knew how fragile she looked, sitting there in a washed-out green hospital gown that shrouded her slender figure like a tent, she'd know better than to ask to be released.

"Your family's in London, right? And you live alone?" At her nod, he patted her good shoulder. "Then you're better off right where you are. We'll talk about going home in a couple of days."

"*A couple of days!*" she echoed in dismay, her green eyes large in her pale face. "You've got to be kidding. I can't stay in here a couple of days!"

"Your body's just experienced a traumatic shock, and you won't feel the full effects of it until tomorrow. Trust me, you don't want to go home today. Tomorrow your muscles will stiffen up and you'll be lucky if you can get out of bed."

"But—"

From the open doorway a mocking voice drawled, "Still bucking the system, huh, kid? It's nice to know some things in this crazy world remain constant."

Lacey stiffened, the blood draining out of her face only to rush back in again. Only one person called her "kid" like that, as if she were a rebellious teenager who shouldn't be taken too seriously. But it couldn't be Tucker. Only days ago, when the news of the coup in Costa Oro had broken, she'd caught glimpses of him on the national news, a flock of reporters hounding him for the details of his daring rescue of the U.S. embassy staff. She hadn't been surprised to learn that he was the nation's latest hero. He could usually be counted on to turn up wherever there was trouble and somehow come out smelling like a rose. He couldn't possibly be in New Orleans. There would be reports to be made, debriefings that could last weeks.

But when she slowly turned toward the door, there was no doubt that the man who stood before her wearing faded jeans, a black polo shirt and a smile that was irritatingly smug was Tucker Stevens. Their paths hadn't crossed in eight years, but she'd have known him if it had been a hundred. A woman didn't forget the first man she'd made a fool of herself over.

Against her will, her eyes roamed over his lean six-foot-two frame, the unfashionably long dark blond hair, the square-jawed, angular face that didn't hold a trace of softness. The boyishness that had clung to his features the last time she had seen him was gone, honed away by time and the pressures of a job that never eased. Deep lines of exhaustion bracketed his sensuous mouth, adding years to his thirty-six years. He was harder than she remembered, tougher, the light in his tired brown eyes cynical and mocking.

The past few days had been hell on him.

The thought came unbidden, the sympathy it stirred unwanted. Her imagination was playing tricks on her, Lacey told herself. The Tucker Stevens she knew of old reveled in his role of troubleshooter. The last thing he would ever want or expect from her was sympathy. "What are you doing here? The last I heard, you were in D.C."

His eyes glinted at her less-than-welcoming tone. "I knew you'd be thrilled to see me," he baited her, giving her a devilish grin. "I even postponed my...*vacation*—" his smile tightened ever so slightly "—when your father called to tell me you were in trouble. Again."

Did he have to make it sound as if she was a child who didn't know when to come in out of the rain? she wondered indignantly. "That still doesn't explain what you're doing here."

"Riding to your rescue," he retorted with an easy shrug. "What else? When Marcus learned I was on my way to Aruba, he asked me to stop in New Orleans and check on you. According to him, you were just a little shook up."

His accusing gaze shifted to the bandage on her forehead and the sling cradling her arm against her body. Lacey felt a guilty flush rise in her cheeks and could do nothing to stop it. Her father was the U.S. ambassador to Great Britain and presently had his hands filled with preparations for an international environmental summit, which the president would be attending the following week in London. When she'd called him earlier in the day to tell him of her accident, she'd deliberately misled him about the extent of her injuries because she'd known he would worry himself sick about her if he knew the truth. She'd simply told him she'd been hit by a hit-and-run driver and luckily all she had to show for it was a few cuts and bruises. He obviously hadn't believed her and had sent Tucker to investigate. She should have known.

"You wasted a trip," she stated coolly. "There was no reason for Dad to drag you into this. I'm fine. Go ahead and take your vacation. I'm sure you need one."

His eyes sharpened at that, impaling her to the bed. Just what did she mean by that crack? Why did everyone suddenly think he needed a vacation? And did she think he wanted to baby-sit her? Eight years ago they'd met at the wedding of his mother and her father and sparks and challenges had immediately flown between them. At nineteen, she'd been headstrong and adventuresome and ripe for a man. She'd also been as innocent as the day she was born, with everything she felt there in her face for the world to see. She'd scared the hell out of him then, and he had a suspicion she'd still be a handful for any man. She was the last thing he needed or wanted. So what was he doing here, stirring up the past?

Doing Marcus a favor. He sighed. Long before he'd become his stepfather, Marcus Conrad had acted as a guide and mentor in his career. They had an unshakable friendship that had only strengthened when Marcus had married his mother, and there wasn't much Tucker wouldn't do for him. When the older man had asked him to check on his daughter, he just hadn't been able to find the words to turn him down.

Now Tucker could see that Marcus had every right to be concerned. When he'd arrived at Lacey's apartment and found it locked and deserted, he'd learned from a neighbor that the story she'd told her father about what had happened last night had been drastically edited. Her attacker had tried to kill her, and from the battered, fragile look of her, he'd nearly succeeded.

Suddenly inexplicably angry at the mess she had gotten herself into, he glared at the iodined stitches that were like a slash of pale blood against her forehead, the pain dulling the laughing green eyes that had haunted him for years, the cuts and scrapes that marred her satiny skin. Her bones were so delicate, so crushable. How had she survived getting run down by a two-ton car?

Never taking his eyes from her, he said to the doctor who stood on the other side of the bed, "I'm Tucker Stevens, doctor. Lacey's...stepbrother." His eyes turned mocking at the term as he silently acknowledged that there had never been anything brotherly about the feelings she had once stirred in him. Thank God that was all in the past! "What is the extent of her injuries?"

"The gash on her head required ten stitches, her right shoulder was wrenched and she's got a bruised thigh," the older man replied promptly. "She's sore today. Tomorrow she'll be stiff. I've recommended that she stay in the hospital at least two more days since she lives alone. When the full effect of the accident hits her, she won't be a happy camper."

"If I'm going to be miserable, then I might as well be miserable at home," she argued stubbornly. "I've *got* to go home!"

Tucker arched a brow at the hint of desperation in her voice. "Why?"

She owed him no explanations, but she gave him one anyway as she rubbed at the headache that started to throb at her temples. "I live over my antique shop, and every time I'm gone for any length of time, I'm robbed. I've already been gone one night. If I'm gone another, I might not have a business to go back to."

"What about an assistant?" Dr. Hamilton asked. "Surely you must have an employee who can watch over the place until you get out of the hospital."

"I had to let her go," she admitted reluctantly. "I even had to drop my health insurance. Sales were...slow." If she hadn't felt so terrible, she would have laughed at her own description, though the situation was hardly amusing. Sales were more than slow, they were practically nonexistent thanks to John Solomon. Ever since the other dealer had moved into the French Quarter last year, his low prices had hurt the sales of every dealer in the area. The loss of revenue, combined with the robberies she had suffered, had driven her to the very edge of bankruptcy.

"I'm sorry, doctor," she said with a sigh, suddenly weary, "but I just can't afford to stay here another night."

Short of tying her to the bed there was little he could do to keep her there. He glanced at his watch. "I've got to finish my rounds. Why don't you think about it some more? If you still want to leave by the time I'm through, then I guess I can't stop you."

Detective Jack Ryan appeared in Lacey's doorway just in time to hear the doctor's last sentence before the older man stepped around him and continued on down the hall. Frowning, the detective tapped on the open door and stepped inside. "I wouldn't do that if I were you, Ms. Conrad." Walking to Lacey's side, he extended his hand, a half smile transforming his craggy, weathered face at the sight of the wariness clouding her eyes. "I can see you don't remember me. I'm not surprised. When we met last night you were a little groggy. I'm Detective Jack Ryan."

Lacey studied the man in the charcoal-gray suit, trying to remember. Her memories of regaining consciousness hours earlier were nothing more than vague and disjointed images of strangers bending over her, prodding her for answers she'd had to struggle to give. Somewhere in the hazy cloud that fogged her impressions lurked a wavering vision of Detective Ryan's thick brown hair touched with gray, the small scar on his left eyebrow, the blue eyes that somehow managed to be both shrewd and kind. He'd questioned her about the robbery, pulling information from her with gentle persuasion until the medication she'd been given dragged her down into sleep.

"Of course I remember, Detective Ryan," she said as she shook his hand, then introduced him to Tucker. "I also remember falling asleep while you were questioning me. How is the investigation going?"

"Better than it has in months, thanks to you."

"Months?" Tucker repeated. "What do you mean, months?"

"The robbery your stepsister witnessed last night was the third armored-car robbery in six months," the detective explained. "The MO is always the same—the holdups occur after a holiday or a major convention weekend, when the hotel, restaurant and shop safes are overflowing. The armored car is disabled on a night run on a deserted street, usually by shooting out one of the tires. We can only assume the driver isn't aware that it's anything more than a flat tire. When he stops and gets out to change it, he's used as a hostage to get the guard in the back to open up. Once he does, both men are killed."

"And in six months' time you haven't arrested any suspects?" Tucker said in disbelief. "Why the hell not?"

The press and citizens had been asking him the same question for months. "Because we haven't had a single witness to lead us to a suspect. Until now. Ms. Conrad gave us a description of the robber last night. If she can pick the man out of one of the mug-shot books I brought, we should be able to make an arrest in a matter of days." He opened the large briefcase he carried, pulled out one of the books and laid it on the tall, wheeled table at the end of the bed. In a matter of seconds he had the table pulled into position across her lap, the book opened in front of her. "Don't be upset if you don't recognize him," he advised quietly. "It was dark and you only got a glimpse of him. Just take your time and do your best."

With fingers that were far from steady, Lacey slowly turned the pages, studying the faces of hard, rough men with soulless eyes that chilled her to the bone. Images of her attacker drifted in and out of focus before her mind's eye until she began to wonder if she would even know the man if he somehow found a way to track her down and finish the job he had started. And then she turned a page near the end of the book and found herself looking down at cruel, blunt features that were horrifyingly familiar.

At her side, Tucker felt her sudden stillness, the almost silent breath she sucked in. Even as he watched, what little blood there was in her ashen cheeks drained away. Protectiveness surged in him, swift and strong and totally unexpected. Telling himself he'd feel the same for any other woman in his family, he moved closer and took her hand. "Lace? Are you okay?"

Fear welling thickly in her throat, she unconsciously gripped his fingers until her knuckles whitened. "That's him," she said hoarsely.

"You sure?" the detective questioned, his narrowed eyes watching her closely. "If you have the slightest doubt, tell me now, Ms. Conrad. We've been beating the bushes for a suspect for six months. We don't want any mistakes at this stage in the game."

"No, I'm sure." Suddenly realizing she was clinging to Tucker like a helpless female, she dropped his hand and tried to pull herself together. She was perfectly safe now, she silently reasoned. She had nothing to fear. But she still couldn't stop the goose bumps that raced over her arms as she stared at the picture before her.

Abruptly lifting her eyes back up to the detective, she said, "The hair's different—last night he had it in a ponytail at the base of his neck—but everything else is the same. The flat nose, the pockmarked cheeks, the cruel mouth."

The detective turned the book so he could read the information under the picture. "Robert Martin, alias Martin Roberts, aka Bob Martinez. He's thirty-five, five foot seven, approximately 175 pounds, with black eyes and brown hair." He closed the book with a snap and returned it to his briefcase. "As soon as we pick him up, you'll need to come down to the station and pick him out of a lineup. Until then, you might want to reconsider your decision to go home. You'll be safer here in the hospital than in your apartment alone.''

Tucker's dark brows furrowed into a frown. ''Are you saying she's still in danger?''

He nodded grimly. ''Unfortunately, yes. As long as this nut's on the loose, there's always a chance he can get to her. Normally I'd station some men around her apartment, but I just haven't got them, not with half the force out on strike for a better contract.'' He shook his head in disgust. While the union was holding out for more money, every crook in the city was coming out of the woodwork. ''I can increase the patrols in the Quarter, but that's about it. I'm sorry, but we're just too shorthanded.''

''It's not as if this Robert Martin or whatever his name is knows who I am,'' she pointed out when she saw Tucker start to voice his disapproval. ''I was just a woman on the street and it was dark. There's no way he could know my name or where I live, is there, Detective Ryan?''

Reluctantly, the detective had no choice but to agree. ''Your name was kept out of the papers, so chances are slim that he's going to be able to track you down.''

''Then there's no reason why I can't go home.''

''Damn it, Lacey, there's every reason,'' Tucker argued. ''Odds don't mean crap when we're talking about your life here. And even if there's not a holy chance in hell of that lowlife finding you, you're in no shape to go home. Look at you! You can hardly move.''

Her mouth set at a determined angle, Lacey struggled to hang on to her temper. If he thought he could still get away with treating her like an eight-year-old who needed a keeper, he was in for a rude awakening. ''I'm going home,'' she said in a sweet voice underlined with steel. ''*Today*. Now that you've done your duty and checked on me, there's really no reason for you to waste any more of your vacation. Send me a postcard from Aruba.''

It would serve her right if he took her up on her suggestion, he thought, staring down at her with hostile brown eyes. He'd blithely go off to Aruba and forget she even existed. Yeah, sure, he silently snorted. Even at nineteen, she hadn't been a female a man could easily put out of his mind. She was like the half-forgotten refrain of a song that clung to the shadows of your memory, never completely there, but never gone, either. Whenever fleeting thoughts of her had slipped through his mind in the past, he'd always told himself she was just a kid, and then he'd distracted himself with work. But the woman who lay on the bed before him was no kid, and he no longer had any work to distract him.

Beneath the sheet that covered her impossibly long legs and the hospital gown that nearly swallowed her, her hips were slender, her breasts small and pert. He could circle her wrist with his thumb and forefinger. But for all her lack of womanly curves, she had a delicacy that any man would be wise to be wary of. Her skin was like the finest silk that tempted a man to stroke, caress. But lightly, so as not to bruise. And her hair, dear God, no wonder he'd had a hard time keeping his hands off her all those years ago. Spun mahogany, shot through with red and gold, it flowed nearly to her waist in a cascade of waves. He didn't even have to close his eyes to imagine it spread out across the bed....

Suddenly realizing where his thoughts had wandered, he jerked them back, cursing himself. Lacey Conrad's hair wouldn't be spread across his bed now or ever. She was a family responsibility, one he couldn't turn his back on just for a vacation he didn't want. Whether she liked it or not, she needed him, and he'd never be able to face Marcus again if he didn't stay to help her.

"Then it looks like I'm going home with you," he retorted, "since you're in no condition to be alone."

Lacey's heart stopped in her breast before it stumbled into an unsteady rhythm. "What? You can't be serious! What about your vacation?"

"It can wait. Family responsibility comes first."

She stiffened, hating the label, telling herself she didn't

want him to feel anything for her, least of all a sense of duty. "We're step relations, Tucker, nothing more. You don't owe me a second thought."

"Maybe not, but I owe your father and I'm staying."

Her eyes flashed at his arrogance. Did he think he could push himself into her life without so much as a by your leave just because she was out of commission for a few days? She opened her mouth to protest, but Detective Ryan didn't give her a chance. Lifting his briefcase from the table, he headed for the door. "Now that that's settled, I'll be on my way. I'll order the increased patrols in the Quarter, Ms. Conrad, and keep you posted on the progress of our investigation."

She only had time to thank him before he was out the door, leaving her alone with Tucker. Silence stretched between them like a chasm, until all Lacey could hear was the thumping of her heart and the echo of her thoughts. She was completely over the silly teenage crush she had had on him all those years ago. Once stung, twice shy. His mocking smile and dangerous good looks would never again tug at her heartstrings. Why then, she wondered in growing panic, did she know spending the next few days alone with him in her apartment would be a drastic mistake?

Resisting the need to hug herself, she struggled for a nonchalance she had never been able to feel in his presence. Lifting her chin, she locked her eyes with his. "I don't want you to stay," she finally managed coolly. "I don't need you."

Stubborn. How could he have forgotten how stubborn she was? "Try telling me that when you're not as white as a sheet and weaker than a sick kitten and I might believe you," he said, striding toward the door. "Close your eyes and take a nap, kid, while I see about getting you released. If you're going to spend the next few days arguing with me, you're going to need your energy."

"I'm not going to spend the next few days doing anything with you! Where are you going? Damn it, Tucker, come back here!''

But she was too late. He was gone.

Swearing at the injuries that prevented her from going after him, she glared at the empty doorway. This couldn't be happening, she thought in growing panic. She knew that stubborn tilt of his chin, the flintlike resolve she'd seen in his eyes as he'd walked out. Bullheaded. His picture was beside the word in the dictionary. Once he made up his mind about something, you could move the World Trade Center before you could move Tucker Stevens. Damn him, what did she have to say to convince him that she didn't need a knight to rush to her rescue? And even if she did, it wouldn't be him! He was too arrogant, too sure of himself, too insistent on having his own way. Somehow she would have to make it clear to him that she just didn't want him there.

But when he returned to her room thirty minutes later, accompanied by a nurse with a wheelchair, there was no reasoning with him. With a charm that set her teeth on edge, he presented her with a yellow cotton gown and robe he'd bought in the hospital gift shop for her to wear home, then waited out in the hall while the nurse helped her change. She might as well have been talking to the wall for all the good her protests did. As soon as she changed, he returned to gently help her sore, battered body into the wheelchair, then whisked her off to the lobby. A taxi waited at the front entrance, and seconds later they were headed for her apartment.

She lived in the heart of the French Quarter in an old-fashioned, one-bedroom flat that could be reached either by an inside stairway from her shop or an outside one that was guarded by an ancient wrought-iron gate. When the taxi dropped them off in front of the gate and Tucker paid the fare, Lacey heaved a silent sigh of relief. Home at last. Now if she could just convince Tucker his help was no longer needed, she could go upstairs and crash in her bed.

Gathering her strength, she turned to face him. "I appreciate you getting me out of the hospital, Tucker, I really do, but—" She gasped, her uninjured arm frantically slipping around the strong column of his neck as he suddenly scooped her up against his chest as if she weighed no more than a baby. "What are you doing? Put me down! You can't carry me!"

"Funny," he teased, grinning down at her as he started up the stairs, "it looks like I already am." He watched her eyes snap at him, and couldn't help but remember another time when he had held her close and the light in her eyes had had nothing to do with anger. His body stirred to life at the memory, and suddenly it was difficult to maintain the light, mocking tone he knew was sure to infuriate her and take her mind off the trauma she'd suffered. "If you're going to have a temper tantrum, I'm going to leave."

"In that case, I'll throw a vase at your head the minute you put me down," she retorted, holding herself stiffly in his arms. "You can leave just as soon as you call another cab."

He chuckled. "Nice try, but it's not going to work. Looks like you're stuck with me, kid, until you're strong enough to throw me out yourself."

Memories, as cutting as barbed wire, hit her in the face, scraping her raw. "Don't call me that!" she said sharply. "I'm twenty-seven years old. I'm not a kid."

No, she wasn't, and that was the whole problem. This was no innocent girl of nineteen, but a woman who felt all too real in his arms. And he was committed to spending the next few days with her. His teeth clenched on an oath, he reached the top of the stairs and held her as she struggled with the key in the lock, then finally pushed the door open.

Carrying her inside, he saw in a glance that the apartment suited her. Art deco in style, with cream-colored plastered walls and ceilings, skylights and arched doorways, it was a romantic's dream. The living room was large, airy, the perfect setting for the powder-blue clawfoot couch and matching chairs that were cozily positioned around a white marble fireplace. A Victorian rug in a rose pattern covered the parquet floor, and plants were everywhere—on antique plant stands, in the flower boxes outside the long windows at both ends of the narrow room, in large urns that stood next to the double French doors in the bedroom that opened onto her rooftop patio.

The bedroom. Too late, Tucker realized there was only one.

Still in his arms, Lacey struggled to force the voice of reason through her suddenly dry throat. "Tucker, I'm sure Dad didn't intend for you to do this, especially when it's not necessary. I'm perfectly capable of taking care of myself. If you'll just put me down—"

Instead, he carried her into her old-fashioned white kitchen, complete with red gingham tablecloth and curtains, and jerked open her refrigerator. A nearly empty half gallon of milk, an overripe tomato and a few eggs were the sum total of its contents.

The baleful look he sent her was laced with amusement. "No wonder you're so skinny. How are you going to take care of yourself if this is all you've got in the apartment to eat?"

"I eat out a lot," she said defensively. "It's hardly worth it to cook for just one person."

"With that bruised thigh, you won't be going anywhere," he reminded her.

He was right and they both knew it. Defeated, she muttered, "It's only a temporary condition."

"Right," he grunted as he strode into her bedroom and carefully laid her on her bed. "So am I. Think of me as the measles. I'll be gone in three days."

Lacey stared up at him as he leaned over to make her more comfortable, his hands brushing over her as he helped her tug down the hem of her gown and robe. Eight years ago she would have thought spending three days alone with

him in a romantic city like New Orleans was nothing short
of heaven. Now it only sounded like her worst nightmare.
She couldn't help but wonder what kind of scars he would
leave behind when he left.

Chapter 2

Exhaustion pulled at her, slowly robbing her of her will as well as her energy, but still she tried to protest. "I really don't think—" she blinked suddenly heavy lids "—that this is such a g-good idea...."

She tried to sit up, but she didn't even have the strength to lift her head from the pillow. Frowning at her stubbornness, Tucker gently held her down until she grew still beneath his hands. "We'll talk about this later," he promised, pulling the sheet over her. "Right now you need to rest."

"No...I've got to..." She squeezed her eyes shut, trying to remember exactly what it was that she had to do. But she was so tired! "My car...got to get it f-fixed." She moved restlessly, trying to escape his hold, but her body was leaden and he could have subdued her with nothing more than the strength in his index finger. "Has to be moved...before it's stripped."

"Relax," he soothed softly, brushing her hair back from her face and trying not to notice the way it curled around his fingers. "Your car's perfectly safe. The police impounded it last night after they found you. Where do you usually have it worked on?''

"Repair shop," she said, yawning. "Albert's."

"Okay, I'll take care of it," he promised. "You just get some sleep."

She wanted to tell him to get an estimate before he had the car fixed—a huge repair bill was out of the question now—but clouds of weariness weighed down her thoughts, dragging her into unconsciousness. With a sigh, she gave up the battle, never knowing that Tucker stood there for a long time, watching her with brooding eyes before he finally turned and walked out of her room.

The sun was just setting, the heat and humidity finally easing, when Lacey awoke hours later. Disoriented, she opened her eyes expecting to see the blank white walls of her hospital room, and found herself safe in her own bedroom instead. Her mind still fuzzy, she blinked in confusion. How—

Tucker.

Memories of his arrival at the hospital rushed into her mind like flood waters, engulfing her. With a groan, she closed her eyes. After the fiasco of their first and only meeting, she could have happily spent the rest of her life without ever setting eyes on him again. She had, of course, heard stories about Tucker Stevens long before she met him. Gossip was traded just as easily at diplomatic functions as it was over backyard fences, and he'd had quite a reputation as a heartbreaker. Even though she'd been forewarned, however, she hadn't, at nineteen, had any defenses against his brand of masculinity. He'd had an air of danger and recklessness about him that had simply bowled her over. From the moment they'd laid eyes on each other, they'd rubbed against each other like chalk on a rough blackboard. Pick a subject, any subject, and they'd disagreed on it, out of sheer perversity if nothing else. She'd been so determined not to let him see how he affected her, and all the time he must have seen through her like a plate-glass window. At the wedding reception they'd argued in the garden and ended up in each other's arms. Woefully inexperienced, she was caught up in the wonder of him when he pulled back suddenly and made it clear that he never got involved with *girls* who still had stardust in their eyes. She'd wanted to die.

And now he was here, in her apartment.

For the next two days!

Wasn't life wonderful?

For the fifth time in two hours, Tucker stepped into the open doorway of her bedroom to check on her. Her head was tilted to the side toward him, her reddish-brown curls spread out against her pillow and sheets in tantalizing disarray, her lashes dark crescents against her ivory cheeks. Unable to draw his eyes away from her, he assured himself she wasn't his type. He liked a woman with some meat on her bones, a woman with soft, rounded curves a man could lose himself in. If one look at Lacey could warm his blood and make his gut clench, it was only because she was damn attractive and it had been a long time since he'd been alone with a woman in her apartment.

She hadn't moved since the last time he'd looked in on her, but something warned him she was awake. Fighting the impulse to move to her side, he stayed stubbornly where he was. "You awake?" he asked in a near whisper.

No! she wanted to cry as his husky voice stroked her senses like a caress. *I'm going to sleep until you're gone, until the only time I hear your voice is in my dreams.*

But she'd never been a coward. Even when she'd been humiliated by him after the wedding, she hadn't run. She'd lifted her chin and stuck it out for the rest of the weekend. Gathering her pride around her vulnerable heart, she opened her eyes and forced herself to coolly meet his gaze. "Yes. I was just resting my eyes. What time is it?"

"A little after eight," he replied without glancing at his watch. "How about some supper?"

For the first time, Lacey became aware of the tantalizing aroma wafting through the apartment. Her stomach growled noisily. A rueful grin slid across her mouth. "I guess that answers your question," she said with a chuckle, struggling to sit up. "Something smells wonderful, and I know it didn't come out of my refrigerator. What'd you do? Go to the store while I was asleep?"

"Actually, I got your neighbor next door to go for me." Two long strides brought him to her side; his frown was fierce. "What do you think you're doing?"

"I'm getting up, of course," she retorted. "I can't very well eat in bed." Ignoring his obvious disapproval, she threw off the sheet that covered her, all her attention focused on her gown, which had somehow managed to work its way halfway up her thighs. Without even looking up, she could feel Tucker's eyes on her, stroking her skin until hot color surged into her cheeks. How could he still make her blush after all these years? she thought wildly. "What are you making?" she asked desperately, hoping to distract him. "It smells fantastic."

"Smothered steak."

Although she didn't look up, she knew his eyes never moved from her legs. "I didn't even know you could cook."

He shrugged. "It was either learn how or starve when I shared an apartment in college with four other guys who didn't know how to boil water." His face impassive, he watched her slowly ease herself over to the edge of the bed and throw one leg over the side. Before the other one could follow suit, he caught her bare ankle in his strong grasp, stopping her in her tracks. At her startled gasp, his eyes locked with hers, his fingers tightening ever so slightly around her. "Think again, Lace. You're not going anywhere. If you're ready to eat, I'll bring you a tray."

She would have swallowed, but her throat was suddenly

too dry to manage even that simple action. "I'm not an invalid," she protested weakly. "I don't expect you to wait on me."

"Then you better change your expectations because that's just what I intend to do," he said bluntly. "Wait on you hand and foot." He jiggled her foot, his grin mocking. "Now do you put this foot back under the covers or do I do it for you?"

A dare. She'd always had trouble walking away from a dare. Unable to stop herself, she moved her gaze speculatively to her ankle and the strong, lean fingers that surrounded it, claiming it with an ease that stole her breath. Her heart drummed against her ribs. She didn't even have to close her eyes to imagine his hand sliding slowly up her leg, caressing her, exploring every inch of her until she melted like warm honey under his touch.

"Well? What's it going to be?"

She blinked, her hot, wayward thoughts jerking to a stop. What was she doing? she thought, horrified. Yanking her ankle free of his burning touch, she quickly slipped her legs back under the sheet and pulled it up to her chest. "All right," she snapped. "I'll stay in bed. For now."

If he'd been a gentleman, Tucker would have accepted his victory with good grace and let the matter drop without comment. But he was no gentleman and never had been. He grinned smugly. "Well, will wonders never cease? Lacey Conrad conceding defeat without an argument. I never thought I'd live to see the day."

"You won't live to see another one if you don't quit pushing your luck," she warned, her lips twitching in spite of her best attempts to appear stern. "The only thing I'm conceding is that you're physically stronger than I am, so you can quit gloating. It isn't becoming."

"You always were a sore loser," he observed, his brown eyes dancing devilishly. "Guess that goes with being the baby of the family." Before she could even sputter a protest, he asked innocently, "Are you ready to eat?"

"No! I mean yes! Damn it, Tucker—"

"Don't cuss, Lace. It isn't becoming," he teased, throwing her own words back at her. "There's no reason to get all bent out of shape just because you're hungry. I'll be right back with your tray."

If she'd had something to throw at him, she would have drilled it into his retreating back. Maddening man! How could she have forgotten how easily he could goad her into losing her temper? From the moment they'd first met he'd known which buttons to push to infuriate her, which ones to tease to set her pulses pounding. And they were only a hairbreadth apart.

She stared unseeingly at the empty doorway through which he had disappeared, trepidation stealing into her heart. Was history repeating itself? Was she arguing with him to fight an attraction that seemed to be tugging her into his arms? No! The cry, never leaving her throat, echoed in the silence of her own thoughts. She wouldn't let him get to her again. Not this time. She was no longer a naive nineteen-year-old, fascinated by a hard, handsome face and a quick wit. She wanted more from a man than that, more than Tucker Stevens had to offer. As long as she remembered that, he wouldn't be able to hurt her.

Convinced she had herself well in hand and her emotions on a tight rein, she deliberately unclenched her hands and willed herself to relax. Then he brought her her tray, leaning over her to carefully set it across her lap, his hands just brushing her hips. At his touch, the air in her lungs just seemed to evaporate. A silent gasp tore through her, but before she could draw a breath he was gone, once more retreating to the kitchen. She almost collapsed in relief. At least he was leaving her to eat in peace.

She'd hardly completed the thought before he was back, this time carrying a TV tray, which contained another plate of food. He set it next to the bed, then drew up a chair in front. When she only looked at him in stunned surprise and made no attempt to pick up her fork, he frowned. "What's wrong? Don't you like steak?"

She loved it, but somehow she knew it would taste like sawdust if she tried to eat now. The scene was too intimate, too cozy, too...*right*. She nodded jerkily and finally found her voice. "No, it's...not th-that. I—"

Understanding dawned across his face. He swore under his breath at his own stupidity. "I forgot about your arm. You can't cut it up, can you? Here, let me."

Setting his tray away from him, he leaned over to cut her meat with his own knife and fork. His dark blond head only inches away from hers, Lacey felt her heart stumble into an irregular beat that seemed to thunder in her ears. She told herself he would do the same thing for a sick grandmother, a hurt child, a stranger on the street, but she couldn't stop her gaze from roaming over his strong, deft hands, the angled line of his jaw, the fascinating curve of his mouth.

"There. How's that?" Looking up from her plate, he found her eyes on his. Tension, thick and pulsing and hot, crawled into the air between them. Time seemed to stop. Too close, Tucker realized. He was too close to something he should be running hard and fast from. But still, it was a long moment before he leaned back and pulled his own tray into place in front of him. "There," he repeated in a voice that had turned rough. "You should be able to manage now."

Manage? she thought wildly as she picked up her fork with trembling fingers and stabbed a piece of meat. Didn't he realize that she managed best when he was halfway around the world?

The meal progressed in a stark silence that was broken only by the clink of flatware and glasses. Their eyes trained on their plates, they both ate without tasting, forcing the tender steak down throats that were as dry as dust. For all the notice each gave the other, they could have been eating in separate rooms, separate apartments. But with every passing moment, awareness coiled between them like a snake preparing to strike.

Studying her set face from the corner of his eye, Tucker decided the next few days were going to be hell if they didn't find a way to declare a truce. They were both adults. Surely they could cohabit for a few days without going for each other's throats. After all, they were family.

Setting his fork down, he leaned back in his chair and set out to charm her. "How about seconds?" he asked suddenly, giving her an easy smile as she finished the last of her steak. "Or dessert? There's ice cream."

Lacey watched his smile warily. A woman would be crazy to trust a man with an angel's smile and the devil's own charm. She shook her head. "I think I'll pass, thanks. I couldn't eat another bite."

Silence fell again as she trailed a finger through the wet ring her iced-tea glass had left on the tray. She seemed perfectly content to let the conversation flounder into nothingness. Frowning, Tucker tried again. "I suppose you realize that the next time I see Marcus he's going to want a complete report on you, since he doesn't get to see you too often. Anything special you want me to tell him?"

"No, just that I'm doing fine."

When she added nothing more, he tried and failed to remember the last time he'd had to pull information out of a woman. Irritation gathered in his eyes, darkening them from brown to black. "Does he know about the robberies?"

"No! And I'd just as soon you didn't tell him," she retorted. "You know Dad. He's never liked the idea of me living here alone over the shop. If he found out I'd been robbed when I was out of town, he'd try to get me to move into one of those apartment complexes that looks like a prison, with a security guard at the gate."

"At least you'd be safer there than you are here," he pointed out. "A woman living alone in an area like this is too damn vulnerable. Why don't you get a roommate?"

"Because the apartment's just big enough for one person. Anyway, all my friends are either married or engaged."

"So why aren't you?"

Startled, she drew back. "What?"

"Married or engaged," he repeated innocently. "You know, if you're serious about anyone, you should let me check him out before I leave. These days it doesn't pay not to be too careful. Give me his name and I can find out everything you want to know about him right down to the shape of his belly button."

"No!"

Struggling to keep a straight face at her horrified tone, he swallowed a laugh. "No, you don't want me to check him out or no you're not seeing anyone?"

"No, I—" Suddenly noting the wicked grin curling the corners of his mouth, she clamped her teeth on the admission that there hadn't been a man in her life for quite some time. Had she lost her mind? Tucker Stevens was the last man she would ever discuss her love life with! "No," she repeated stiffly, "I don't need you to check out anyone for me."

"That bad, hmm?" he teased. "Well, don't despair. You've got a lot of good years left yet to find a man. Maybe I could introduce you to some of my friends?"

From what she'd heard about his friends, they were as rough and hardened as he was. "Don't do me any favors," she said dryly. "I like my life just the way it is. If you want to worry about someone's love life, worry about your own. You're pushing forty, you know. Already past your prime sexually. If you're ever going to find a wife, you better start looking while you're still young enough to enjoy her."

His eyes gleamed dangerously. He was tempted, damn tempted, to pull her into his arms and show her that he was more than capable of satisfying her or any other woman. But he knew from experience that she wasn't the kind of

woman a man could enjoy, then casually walk away from.
And he was a man who went out of his way to avoid ties.

He arched a mocking brow that was sure to infuriate her.
"Who said anything about marriage? I can have a love life
and still not have a wife clinging to me when I get orders
in the middle of the night to head for some hot spot in a
country most people have never heard of."

As far as warnings went, it wasn't very subtle. It was
also unnecessary. He'd effectively killed any dreams she'd
had about sharing happily ever after with him years ago.
Wadding up her napkin, she dropped it onto the tray still
stretched across her lap and leaned her head back against
the pillows propped behind her. "Then neither one of us
has a problem, do we? Now that that's settled, I think I'll
call it a night. It's been a long day."

His brows drawing together in a heavy frown, Tucker
could almost see the last of her energy drain out of her,
leaving the circles under her eyes darker than ever. As fragile as hand-blown glass, she looked as if it would take little
more than a harsh word to shatter her. He bit back an ex-
pletive, wanting to kick himself for not noticing sooner that
he was tiring her. He was supposed to be taking care of
her, not wearing her out! Quickly lifting her tray, he set it
on top of his own and turned to leave. "I'll get you one of
the pain pills the doctor prescribed. It'll help you sleep."

"No!" Her sharp cry stopped him before he could take
more than a step away from the bed. Just the thought of
darkness descending on her again as it had when she'd been
struck down, defying her control, was enough to make her
palms grow damp. "No...I don't need anything," she said
quickly when he lifted a brow questioningly. "I can hardly
keep my eyes open now."

The pain pill would ensure her a good night's sleep, but
the last thing Tucker wanted to do now was argue with her.
He hesitated, his gaze roaming over her pale cheeks, the
bandage on her forehead, the vulnerability that she rarely
allowed anyone to see. "All right," he reluctantly agreed

as he switched off the bedside lamp, then picked up the trays. "But if you change your mind during the middle of the night, I'll be right there in the living room on the couch. Just call me and I'll hear you."

"I will," she promised, even though she knew she wouldn't. Standing in the darkness, silhouetted by the light that spilled into the bedroom from the living room, his shoulders impossibly broad as he towered over her, he was a man a woman could easily turn to in the night. But in the light of day, he'd be gone just as soon as the opportunity presented itself. She couldn't allow herself to forget that. She pulled the sheet up to her breasts, as if to shield her heart. "I'm sure I'll be fine."

Unconvinced, he fought the inexplicable urge to linger. *She's made it clear she wants to go to bed,* a disgusted voice growled in his head. *Get out of here before you do something stupid!* Heeding the warning, he turned abruptly toward the door. "Then I'll let you get some sleep," he said gruffly. "Good night."

An hour later the apartment was dark, the only light that crept in through Lacey's bedroom blinds coming from the streetlight on the corner. Still awake, she'd grown drowsy listening to Tucker do the dishes, then search the closet next to the bathroom for sheets and blankets to make a bed on the couch. The blankets had been folded with only a whisper of sound, the sheets snapped into place. She'd almost been asleep when the last light had been switched off and she'd heard him crawl onto his makeshift bed. Silence, thick and relaxing, had lasted all of five seconds when he'd muttered a curse.

The couch was too short.

Slowly drifting into sleep, she was aware of images playing before her closed eyes. Tucker, his six-foot-two frame stretched out on the five-foot-two sofa. His feet were no doubt sticking out over one end, his head crammed up against the arm at the other. She heard him give his pillow

a savage punch, then wish the couch to hell and back as
he struggled to get comfortable. But Lacey had slept on
that couch when her father and Tucker's mother, Elizabeth,
had visited her last year, and she knew from experience
there wasn't a comfortable position on it. In spite of the
sympathy she felt for him, she couldn't stop the mischie-
vous smile that tugged at her mouth as she sank deeper into
sleep.

The dream, when it came to her, slipped into her mind
like a creature of the night lurking undetected in the shadows. Darting past her slumbering defenses, it took refuge
in harmless memories—the Quarter at night, the beat of
jazz stirring the humid air until it throbbed with life, the
aged and graceful architecture that linked the present with
the past. With a nearly soundless sigh, Lacey relaxed in her
sleep and never thought to be wary of the dream images
that were as safe and familiar as the lines on her palm.

Suddenly the shadows surrounding her shifted, envel-
oping her. Terrified for reasons she couldn't name, she ran,
stumbling into an alley. An all-too-familiar alley. Her blood
turned to ice. The two armored-car guards lay dead on the
pavement.

No! She wouldn't relive what she had seen! She tried to
scream the denial, but the words lodged in her throat as the
man who had tried to kill her rose up before her like the
specter of death. Eyes as black as coal glowed red with
hatred. She whimpered, unable to move as he bore down
on her in a black hearse. Closer, closer, until she could feel
his fury burning the back of her neck....

She woke with a start, her heart slamming painfully
against the walls of her chest, her face damp with sweat.
A dream, she thought in relief, swallowing a sob. It was
nothing more than a dream. Dragging in a calming breath,
she stared at the dark ceiling as her pulse gradually slowed
and the panic subsided. But when she closed her eyes again,
her tormentor stared back at her from out of the blackness
of her own subconscious. Watching. Waiting.

Chilled despite the heat of the night, she snapped open her eyes. She was, she told herself in disgust, perfectly safe. Her attacker couldn't possibly know her name or where she lived—she was just one among thousands of nameless women in New Orleans. He, on the other hand, was well-known to the police. For all she knew, they could be arresting him this very moment. She had nothing to be afraid of.

Except a stupid dream that refused to go away. Her pulse racing madly, she threw off the covers. She might as well get up for a while. It would be hours before her overactive imagination let her rest.

From outside, the soulful wail of jazz floated on the night air, drawing her from the bed. With painstaking slowness, she rose to her feet and almost groaned when her muscles suddenly tightened in protest. Biting her bottom lip, she froze, her eyes flying to the darkened living room. Had Tucker heard her? But the only sound that disturbed the quiet was the curse he muttered in his sleep as he shifted positions on the couch. Relieved, she released the breath she'd unconsciously been holding, and haltingly made her way to the window seat that overlooked the street.

Something wasn't right. The thought nagged at Tucker, pulling him out of a troubled sleep. Turning on his side, he inadvertently kicked the end of the couch and swore. From Lacey's room he heard the creaking of the bed, then a stifled gasp. Lying perfectly still, he stared at the dark doorway, listening. Footsteps shuffled across the carpet at a snail's pace. What was she doing out of bed? Was she in pain? Pushing aside the sheet that covered him, he reached for his jeans.

Barefoot and bare chested, he strode quickly into her room, only to stop short when he finally spied her sitting in the dark in the window seat, hugging her drawn-up knees to her chest as she stared out at the night. Heat curled into his loins. In the weak light that streamed in through the blinds, she was soft and mussed from sleep. Touchable, he decided, his gaze drawn to the dark curls that fell over her slim shoulders like a cloak. Too damn touchable.

Ordering himself to stay where he was, he crossed his arms over his chest and studied her for a long moment before saying quietly, "I thought I heard you moving around in here. Are you all right?"

Lost in her thoughts, she jumped. Glancing back over her shoulder, she found him in the doorway, standing there dressed in nothing but jeans as if he'd just stepped out of her dreams. Her eyes quickly returned to the window as she felt her heart slowly pick up its pace. *Go back to bed*, she wanted to cry, feeling naked and defenseless. *I can't deal with you now!* Instead, she said shakily, "I'm f-fine. I just couldn't sleep."

Even in the darkness, with half the room between them, he'd seen enough of her face to catch a glimpse of the pain tightening her mouth and the fear lingering in her eyes. Something twisted inside him, a need to hold her. Unable to stop himself, he crossed the room to her, all the while asking himself if he'd lost his mind. He had no business being in her room at this hour of the night when they were both half dressed.

But that didn't stop him from taking a seat at the opposite end of the wide window seat from her. "Bad dream?" he guessed shrewdly.

She didn't want him there, so close she had only to stretch out her leg to touch his thigh. "No," she started to lie, but the hard look he gave her stilled the word on her tongue. She sighed in defeat. "Okay, I had a dream. It's no big deal. I'm sorry if I disturbed you."

She'd disturbed him, all right, but not by waking him. "I was half awake, anyway."

"I was just going to listen to the music awhile, then go back to bed. You don't have to keep me company."

She couldn't have been much blunter, but he didn't take the hint. "No problem." He shrugged. "I'm not all that anxious to torture myself with that couch again.'' Settling back against the window frame behind him, he stretched his legs out next to hers as if he intended to stay there all night. ''How about a story?'' he suggested lightly. ''I've got one that'll make your nightmare look like a fairy tale.''

Lacey laughed in spite of herself. ''Tucker, this isn't necessary—''

''Be quiet, woman, and listen.'' Crossing his ankles, he began. ''Once upon a time, there was this baby-sitter—''

''Not a baby-sitter story!'' she groaned. ''I outgrew those when I was fourteen!''

''Who was baby-sitting a little girl on New Year's Eve,'' he continued, throwing her a quelling glance. ''Everything was fine until the TV program she was watching was interrupted by a news bulletin. A maniac was on the loose and everyone should stay safely indoors.''

''What?'' Lacey teased. ''You mean there's no ax murderer? I'm disappointed.''

''That's another story,'' he growled. ''The baby-sitter was nervous, so she checked the house to make sure it was locked tight, then took the little girl upstairs to put her to bed. They just got upstairs, though, when they heard a noise downstairs and the lights went out.''

''Uh-oh,'' Lacey murmured. ''Here it comes.''

''You're damn right,'' he agreed, grinning. ''The baby-sitter knew it was the maniac, so she told the little girl to lock herself in the bathroom while she sneaked back downstairs to call the police. The little girl did as she was told, waiting and waiting for the baby-sitter to come back. But she never did, and then she heard a strange noise on the stairs.'' He lowered his voice to a deep, ominous whisper, dragging out the words. ''Thuump, thuump, draaag.... Thuump, thuump, draaag....''

Caught up in the story, Lacey didn't even realize she'd leaned forward. ''What was it?''

Tucker bit back a smile at her whispered question. ''It was the baby-sitter,'' he whispered back. ''The maniac had cut off her legs and she was pulling herself up the stairs by her elbows. Thuump, thuump, draaag!''

"Oh, that's *awful*!" she cried, laughing as she covered her ears as if the three words still echoed in her head. "Where did you hear something so terrible?"

"Camp," he replied smugly. "When I was twelve. Isn't it great?"

"No, it's sick!"

"But you loved every minute of it, didn't you?"

"Well, of course I did." She chuckled. "You were right—my nightmare was nothing compared to that."

But the fear that stalked her in her dreams had originated in reality. Tucker's smile faded, and his eyes probed hers. For a moment he'd almost forgotten that it was only his need to protect her that had drawn him to her, nothing more. Closing his mind to her nearness in the small enclosure and the way her cotton gown draped her slender body, only hinting at what was beneath, he asked gruffly, "How are you feeling now?"

Trapped in his gaze, she tried to hang on to the laughter they'd shared, but she couldn't stop it from slipping away. "Better," she admitted in a voice that sounded nothing like her own. "Thanks."

"Think you'll be able to sleep now?"

Not without dreaming of you.

The thought hit her in the face before she could see it coming, horrifying her. Had the nightmare scrambled her brain? She knew he wasn't the type of man a woman could sit in the dark and share laughter with, not without leaving herself wide open to hurt. Retreating into herself, she nodded. "Yes, of course. I didn't mean to keep you up so long."

He frowned in confusion at her sudden reserve. "You didn't keep me up," he began, but she'd already edged her legs past his and forced herself to her feet. "Damn it, Lacey, what do you think you're doing? Let me help you."

But she didn't want his help, and she certainly didn't

want his touch. Not now, when she was feeling so vulnerable. Desperate to reach the safe haven of her bed, she ignored her bruised muscles and hurried across the room. By the time she collapsed on the side of her bed, her legs were trembling and her face was as white as her sheets.

If she hadn't been in obvious pain, Tucker would have been sorely tempted to throttle her. What the devil was the matter with her? He glowered down at her, making no attempt to help her when she tiredly swung her legs up on the mattress and pulled the sheet over her. "You made your point. You don't want me to touch you. Would you like a pain pill? You look like you could use it."

If he was expecting an argument, he didn't get one. "I think you're right," she agreed.

Without a word he went to the kitchen for her medicine and a glass of water, finding his way in the dark as if he'd been doing it for years. Returning on silent feet, he stood at her side while she downed the pill, then set the glass of water on the nightstand.

He was irritated with her. Lacey could almost feel the frustration seething in him. Half expecting him to stalk off to his bed on the couch any second, she knew she had to find a way to break the tension she herself had created. "I'm sorry," she said huskily. "It isn't that I don't want you to touch me…I mean I do…" She floundered to a stop, groaning. Oh, God, what was she doing! "What I mean—"

He cocked a brow at her and made no attempt to conceal the grin that stole across his mouth. "Yes? I can't wait to hear the rest of this."

Damn him, he was enjoying this! "I mean I really do appreciate you taking care of me when you really don't have to," she said quickly. "If I seem ungrateful sometimes, it's just because I'm not used to anyone waiting on me."

"Are you sure that's all there is to it?"

"*Yes!*"

Her answer was too quick, too desperate, and they both

knew it. But he leaned over her only to tuck her in. "If you need anything, even if it's just someone to chase away another bogeyman, call me."

He should have pulled back then. There was no reason to linger. But his eyes dropped to her mouth and all he could think of was how long it had been since he'd kissed her. *Eight years!* Did he even remember what she tasted like? Suddenly it was imperative that he find out.

Lacey watched his mouth draw nearer and knew she should push him away. But her arms clutched the sheet to her breasts, refusing to move. Then his lips brushed hers and suddenly it was difficult to breathe, let alone think. His kiss was hardly more than a promise of things to come, a whisper of heat, a stroke of need, a tangling of breaths that lasted only an instant. It was an instant too long. In the time it took two hearts to beat in unison, they both realized that nothing had changed. He was lightning; she was kindling. They had only to touch to ignite.

Chapter 3

The pain pill did everything that Lacey had hoped it would do. It numbed her senses and clouded her mind, dragging her down into a bottomless void that was dark and dreamless. Exhausted, she slept like the dead, never moving so much as a muscle. But when she woke the next morning to bars of sunlight filtering through the blinds and shining directly in her eyes, her brain was fuzzy from the drug and just barely functioning. Work, she thought groggily, pushing her tousled hair from her eyes to stare blearily at the clock. It was already eight-thirty. She had to get up...get dressed...open the shop....

Without another thought, she rolled out of bed just as she did every morning, only to cry out as pain clawed at her with razor-sharp talons. Too late, the doctor's warning that she wouldn't feel the full effects of the accident for twenty-four hours came flooding back to her in a black wave of pain. Staggering, she sank back down to the edge of the bed, sweat beading her brow.

Tucker shot up off the couch at her first cry, his heart

pounding. Instinct had him running into her room before
he'd even blinked the sleep from his eyes. "What?" he
demanded hoarsely when he found her struggling to rise
from the side of the bed. "What's wrong?"

"My legs..." she began, only to have the rest of her
words turn to dust at the sight of him.

He wore white jockey shorts. Nothing else. And he
looked magnificent. Later, Lacey was sure, she'd amend
that description to something less flattering, but for now all
she could do was stare at him. His angled jaw dark with a
night's stubble of beard, his brown eyes heavy lidded and
sexy, he was every woman's fantasy of what was masculine. Broad shouldered and lean hipped, he had a muscled
chest splattered with golden hair that the darkness had hidden from her last night. With a will of their own, her eyes
followed the sensuous path that arrowed down his hard
belly until it disappeared into the elastic waistband of his
shorts.

Tucker felt the touch of her gaze as surely as if she had
reached out and trailed her fingers across him, making him
ache with just a look. Suddenly realizing that his arousal
must be blatantly obvious to her and that her gown, for all
its demureness, was as revealing as tissue paper in the
morning light, he bit out a terse oath and pivoted sharply
on his heel. "Put something on," he grated, and disappeared into the living room.

Shaken to her core, Lacey blindly closed her fingers
around her pale yellow robe. He'd kissed her, she thought,
staring after him and wincing. He'd leaned over her and
brushed her mouth with his, and she'd wanted to melt. Just
like chocolate in the noon sun. Mortified, she closed her
eyes and clutched her robe to her wildly racing heart. Oh,
God, how could she still be so susceptible to him? At just
the touch of his lips, she'd wanted to pull him down to her,
into her, as if the past had never happened, as if nothing
mattered but satisfying the longings that he fanned to life
without even trying.

It had to be the pain pill she'd taken, she told herself, grasping for excuses. The drug had lowered her defenses, dulled her reasoning, destroyed her inhibitions.

Oh, come off it, Lacey! a voice in her head jeered. *It wasn't even in your bloodstream yet. Face it. You wanted Tucker Stevens eight years ago and you still do.*

As a child she'd wanted chocolate chip cookies, too, she reminded herself in growing desperation. Until she'd made herself sick on them. She wasn't going to make that same mistake with Tucker. Not this time. They might strike sparks off each other like exploding Roman candles, but he wasn't the man for her and he never would be. He belonged to the regimented world of her father, a world she knew from experience she had no place in.

Oh, she'd tried, she ruefully admitted. She'd spent most of her childhood struggling to conform to the protocol expected of the daughter of a diplomat. The only trouble was that she never quite got the hang of it. She was too curious, too impetuous, too outspoken. She seemed to constantly jump from the frying pan into the fire, much to the disgust of her three older sisters, who always knew what to say, how to dress, which fork to use. She'd chafed at rules that made no sense to her, until she'd gradually come to realize that she would always be something of a nonconformist.

She hadn't come to that conclusion easily. Even after she'd left home and gone out on her own, she'd found herself still trying to conform, trying to follow in her sisters' footsteps. Without the least bit of trouble they had all finished college, fallen in love with men Marcus Conrad heartily approved of, then settled down into domesticity without a whimper of protest. When she'd tried college, she'd changed majors a half dozen times, not to mention colleges. After four years she'd decided she was only throwing away time and money because all she really wanted to do was buy and sell antiques. With her father's blessing and financial assistance, she'd moved to New Orleans and opened her shop.

When she met Fred Parker and fell in love with him, she'd thought she had finally found her niche in life. He was a doctor, a member of one of the city's oldest families, someone her family would approve of. Convincing herself that her rebelliousness against other people's expectations was just a phase she'd finally outgrown, she'd thought she loved him enough to deal with what would be required of her as his wife. Then, the night he proposed to her, he'd made it clear that he expected her to give up her business and devote herself to the causes that his mother had always championed. She would be the perfect doctor's wife, and one day he would follow in his father's and grandfather's footsteps and become chief of staff at the hospital his family had founded.

What had sounded like heaven to him was anything but that to her. After spending her childhood trying to force herself into a mold that never fit, she'd known she couldn't do it. She couldn't be anything but what she already was. She'd turned him down and never once regretted it.

After all that, how could she have forgotten that men who belonged to neat, structured worlds were to be avoided?

Dressed in stone-washed jeans and a mint-green shirt, his jaw still shadowed and in need of a shave, Tucker approached the door to her bedroom with a caution that irritated the hell out of him. You're not walking through a mine field, he told himself angrily. But then he remembered the way she'd looked sitting on the side of the bed, her hair catching the morning light, the soft, womanly curves of her breasts peeking out at him from the gossamer folds of her nightgown. His body instantly hardened in reaction, drawing a curse from him.

It's your own fault, he told himself coldly. When you charge into a woman's bedroom first thing in the morning, you can't expect to find her dressed for church. Next time have the sense to knock. No, he amended, next time don't insist on playing big brother to someone who's not your sister. Then don't compound the problem by sitting in the dark telling her stories so you can hear her laugh the way you remembered. And don't kiss her, damn it! That was really smart, Stevens! Maybe you really do need that vacation on Aruba after all, because your judgment stinks. You keep playing with dynamite and it's going to blow up in your face.

Stopping two feet from her bedroom door, he reached out and rapped curtly on the door frame. "Do you need help getting dressed?" he called to her and prayed that she didn't. After the way he'd reacted to the sight of her in that gown, he didn't know if he'd be able to keep his hands off her if he had to help her take it off. What a mess!

Still hugging her robe, Lacey jumped like a scalded cat, her widened eyes flying to the doorway. But he was standing well back, out of sight. "No! I can do it…I'm perfectly capable…" She cringed at her high-voiced stuttering, swallowing the panicky words before they could collect in her throat and choke her. She didn't sound as if she was capable of stringing two coherent sentences together, let alone dressing herself!

Sternly ordering herself to stop acting like a blushing teenager, she struggled into her robe, ignoring the needle-like pricks of pain that stung her stiff muscles. Her hand at her throat, checking her buttons, she drew in a bracing breath. "You can come in."

She thought she was ready to face him again, to pretend that the attraction between them was as invisible as the silence that began to vibrate in the air the second he stepped into the doorway. But when her gaze intersected his, she knew it wasn't going to work. She had never been any good at hiding her feelings—her face was too expressive, her emotions too close to the surface. She couldn't look him in the eye and not see him standing over her in his underwear. She couldn't see his smile without recalling the feel of his mouth on hers, the taste of him seeping through her.

Her cheeks fiery, she brought her thoughts up short, but she wasn't able to stop the panic racing through her. She wanted him gone, needed him gone, her life back to normal! And the only way she was going to do that, she decided, was to convince him that she was well on her way to recovery.

Her face carefully devoid of expression, she rose to her feet with a steadiness that never hinted at the pain it cost her. Forcing a smile, she said lightly, "Unless you've got first dibs on the bathroom, I think I'll take a bath."

"No, I—" Expecting her to be too stiff to move, he started forward to help her when she stepped toward the bathroom. "Wait! You shouldn't be walking on that bruised leg. You should be in bed."

"Actually, I should already be in the shop getting ready to open," she contradicted him without slowing her pace. "Looks like I'm going to be a little late today."

His arms out to catch her if she so much as swayed, Tucker raised his brows. She had to be kidding! "You were almost killed two days ago. You can't go back to work yet."

He knew it was the wrong thing to say the minute she glanced over her shoulder at him and arched a brow. "Oh, no? Watch me!"

"You're damn right I'll watch you," he growled as she reached the bathroom. "I'll watch you fall right on your face if you're not careful—"

But instead of falling on *her* face, she sharply shut the bathroom door in *his*. His nose almost flattened by it, he glared at the wooden panels, muttering a curse that should have blistered the paint. He reached for the door handle, intent on pushing his way in after her, when he suddenly remembered his vow to knock on a door before barging in and making a fool of himself again. Abruptly lifting a clenched fist, he pounded against the door in a way that was sure to strain the wood. "Lacey, this conversation is *not* over!"

She jerked open the door, not the least bit intimidated by his thunderous expression as she asked suspiciously, "You're not one of those men who thinks a woman needs a man to tell her how to run her life, are you?"

He scowled. Did he look like a chauvinist to her? "No, of course not—"

"Good. Then you agree that when I go back to work is my decision, not yours." Patting his arm as if he were a little boy who had to be consoled when he lost an argument, she gave him an innocent smile. "Now that we have that settled, would you be a sweetheart and get me some clean clothes? Just grab my blue jean skirt and white eyelet blouse out of the closet and some underwear from my dresser. You can leave them on the chair here by the door."

When he didn't budge but continued to frown down at her as if he couldn't quite figure her out, she knew she was teasing a cat, a very large cat who could pounce on her at any moment. But for the first time since he'd come back into her life, she felt as if she were holding her own with him. Exhilaration flowed through her. "I may be a while— I'm going to see if I can soak some of the stiffness out of my muscles—so don't wait breakfast for me. I'll eat later."

"Damn it, you're in no shape—"

The door shut smartly in his face. This time it stayed closed.

Gritting his teeth, Tucker gave serious consideration to breaking it down. The woman was driving him right up the wall, and he had a feeling she knew it. Did she think she only had to widen her eyes at him and give him a sweet smile to get her way? Well, he had news for her! He wasn't such a soft touch. She might have been able to get away with murder when she was a kid—he'd heard the stories of how, as Marcus's favorite, she'd wrapped him around her little finger—but he wasn't her father. Her little tricks weren't going to work with him, he promised himself as he strode to her closet. The only reason he was getting her clothes for her was that he wouldn't want to touch her nearly as much if she was dressed in some decent clothes. Preferably something that covered her from neck to ankle like a sack. What the hell was an eyelet blouse, anyway?

Hot water swirling about her shoulders, Lacey leaned her head back against the edge of the tub and closed her eyes, letting her mind empty. A sigh of contentment rose in the thick, steam-clouded air that fogged the mirror over the sink. Heaven, she thought dreamily. This was nothing short of heaven. One by one her tight muscles loosened, then relaxed completely. Feeling boneless, she could have slid down the drain without a word of protest. With very little urging, she could have stayed there all day.

But she had a business to run. If that wasn't enough to pull her from her bath, the thought of Tucker was. She wouldn't let him think, even for a minute, that she was hiding from him in the bathroom.

Reluctantly she left the tub and reached for a towel. Wrapping it around her, she made sure it was snugly tucked between her breasts before she moved to the door. Would her clothes be waiting for her on the other side? she wondered, her green eyes suddenly twinkling. Somehow she doubted it. It wasn't often that Tucker allowed himself to be outmaneuvered. If he could have gotten his hands on her—

Images played before her mind's eye—strong, knowing hands sliding over her, removing the towel with an ease that left her gasping, wanting something she couldn't even put a name to.... Suddenly realizing what she was doing, Lacey brought her wayward thoughts to a bone-jarring halt, the flush her bath had brought to her cheeks deepening. This had to stop! she told herself sternly. She couldn't afford to let Tucker invade her thoughts at will, teasing her with fantasies that she had no intention of allowing to come to pass.

Cautiously easing the door open, she glanced around, half expecting Tucker to be lying in wait somewhere to resume their argument. But the bedroom was empty, and from the kitchen she caught the sound of pots and pans clattering, the scent of bacon frying. And her clothes were neatly piled on the ladder-back chair right next to the bathroom door.

She reached for them, a slow smile of surprise flowing across her face. She didn't kid herself into thinking that she'd won anything more than a minor skirmish, however. No one bested Tucker that easily. Mind games were his specialty, his patience and cunning two of his biggest strengths in his job. He knew the advantage of retreat, the value of the unexpected. He could take a step back, even two, and still manage to come out on top. A wise woman wouldn't underestimate him.

Fifteen minutes later, when she stepped from the bathroom into her bedroom, she discovered to her relief that he'd already eaten and she wouldn't have to share another intimate meal with him. But he was waiting for her nonetheless. The breezy smile she had intended to give him never materialized as her gaze drifted past him to the TV tray set up next to her bed. The single plate it held was piled high with enough scrambled eggs and bacon to feed a marine.

Lacey swallowed, her eyes shifting back to his. "Is all that for me?"

"Every bite," he replied. Dropping down onto the window seat, he stretched his long legs out before him and crossed his ankles as if he were prepared to sit there as long as it took her to clean her plate. The grin he shot her was every bit as wicked as the one she'd given him just before she'd disappeared into the bathroom. "Dig in," he said, motioning for her to take a seat on the side of the bed. "You could use some fattening up. You're as thin as a toothpick."

She hesitated, wanting to protest, her confidence slipping a notch. For just a moment Tucker let his eyes feast on her without ever taking his gaze from hers. She was beautiful, he acknowledged, in spite of the circles under her eyes and the sutured cut that colored her forehead a bruised yellow. But she had something more than that, a freshness, a lack of artifice, an easiness with who and what she was that was far more potent than beauty. A man had only to look at the wild, mahogany curls that fell to her waist to want to touch, while the sight of her mouth alone could make him ache.

Dangerous, he silently warned himself as he reeled in his straying thoughts. He doubted that she even knew her own power, and that was all the more reason for him to be leery of her. But if she thought he was going to sit back and let her go to work without lifting a hand to stop her, she was in for a rude awakening.

With eyes that missed little, he followed her progress to the bed. She was moving better than she had been before the bath, but there was little chance her increased mobility would last. Once the effects of the hot water had worn off, she'd be stiff again and no doubt hurting. Waiting until she was seated on the bed and reaching for her fork, he asked, "How are you feeling?"

"Terrific," she said brightly. Too brightly. "The bath really helped." Scooping up a forkful of eggs, she looked up to find his gaze trained on her, noting her every move. The fork stopped midway to her mouth. How could she eat with him staring at her that way? "You know, you don't have to sit with me every moment. Why don't you do some sight-seeing? You should go this morning while it's cool. The humidity in the afternoons can be a real killer."

"Not today," he said easily, biting back a grin at her ploy. "I can't leave you."

She hadn't expected him to give in easily, so she only shrugged as if she didn't care in the least where he spent his day. "If that's the way you want it," she said easily, taking a bite of the egg. "But you're going to get awfully bored watching me work."

So the gloves were off and the game was on. He grinned,

relishing the clash of wills. "You'll never make it down the stairs," he predicted.

Her eyes glinted at the challenge. "Never say never," she warned. "You may have to eat it."

With renewed determination she dug into the bacon and eggs as if she hadn't eaten in a week, knowing she would need all her strength to prove to him that she really didn't need him. But even then she could eat only half of the food he'd cooked for her. "Enough," she groaned, setting the tray away from her. "If I eat all that, I'll soon be the size of a barn."

His gaze swept down her, then up again. "I don't think you've got anything to worry about," he said dryly.

Lacey felt her skin heat at the stroke of his dark eyes. Repressing the shiver of awareness that skated down her spine, she jumped to her feet, catching back a gasp of pain as her body protested the too-quick action. "I need to put on some makeup...fix my hair..."

She didn't need it, but Tucker didn't want to notice that. He rose to his feet to take her tray to the kitchen. "No one's going to see you but me, but I'm not going to object if you want to make yourself beautiful for me," he teased, throwing her a wink as he walked out with her breakfast tray in hand.

He was incorrigible. Shaking her head, Lacey moved to the old-fashioned vanity dresser where she kept her makeup. Sinking down to the matching stool, she wrinkled her nose at her pale, reflected image. With her damp hair wild and curly on her shoulders, violet shadows lining her eyes and the ugly gash on her forehead, she could easily have passed for the star attraction in a fright show. No wonder Tucker had teased her about making herself more beautiful. If she went downstairs the way she was, she'd scare away the customers!

With quick, sure strokes, she applied concealer, then foundation. After a light brush of blush and a few strokes with the mascara wand, she felt infinitely better. Her hair, however, looked as if it hadn't been combed in a week. Deciding it would be much cooler and less trouble if it was swept up, she pulled a banana clip from her top drawer, then reached for her brush.

Forgetting her injury, she lifted her right arm to run the brush through her hair, but it never connected with her scalp. Pain, as white and hot as a streak of lightning, flashed out from her shoulder. Grabbing at the top of her arm with her left hand, she gasped, the brush falling from her fingers.

In the living room Tucker was folding the blankets he'd used to make his bed when he heard the brush clatter to the floor. "You all right?" he called out.

"My shoulder..." Lacey grimaced, drawing a deep breath and slowly releasing it. Gradually the burning pain eased. When Tucker suddenly appeared behind her, his worried eyes zeroing in on hers in the mirror, she explained, "It's nothing, really. I just forgot about my shoulder and tried to brush my hair."

He glared down at the brush as if it were to blame for her pain, then scooped it up. "How could you forget about it?" he demanded. "It had to hurt when you got dressed."

"No, I didn't have to lift my arm above my shoulder." And both her bra and her blouse fastened in the front, reducing any strain on her injury. She held out her left hand for the brush. "I guess I'll just have to do it left-handed."

In answer, he framed her head in his hands and turned her eyes back to the mirror. "I'll do it," he said gruffly and stopped the objection he could see forming on her lips by simply pulling the brush through her hair.

Letting his hands come in contact with her mass of reddish-brown curls was a mistake. Tucker realized that the minute his eyes met hers in the mirror, but he wasn't surprised. He'd done nothing but make mistakes with her from the moment he'd stepped into her hospital room. If he had any sense, he'd accept her insistence that she didn't need his help, then get his butt on the first plane to Aruba. But then he remembered her white face drawn with pain when she'd tried to get out of bed this morning, her startled cry just now. Without the slightest hesitation he lifted the brush and brought it down with a long, slow, sweeping motion.

Silk. Her hair was like silk under his fingers as he lifted it off her neck and ran the brush through it. What would it feel like flowing across his chest, his thighs? A man could lose himself in all that softness and die happy. Seduced by the thought, he gripped the brush handle as his body tightened with need.

Mesmerized, Lacey watched his every movement, his every change of expression in the mirror. What was he thinking? Feeling? He was so close her back and hips were scorched by his nearness. Did the heat burn in his stomach as it did in hers? Did he want to melt with it? Did he know that with every tug of the brush, she found it harder not to lean back against him and close her eyes and place herself trustingly in his hands?

Of course he did, a voice in her head retorted. Tucker Stevens was a master at seduction. How many times was she going to let him hurt her before she realized that?

Pulling forward abruptly, she picked up the hair clip and held it out to him. "If you'll just pull it all back and secure it with this, it should be fine," she said coolly, and had no idea how she managed to find her voice.

Tucker stared at the clip, the set of his jaw tense when he finally reached for it without saying a word. But securing the ornament wasn't nearly as simple as she'd made it sound. He fumbled with it awkwardly, cursing when his fingers brushed the back of her neck and she stiffened. Seconds stretched into an eternity. Finally, just when he thought he'd never get the hang of the blasted thing, it latched in place.

Lacey, her heart thundering as if she were balanced on the edge of a cliff, immediately rose to her feet with a murmured "Thank you," and stepped away from him. Work, she thought, anxious to put some space between them. She needed work to distract her. "I'd better see about

opening the shop,'' she said quickly and started toward the
door.

Tucker strode after her, his long legs making short work
of the distance she had covered as he quickly caught up
with her at the head of the stairs. "You're really going to
go through with this, aren't you?" he demanded in annoyance. "Just to prove to me that you can. Well, go ahead."
Irritated, he gestured to the narrow steps that dropped
sharply before them, motioning for her to precede him. "I
can't stop you. I'm not even going to try. I'm just here to
pick up the pieces at the bottom."

"Oh, quit being a crepe hanger," she replied, starting
down the stairs. "I'm not independently wealthy, you
know. I can't afford to just close everything up when
there's not that much wrong with me. I've got bills to pay.
I've got to work."

"What you're going to do is break your pretty little neck
if you're not careful," he grumbled, watching her like a
hawk as he followed her down the stairs. "Then how're
you going to work, huh? Have you thought of that?"

"Of course not. Because I'm not going to—"

Her boast ended on a gasp as her badly bruised thigh
chose that moment to tighten up. Caught in the act of stepping down to the next step, all her weight on her injured
limb, her leg started to crumble.

Close behind her, his curses turning the air blue, Tucker
snatched her up against his chest with a speed that left her
head spinning. As the world dropped away from her feet,
she clutched at him, her arms flying around his neck. Her
eyes lifted to his. Stunned by his closeness and the sudden
turn of events, she felt her heart stop. For the life of her,
she couldn't think of a thing to say.

Tucker didn't have any such problem. He bit out a word
that was better left unspoken. "Stupid," he lashed out at
her from only inches away, "that was really stupid! Of all
the stubborn, pigheaded—" Furious, frustrated, so angry
he couldn't think of another printable adjective, he glared

at her and made the mistake of dropping his eyes to her mouth. His hands bit into her; his control snapped. Groaning in defeat, he crushed his mouth to hers.

This was no mere brushing of lips, no teasing reminder of a kiss from the past that was better left forgotten. He wanted more than that, intended to have more than that. Roughly forcing her lips apart, his tongue dove into the dark, hidden recesses of her mouth, taking, seducing, stealing her sweetness like a man who had gone too long without the taste of honey. No one was more surprised than he when it wasn't enough. He muttered against her mouth and didn't know if it was a curse or a prayer. All he knew was he had to have more. Gathering her closer, he took the kiss deeper.

Senses whirling, her heart galloping like a thoroughbred heading for the finish line, Lacey tried to summon up all the reasons she couldn't be in Tucker's arms being kissed as she hadn't been kissed in eight impossibly long years. But her mind had emptied at the first touch of his lips. She couldn't think, couldn't move, couldn't do anything but feel. And Lord, how he made her feel! Her blood flowed like warm molasses, slow and hot through her veins, igniting little flames deep inside her that set her burning. She strained against him, wanting to wrap her arms around him, aching for him to fan the flames of the fire higher and higher until they were both consumed by the heat.

Her breasts rubbed against his chest as she pressed against him, driving him wild. Too fast, he thought, the fire in his blood pushing him to madness. Time was spinning too fast, the world turning upside down. His body was already hot and hard for her, urging him to take her then and there, on the stairs, like a savage claiming a prize. After nothing more than a kiss.

The thought sobered him as nothing else could. Wrenching his mouth from hers, he swore. What the hell was he doing?

At the murderous look in his eyes, Lacey plummeted

back to earth with a jolt. Dear God, had she lost her mind? This was the same man who had once broken her young heart, the same man who had rejected her because her experience was so far inferior to that of the other women in his life. *You're too young, Lace. You don't even know what you're asking for.* Just the echo of his words still had the power to make the steam rise in her ears. If he thought she was going to give him a second chance to reject her, he could think again!

Still held tightly against his chest, she crossed her arms over her breasts and looked him right in the eye. She knew her rejection would have been a heck of a lot more effective if she hadn't just practically dissolved in his arms, but it was too late for regrets. Fighting a blush, she said coldly, "We better get something straight right now. You may be on vacation and looking for a good time, but I'm not it. If you want a fling, then you'd better catch the first plane to Aruba."

He eyed her irritably. "Just because I kissed you doesn't mean I'm looking for an affair."

She snorted at that. "This from the man who has women in countries I've never even heard of?"

"If you believe that, I've got some swampland in Florida you might be interested in. Anyone who fools around that much in this day and age is asking for trouble." Stomping down the stairs, he pushed open the door to the shop and crossed to an antique chaise longue positioned near the counter in the middle of the shop. "For your information, I'm not looking for a good time or even a vacation, for that matter," he said flatly as he eased her down onto the chaise, then stood over her like a furious grizzly. "I've been ordered to take some time off. I don't want it, but I didn't have any say-so in the matter. All I want to do is go back to work. Since that's not possible right now, Marcus asked me to check on you. He was worried. It looks like he had reason to be."

Just listening to his voice, she could almost have believed he wanted nothing to do with her. But the heat of the kiss was still between them every time their eyes met. "If Dad were here, I'm sure he would agree I'm perfectly capable of working," she said, deciding it was best to let him change the subject. "Now if you'll excuse me, I've got things to do."

She started to get up to open the shop, but Tucker stopped her in her tracks. "You stay put. I'll do it. Just tell me what you want done."

She should have insisted that she could do it herself. Now, more than ever, it was imperative that she get him out of her life as soon as possible. But her energy was quickly flagging, her muscles once again constricting. She gave him the key to the front door and told him how to raise the retractable metal bars that protected the front of the store.

He did as she instructed, then perched on a stool behind the counter, waiting for the first sale of the day. Over the course of the morning several people came in, but no one bought anything. A few people told Lacey they were checking prices and would probably be back later, but they didn't come back. Puzzled, Tucker watched a man and woman whisper to each other over a lamp, then leave without even bothering to haggle with Lacey over the price. "Are your mornings always this slow? How come no one's buying anything? I would have sworn that couple that was just in here was interested in that lamp."

"Some weekdays are slower than others, but that's not the problem. It's John Solomon." At his inquiring look, she explained, "He's a competitor. The couple that was looking at the lamp didn't buy mine because they probably saw one in his shop that was much cheaper. He's cut into my walk-in sales, as well as those of every other dealer in the area, by selling his merchandise at nearly wholesale prices."

"How can he manage to stay in business at that rate?"

She shrugged. "If he gets the merchandise cheap

enough, he could get by on sheer volume alone. I wouldn't be worried if that was all he'd done, but that's just the beginning. I make most of my money from estate liquidation sales, but that's all but dried up over the last six months.''

He frowned. "Why?"

"In order to get the estate, different dealers bid on it, and Solomon keeps getting the bid. Or he did until last week," she amended, a satisfied smile stealing across her mouth. "I outbid him on the St. John estate. The St. Johns were in shipping, and the family plantation was filled to the brim with the most fantastic antiques I've ever seen in my life. Every dealer in town fought to get his hands on that estate, including Solomon. And I got it! He's probably still gnashing his teeth over it."

The sound of a truck grinding to a stop in the alley cut through the conversation. Tucker stepped into the storeroom at the rear of the shop and pushed open the back door. "You expecting a delivery?" he called over his shoulder.

"My furniture!" Lacey exclaimed in delight, struggling to her feet. "From the estate. The sale's already been advertised for this weekend, and the furniture was supposed to arrive today or tomorrow. I can't wait to see it!"

"Neither can I," the man who stepped through the front door said mockingly. "I hope you don't mind if I watch the unloading."

Lacey turned slowly, but she already knew who stood in her doorway casting a long, unwelcome shadow. John Solomon.

Chapter 4

For all her dislike of him, Lacey recognized Solomon as one of the shrewdest businessmen she'd ever had the misfortune to come into contact with. In the two years he had been in New Orleans, he'd managed to establish himself as one of the best known and most successful dealers in the city. Some of his resentful competitors had maligned his business practices behind his back and called him a cutthroat. Lacey didn't doubt for a minute that Solomon would have taken the label as a compliment. Ambitious to a fault, he was a man who had little use for scruples.

Not that you could tell it to look at him, Lacey thought as she watched him walk toward her with long, sure strides. Dressed in an Italian suit that was as black as his conservatively cut hair, he had a confidence about him that seemed to say "Trust me." Lacey didn't. He was tall and thin to the point of gauntness, with an olive complexion and black eyes that were sharp as a buzzard's, and there was something about his easy smile and smooth friendliness that grated on her nerves. He was, she decided, just a little too smooth, too perfect, to be real.

"That's it, isn't it?" he boomed in his big, thundering voice, his smile wide as he looked past her through the storage area to the delivery door standing open at the back of the shop. "The St. John estate? I saw the truck turn the corner into the alley and figured that had to be it." Apparently unperturbed that she had bested him in acquiring the estate, he stopped before her, his eyes bright with excitement. "I saw your ad in this morning's paper for the sale. It was terrific! That and the St. John name are bound to bring buyers in from all over the state." He practically rubbed his hands together in anticipation. "This weekend's going to increase all our sales!"

She seriously doubted if he was interested in increasing anyone's sales but his own, but she only said, "I hope so. It's been a slow summer." She wanted him out of there, his prying eyes away from her merchandise, but Tucker walked up just then and she had no choice but to introduce the two men.

His face impassive, Tucker offered the older man his hand. "Lacey tells me you're a dealer, too."

"That's right," Solomon replied. "My shop's a couple of blocks over, by the church." Returning his gaze to Lacey, he suddenly noticed the cut on her forehead and the paleness no amount of makeup could hide. His smile abruptly turned to a frown. "Hey, what happened? Are you all right?"

Considering how he'd done everything he could to drive her out of business, his concern for her health was a little hard to swallow. She certainly had no intention of telling him about her run-in with the armored-car robber. "I'm fine," she hedged. "I just…had a little accident."

"Then I'd hate for you to have a big one," he retorted. "You look like you ought to be in bed."

"I told her the same thing," Tucker said, giving her an I-told-you-so look. "But it didn't do much good."

"What about the sale Saturday?" Solomon asked, frowning as if he were truly worried about her. "Are you sure you're going to be able to handle it? You're going to have a real crowd on your hands. Maybe you should consider rescheduling it or get some help...."

If he was hinting that he'd be happy to offer his services, he could have saved his breath. She'd rather have turned to a water moccasin for assistance! "That won't be necessary," she said stiffly. "I'm fine. Really. And Tucker's here to help me with the heavy moving. I should be back to my old self by Saturday."

The older man had no choice but to accept her refusal with easy grace. "If you change your mind, just give me a call." He looked longingly at the furniture the truck driver was just starting to unload. "You've got some damn fine merchandise there. I'd like to get a better look at it, but I can see you want to get it unloaded and go over it yourself. Maybe some other time."

Lacey didn't commit herself. "Maybe."

If he noticed her reticence, he gave no sign of it. "I'll let you get to it, then. Good luck with the sale."

He was gone as quickly as he'd appeared, leaving behind a tense silence. Tucker stared after him, wanting to ask Lacey what that was all about, but the truck driver appeared in the back door with a delicate three-legged embroidered fire screen that looked incredibly fragile in his large hands. "Where do you want this put, Ms. Conrad?"

"Over here—"

She had time to take only a single step away from the chaise longue before she found Tucker standing in her path. "Sit," he ordered. "If you're determined to wear yourself out working, you're going to do it sitting down. You tell me where you want the stuff. I'll do the manual labor."

She gnawed her bottom lip, considering. The St. John estate was the biggest and most exquisite collection she'd ever handled. She was dying to get her hands on it, to inspect every piece, to feel the old but beautifully finished

wood under her palms. But from the set of Tucker's jaw
she knew she'd have to fight him every step of the way.
Even if she'd had the strength, she was suddenly tired of
arguing, of constantly pitting her will against his.

Without a word of argument, she sat back down on the
chaise. "Just put everything in the storage room for now.
Later I'll want to switch it with the furniture I already have
on the floor, but for now we just need to get the truck
unloaded."

He nodded, then strode off to help the driver, but not
before Lacey saw the amused satisfaction twinkling in his
brown eyes. He obviously felt this was one skirmish he'd
won. They were even.

The next hour was spent unloading one treasure after
another. Tucker didn't know he was handling the work of
such masters as Hepplewhite, Chippendale and Sheraton,
but as one piece after another was carefully placed in the
storeroom, he recognized quality when he saw it. The de-
signs were classic, the woods rich walnut and oak and
cherry. Now that he had seen it, Tucker could understand
why John Solomon had come running when he'd seen the
delivery truck. There wasn't one piece that couldn't have
belonged to a museum.

After the last table was carried inside and the driver rattled off in the truck, Tucker surveyed the crowded storeroom in amazement. "All this was in one house?" he asked
Lacey. "That must be some house."

"It is." Lacey chuckled as he left the storeroom and
rejoined her in the shop. "A plantation out on River Road.
Normally I'd have the sale there, but the house is being
sold and the heirs don't want the grounds trampled by the
crowd this sale is expected to draw. Lord, I hope they're
right. About the crowd," she explained. "I'm counting on
this to get me out of a real bind."

Pulling the stool behind the counter closer to the chaise,
he sat down and hooked his heels on the bottom rung, his

brows knitting. "Does Marcus know you're having financial trouble?"

"No."

"Why the hell not? You know he'd help you."

She nodded. There wasn't a doubt in her mind that her father would wire her whatever she needed and never expect her to pay him back. But she couldn't ask him. "Dad loaned me the money to start the business," she admitted quietly. "At the time, I promised myself that I would stand on my own two feet, or I'd go down fighting, but I wouldn't ask him for more."

Pride. He hadn't expected the spoiled, willful girl he remembered to have so much pride. "Then sell out," he suggested. "Move out of New Orleans. Somewhere safer. You can start over."

"Move away from New Orleans?" she repeated, stunned. "No, I couldn't." She'd traveled all over the world with her father and never truly felt as if she belonged anywhere until she'd come here. "This is home. And even if I was willing to move, I couldn't sell out. I know it doesn't look like it now, but I was really making a go of it before the robberies and John Solomon pulled the rug out from under me. This is the only thing I've ever succeeded at. If I sell out now, I'd be admitting I just couldn't hack it."

And that was something her pride would never let her do. He knew that because he would feel the same way if he was in her shoes. She was a fighter, just as he was. She wouldn't accept defeat any more easily than he would. And that disturbed him more than he wanted to admit.

"Then you'll just have to make sure your sale's a success," he said, and promised himself that he wouldn't be there to see her do it. He didn't want to find another reason to like Lacey Conrad. And he sure as hell didn't want to take on her battles as his own. He had enough problems as it was.

* * *

That day and the next fell into a pattern that they both welcomed with a sigh of relief. The approaching sale, the pricing of the furniture and then the arrangement of it in the shop filled the long hours between morning and sunset and gave them little time to think of anything but the work that needed to be done. Impatient with her sore muscles, Lacey found herself jumping up off the chaise to help Tucker move the heavier pieces before she remembered her injuries. The pain would catch her by surprise, but then she'd push it aside and help him anyway. Tucker grumbled but didn't try to stop her. And when Marcus called several times to make sure she really was all right, neither her sore muscles nor her precarious financial position was mentioned. Gradually Lacey's strength returned.

The tension between them never completely evaporated, but they learned to ignore it as they discussed everything from where to put a banjo clock to show it off to its best advantage to how the weather would affect the sale. If the memory of the two kisses they'd shared sometimes rose before them at unexpected moments and set the air humming, they didn't by so much as a glance allow the other to see a need each refused to acknowledge. The nights, however, were a different story.

Once they went upstairs each evening, everything changed. There was no work to distract them, and with its absence the surprisingly friendly conversation they'd shared downstairs dried up like a shallow pond in the desert. Silence stretched and grew. Tension returned, uninvited, and their eyes refused to meet. They both escaped to their separate beds as soon as possible, but the darkness that engulfed the apartment only seemed to sharpen their awareness of each other. Every breath, every whisper of movement was exaggerated by the quiet of the night. Sleep was a long time coming.

Despite that, Lacey woke the third morning feeling much better. She was still stiff and bruised and haunted by an occasional twinge, but as she dressed in a pale yellow blouse and white slacks, she didn't ache as she had the two previous mornings. And her energy was back. Her shoulder throbbed when she lifted her arms to braid her hair in a long ponytail, but the mild discomfort she experienced was something she could deal with. She was confident she could manage just about anything now, including the stairs, which she'd insisted on taking under her own power even after her near-disastrous first attempt.

Shying away from that memory, she stepped from the bathroom and knew it was time to confront Tucker. Somehow she had to convince him that there was no longer any reason for him to postpone his vacation. Remembering how she'd tossed and turned last night during a dream in which he'd played havoc with her senses, she knew it was none too soon.

She didn't broach the subject, however, until after breakfast. She had planned to wait until they were downstairs and on less intimate ground, but he looked too comfortable, too *right* sitting across the table from her in a pair of old jeans and a tan-and-white-striped shirt. He'd been watching her all morning, his thoughts concealed behind the dark, enigmatic shutters of his eyes. Setting her coffee cup back in its saucer, she stifled the urge to wipe her suddenly damp palms down her thighs. When she lifted her eyes, she found his waiting for hers, just as she'd expected.

"Now that I'm feeling better, there's no reason for you to stick around here baby-sitting me," she said as she met his gaze unflinchingly. "When did you plan to leave for Aruba?"

So she wanted him gone. He wasn't surprised. From the very beginning she'd fought against his help, against his intrusion into her life, tolerating him because he'd given her no choice in the matter. He should have been relieved that over the course of the past few days she'd needed less and less of his assistance. Ironically, her growing self-sufficiency had only made him want to touch her more. It wasn't logical, damn it!

Setting his own cup down, he stared at her shoulder as if he could see through the lightweight material of her blouse. "How's the shoulder?"

"Better. I can even put my hair up now."

He'd noticed. With a will of their own, his eyes trailed across her shoulder to the graceful line of her naked neck. He stood abruptly and carried his plate and coffee cup to the sink. "And the thigh? The doctor said that was an ugly bruise you had. I know you've been going up and down the stairs by yourself, but I've always been right by you to catch you. Are you sure you're ready to be on your own just yet?"

It would have been easy to say no, she wasn't sure of anything, especially where he was concerned. But she couldn't allow herself to become dependent on him, to grow used to his presence in her life, not without being devastated when he left. "I'm sure," she said firmly as she, too, rose to her feet. Flexing her knees, she grinned gamely. "See, nothing to it. The leg works, the shoulder works, everything works. I could run a marathon if I had to."

He snorted. "I wouldn't try it if I were you—"

The phone rang, cutting him off before he could tell her that he was as convinced as she was that there was no longer any reason for him to stay. Lacey moved to answer it. "I'll get it."

At the sound of her voice Jack Ryan said, "Ms. Conrad? This is Detective Ryan. How are you feeling?"

Surprised, she said, "Much better, thank you. How is the investigation going?"

"That's why I'm calling," he replied in satisfaction. "We arrested Robert Martin this morning. Can you come down to the station this morning and pick him out of a lineup?"

Unconsciously, Lacey's fingers tightened on the phone. "Yes, of course," she said huskily. "I'll come now, before I open the shop."

* * *

She'd thought it would be easy. All she had to do was walk into the police station, pick the man who'd tried to kill her out of a group of other men, then walk out. It should have been that simple. It was anything but.

The minute she stepped into the police station with Tucker at her side, unwanted memories of her attack hit her in the face—sirens somewhere in the distance, fear clutching at her throat when she regained consciousness in the hospital, strangers bending over her asking questions, probing at her memory when she was too numb to think, too hurt to want to relive it all again.

She could have gone the rest of her life and gladly forgotten everything about that night. But now it was back, hovering there before her eyes in vivid detail. Without even realizing it she slowed her pace, dreading what was to come.

Tucker was almost three steps ahead of her before he realized she was no longer at his side. Stopping abruptly, he turned back to wait for her, his eyes narrowing in concern at the sight of her pale cheeks and haunted expression. The station was busy at that hour of the morning, but he didn't notice the organized chaos surrounding them. "Are you all right?" he asked worriedly. "I know this can't be easy for you, but it's got to be done."

A sorry excuse for a smile pushed up one corner of her mouth. "I know. I just didn't expect to be so nervous." Stiffening her spine, she lifted her chin and headed for the front desk. "Come on, let's get it over with."

Tucker would have taken her hand and given it a squeeze of moral support, but she no longer appeared to need him. She crossed to the desk, asked for Detective Ryan, then sat impatiently on a nearby bench while they waited for him. They didn't have long to wait. Within minutes he was striding down the hall toward them, looking as if he'd been up all night, with his tie askew, his jaw unshaven and his blue eyes tired.

But the smile that slid across his mouth was downright

smug as they rose to greet him. "Ms. Conrad, Mr. Stevens, glad you could get here so fast. I don't have to tell you how anxious we are to get this case wrapped up. We've been trying to nail this guy for months while the press has been nailing us to the wall for not doing anything. No one seemed to care that all we had to work with were two armored cars wiped free of fingerprints and four dead guards. Until you came along."

"If I had it to do over again, Mr. Ryan, I wouldn't have come along," she said dryly. "I hope this isn't going to take long."

"No, actually, there's not much to it," he assured her as he escorted them down the hall and opened the door to a dark, windowless room whose only light was provided by the row of floodlights that shone against the elevated platform against one wall. "We'll stand here in the back," he explained, stopping in the darkness and facing the stage. "Five or six suspects will file in and line up against the wall. Don't worry about them seeing you—they won't be able to see anything with those lights shining in their eyes. Each man will step forward, show a profile, then step back. If you need a second look, all you have to do is ask. *Don't*," he stressed, "make an identification if you've got even the slightest doubt. The last thing we want at this point is a mistake, so take your time and be sure."

Lacey nodded, her throat dry and scratchy as she said thickly, "Yes, of course. I'll be careful."

In the shadowy recess that engulfed them, his steely-blue eyes watched her closely. "We can start whenever you're ready."

Her stomach twisted into a knot, but she didn't turn and run as she longed to. Instead, she linked her fingers together and squared her shoulders, the small twinge of pain reminding her of what the man she was about to identify had done to her. Anger burned in her eyes. He wasn't going to get away with it! "I'm ready," she said coolly.

While the detective turned to the intercom on the wall

and spoke quietly into it, Tucker moved closer to Lacey, offering his support without saying a word. She shot him a grateful look, then stiffened as the door at one end of the platform opened and a uniformed police officer walked in. Five men filed in behind him and lined up against the wall.

At first glance, they all fit the description of Lacey's assailant. Their faces lined with boredom and indifference, they were all of medium height, with chunky builds, long, unkempt brown hair and fair complexions. But only one had tried to kill Lacey.

She saw him immediately. Second from the far end, he lounged against the wall as if he didn't have a care in the world, his black eyes insolent, his mouth mocking. He stared out into the darkness, and if Lacey hadn't known better she would have sworn he stared right at her, daring her to identify him.

Hate. It came at her in waves, easily penetrating the protective darkness that shielded her, washing over her, smothering her. Once before he'd stared at her in much the same way, his all-seeing eyes finding her in the night as he hunted her down like a helpless rabbit. Her blood turned to ice, chilling her very soul. Her common sense reminded her that she was safe; she was at the police station and there was no way he could get to her now. But the fear gripping her by the throat had nothing to do with reason. Without even realizing what she was doing, she stepped back, her entwined fingers tightening until her knuckles ached.

Tucker had been watching her, expecting her reaction. She was a strong woman, but no one could expect her to face the man who had tried to kill her without feeling something. What he hadn't been expecting, however, was his own need to hold her, to somehow protect her from the memories that still had the power to terrify her. Before he gave himself time to question what he was doing, he stepped back until his shoulder brushed hers. Covering her clinched hands with one of his own, he leaned close and whispered, "Easy, honey. He's in no position to hurt you now. You're safe."

Wordlessly, she turned her fingers into his, the endearment warming her as nothing else could have. He was right, she told herself, and concentrated on the feel of his large hand surrounding hers. Strong. She could feel his strength seeping into her, banishing the darkness threatening to close in on her. She wasn't a clinging vine—she'd gone her own way for too long to need a man to cling to—but just this once she needed someone. No, not just anyone, she thought, refusing to lie to herself. She needed him. Later there would be time to worry about that, but not now.

On her other side, Detective Ryan watched her regain control. "Do you see the man who tried to kill you?" he asked quietly.

Still holding Tucker's hand, she nodded. "The second man from the left."

Only someone who knew Jack Ryan well would have known he was pleased by her response. His expression remained unchanged. "Are you sure?"

She stepped away from the wall, releasing Tucker's hand with a grateful squeeze as she faced the detective confidently. "There isn't a doubt in my mind."

This time he grinned broadly. "Good." Turning to one of the officers at the door, he said, "That's it, Mike. Take 'em out."

It was over.

Her part in the proceedings finished for the moment, Lacey returned to her apartment with Tucker, feeling as if a ten-ton weight had been lifted off her shoulders. For the first time since her eyes had locked with Robert Martin's all those nights ago, she was safe. Any fears she had that he would be back out on the streets as soon as he could post bail were eased when Detective Ryan called several hours later to inform her that the suspect had been formally charged with murder, attempted murder and armed robbery, then denied bail.

No one was surprised that Martin had claimed innocence and refused to talk to anyone but his attorney. Anyone who had the cunning to commit three armored-car robberies that had stumped the police for months wasn't about to confess, especially when the only evidence against him was the testimony of a woman who had claimed to have seen him on a dark night. The police couldn't even use the money against him. A search of his home had turned up nothing, and half a million dollars was still missing. Despite that, Detective Ryan was convinced he had the right man. Because of all the pressure to solve the case, the trial was being pushed up to the end of the month. The D.A. wanted Martin in prison just as soon as possible.

When she finally hung up, Lacey was almost weak with relief. She turned to Tucker with a smile and quickly gave him all the latest information. "The trial's set for the end of the month, thank God! I was afraid this thing was going to drag out for months."

"You lucked out," he agreed, his answering smile not quite reaching his eyes. "Now that you're safe, you can get on with your life, and I guess I can go on to Aruba since you don't need me anymore."

The excitement glistening in her eyes dulled, though her own smile stayed firmly in place. She'd known from the moment he decided to stay that his presence in her life was only temporary. She'd never wanted him there anyway, she reminded herself. "You must be anxious to get on with your vacation," she said with forced lightness. "I never expected you to give up so much of your time for me. And I'm sure Dad didn't, either. Thank you," she said huskily. "For everything."

He shrugged. Gratitude was the last thing he wanted from her. "Like I said before, this vacation wasn't my idea anyway. Aruba wasn't going anywhere, and you needed help. Everyone does at one time or another. Forget it."

Swallowing the sudden lump in her throat, Lacey nodded. Hadn't she known all along that she was just a responsibility to him? Why was she so hurt when he said as much to her face? "All the same, I appreciate it."

"And I thought you couldn't wait to get rid of me," he mocked teasingly, wishing just for a moment that the old hostility was between them again. Maybe then it wouldn't be so hard to leave her. How had he let himself get in this position? He should have been anxious to get out of there and on to Aruba. The faster he got the damn vacation over with, the sooner he could return to work. Frowning suddenly, he moved to the phone. "Since it's so early, I might as well see if I can get a flight out this afternoon and get out of your hair."

"You're not—" Lacey bit back the rest of the denial, telling herself to let him go. If the apartment later seemed empty without him, if she found herself looking for him down in the shop, she would get used to it. Out of sight, out of mind. He would go back to his life and she would settle into her old routine and eventually forget the scent of after-shave in her bathroom and the strength of his powerful arms as he'd carried her downstairs. Smoldering glances and kisses that were better left forgotten would be remembered only in her dreams. With the passing of time they, too, would fade into nothingness. And that was just the way she wanted it, she told herself and tried to believe it.

Then he hung up the phone and turned to her to announce, "I can't get a flight out until the morning. Looks like you're stuck with me for another night."

When relief almost weakened her knees, she knew she was in trouble. When she noticed the irritation darkening his eyes, her heart constricted painfully. He was obviously anxious to be on his way. Why did that hurt so much when she didn't want him there any more than he wanted to be there?

Refusing to dig too deep for the answer, she strode into

the kitchen. "What's one more night?" she said with a nonchalance she was proud of. "Don't look so glum. By this time tomorrow you'll be lying on the beach fighting women off with a stick. Then again," she said, frowning as she remembered his well-earned reputation, "maybe you won't be fighting them off. You'll probably be in hog heaven. No wonder you're so anxious to leave." She jerked open the refrigerator and scowled at its contents. "What do you want for dinner?"

Tucker lifted a brow in surprise, amusement mixing with the annoyance in his eyes as he followed her into the kitchen. Leaning against the counter, he crossed his arms over his chest and watched her every move. He'd never known a woman who was so easy to watch. "I don't care. Anything. And I have no intention of lying on the beach."

"Or fighting off women," she added. "You'll probably be black and blue when you get back, poor baby."

His lips twitched. "Will you forget the damn women?" he growled. "There aren't any." There hadn't been for some time but he doubted that she'd believe that. "If I had my way, I'd already be on another assignment, probably in some jungle in South America. What the hell am I supposed to do on a tropical island?"

"Relax. Go fishing. Play." Not liking the images that word conjured up, she slammed the refrigerator door and turned to face him. "I'll have to go to the store. I don't see a thing in there worth eating. If you don't want the time off, why are you taking it? Go back to Washington and find yourself another assignment."

"It isn't that easy."

"Why not?"

"Because..." He hesitated, memories of the coup flashing before his eyes, turning his expression grim. It wasn't something he was ready to discuss with anyone. "I haven't taken a day off in three years," he admitted finally. "Let's just say my boss thought it was time I had a vacation."

There was something he wasn't telling her. She caught

only a glimpse of it before he turned away, shutting her out. She knew him well enough now to know that no amount of probing would get him to open up to her if he didn't want to talk. "Maybe he's right," she said quietly. "Everyone needs some time off once in a while just to get away from the pressures of—"

Outside, a car backfired almost directly in front of the shop, cutting her off in midsentence. Tucker heard only the explosion. In the blink of an eye, instincts that had been honed and sharpened by the years he'd spent living on the edge of disaster kicked into place. As quick as a slash of lightning ripping through the sky, he grabbed Lacey and pulled her to the floor, protectively covering her body with his. His body tense and ready to spring into action, the sounds of the coup echoing in his ears, he waited for the next explosion.

Frozen beneath him, her heart thundering, Lacey stared up at him and saw a side of him she had never seen before. His face was set in hard, unrelenting lines, his eyes cold and deadly. He was as taut as a bowstring ready to snap, and Lacey was suddenly afraid to move. Caught up in a waking nightmare, he hardly seemed aware of her at all.

Quelling the urge to shift into a more comfortable position, she called his name in a voice that was little more than a whisper. "Tucker? What's wrong? It was only a backfire."

Her soft words pulled at him, penetrating the red haze of remembered gunfire and bloodshed that held him in their grip. His fingers still biting into her slender shoulders, he stared down at her, blinking as awareness returned in a rush. "What?"

"It was only a backfire," she repeated gently, her eyes searching his. "Are you all right?"

His full weight pinned her to the floor and she was asking if he was all right. Suddenly realizing what he had done, he got stiffly to his feet and helped her up. "I'm fine," he replied shortly. "Are you all right?" His fingers gently ran over her injured shoulder. "Did I hurt you? God, Lace, I'm sorry!"

"I'm okay," she assured him, sweeping her hair back from her face, her eyes worried as they studied his. "Just surprised. Would you like to tell me what that was all about?"

He owed her an explanation, if nothing else. "I thought the backfire was a gunshot. I overreacted."

"But why would you think someone was shooting at us? Robert Martin is in jail."

Because maybe my boss was right. I'm too close to the edge. "In my job, you learn to react first and ask questions later," he replied. "Better safe than sorry."

Unconvinced, Lacey tried to see past the guards that shielded his thoughts from her, but he had given her the only explanation she was going to get. He was determined not to let her get too close, see too much. Maybe that was why he was still a bachelor at thirty-six. He had secrets, a whole other world of work, of danger and intrigue, that no woman could hope to compete with.

Forcing back the questions she knew he wouldn't answer, she deliberately changed the subject. "I think we both need a change of scenery. You've been here almost a week and haven't even done any sight-seeing. And I could get by without opening the shop today."

He nodded, adrenaline still pounding in his blood. "Sounds good to me. The way I feel right now, I wouldn't mind spending a few hours on Bourbon Street. I could use a drink."

Chapter 5

Less than an hour later Lacy stood outside the entrance to a gun shop and planted her feet, refusing to go in. "This is ridiculous! We should be getting ready to go out, not shopping around for a gun. I don't *need* a gun," she told Tucker for the tenth time in ten minutes when he just patiently held the door open for her. "And even if I did, I haven't the foggiest idea how to use one. With my luck, I'd probably end up shooting myself in the foot or something."

"You're not going to shoot yourself," he argued with maddening calm. "I'll make sure of that." He was also going to make sure that he didn't leave her unprotected in the crime-ridden French Quarter. "Considering the number of times you've been robbed, I'm surprised you didn't get yourself something months ago."

"The robbers weren't trying to hurt me, just steal me blind. Besides, I wasn't even home at the time."

"But what if you had been? What if you'd been in bed and someone thought you were gone?" he taunted. "You could have come face-to-face with a gun-toting thief who didn't give a damn about adding murder to his rap sheet. What would you have done then, huh? Hit him over the head with a frying pan? Unless you sleep with one under your pillow, you'd be as helpless as a baby and you know it.''

Why, she wondered in disgust, did he always have to be right? "All right, so I wouldn't be much of a threat to a burglar. A gun's not going to change that.''

"Probably not," he conceded, "but I'll sleep better at night knowing you're not completely unprotected, okay?''

"That's not much consolation when I'm the one who's going to have to shoot the thing,'' she retorted, shuddering. "They're so…ugly.''

For the first time since he'd pushed her to the floor after the backfire, he grinned. "Then I'll get you one with a pearl handle. That's the best I can do. They don't come in pink.''

She withered him with a glance. "Cute, Tucker, real cute.''

"I can only try.'' He chuckled, pulling the door wider. "Come on, let's go. We're wasting time.''

The shop was well stocked with handguns, rifles and automatic weapons, offering the hunter or serious gun collector everything he could possibly need or want. Lacey took one look at the black pistols in one of the display cases and felt her hands turn cold. She never had and never would like guns.

As if reading her mind, Tucker said, "You don't have to like it, just know how to use it.'' Glancing at the clerk behind the counter, he said, "The lady needs a pistol. Something small she can handle easily.''

"Well, let's see what I've got," the tall, balding clerk mused as he stroked his mustache and stared down at the contents of the case. "I've got a .357 Magnum that's a real beauty—''

"She doesn't need anything that powerful,'' Tucker cut in.

"Then how about a .38 Special?" he suggested, removing the snub-nosed revolver from the top shelf and laying it on the counter. "This one's specially designed for a woman's hand. It's got a slim, rosewood stock and a stainless-steel barrel, and it's light. It wouldn't do at all for a man, but a lot of my women customers just love it."

Lacey couldn't imagine anyone loving a gun. Even if it had been designed for a woman, though she didn't see anything feminine about it. Staring down at the glistening barrel, she couldn't bring herself to touch it. How could something so small look so sinister?

"Don't you have anything smaller?" she asked. "Something less...threatening."

"Lace, it's not going to do you any good if you can't threaten an intruder with it," Tucker pointed out reasonably.

"I think I have an idea of what she wants," the clerk said with a smile. "I've got something in the back you might be interested in." He hurried into the back and returned with a small, pearl-handled derringer that looked ludicrous in his large hand. "An old lady brought it in last year for cleaning and repair and never returned for it. I tried to contact her, but her phone had been disconnected and I don't know what happened to her. The bill was never paid, and we usually only keep things for six months, then get rid of them if the owner doesn't return. It's only one shot, but if you want it, you can have it for the cost of the repairs."

When he held it out to Lacey, she took it gingerly, prepared to hate it. But it was hardly bigger than her palm, nickel plated, and anything but the deadly weapon she'd expected. She didn't doubt for a moment that it could be used to kill at close range, but it looked far more like something a woman would have carried in her reticule at the turn of the century than something used to hold up a convenience store. If she had to have a gun, she'd rather it be an antique than the latest thing in firearms.

Observing the emotions flickering across her expressive face, Tucker said, "I take it you can live with that one?"

She glanced up. "If you insist. But I still don't like guns."

"Then I won't buy you another one for Christmas," he replied, grinning, then turned to the clerk. "We'll take it."

There was no waiting period, so as soon as the gun was paid for and the paperwork for a permit filled out, they went to a shooting range on the edge of town. Lacey wasn't thrilled at the idea of actually firing the derringer, but there wasn't much point in having it if she didn't know how to use it. Thankfully, however, the outdoor range was virtually deserted in the middle of the afternoon on a weekday. If she was going to make a fool of herself, she'd just as soon the whole world wasn't watching.

She followed Tucker down to the end of the covered area provided for the marksmen, and set the bullets they'd bought on the rough wooden counter in front of them. She frowned at the target that seemed a hundred miles away. "I hope you're not expecting me to hit that," she said wryly, cutting her eyes to Tucker. "You're bound to be disappointed."

"If you can hit that with this popgun, you're a better shot than I am," he said with a laugh. "Relax. Right now, all you're going to do is learn how to load it and pull the trigger. You can worry about hitting something later." Stepping closer, he held the gun between them and showed her how the weapon broke open like a shotgun for loading. "The bullet goes in here," he explained, demonstrating. "It only holds one, but you're only going to need one. It's a large caliber, so if you hit someone at close range with it, you're going to do some damage. It's not meant for distance."

Unloading the gun, he held it out to Lacey. "Okay, your turn."

Her bottom lip caught between her teeth, she did as he'd done and loaded the bullet in the chamber. Clicking it closed, she was careful not to point it at anything. "Now what?"

He moved behind her and turned her shoulders square with the target in the distance. "Okay, take a shot at the target. And don't worry about hitting it. You won't."

She nodded, sucked in a bracing breath, then aimed the small derringer at the bull's-eye a hundred yards away. The gun wasn't even the slightest bit heavy, but her hand shook with nerves. "Damn!" she whispered under her breath. Just the thought of pointing a gun at anything and pulling the trigger was enough to make her shake in her shoes! "I told you I didn't like guns," she told Tucker ruefully without taking her eyes off the target. "I'm shaking like a leaf."

"Here." He moved until he stood directly behind her. Reaching out to cover her left hand with his, he lifted it to the gun, then brought up his right hand to support her right one. In the blink of an eye, she was in his arms, his powerful chest heating her back, his breath stirring the hair at her temple as he spoke near her ear. "Use two hands if it'll help steady you."

Lacey would have laughed if she'd had the breath. Steady? He had to be kidding! Couldn't he feel the pounding of her heart? "I sh-shouldn't need two h-hands to hold this tiny thing. I bet it doesn't even weigh a pound."

"You're not using both hands to hold it, only to steady your aim," he replied huskily, and wondered how a simple shooting lesson had suddenly turned into something far more dangerous. He hadn't meant to hold her; he hadn't even meant to touch her. He'd been tense ever since that damn car had backfired, but the tension churning in his belly now had nothing to do with that and everything to do with Lacey. What was that scent she wore? It was sweet, but not too sweet, subtly intoxicating, no doubt designed to slowly drive a man out of his mind. It was working.

Underneath his hands her fingers clutched at the gun, every nerve in her body tingling with awareness. "Now what?" she asked thickly.

Now what, indeed? his mind repeated cynically. Have you forgotten you're leaving in a matter of hours? And even if you weren't, you really are in need of a vacation if you think you can start something with Lacey. She's not your type. She deserves a husband and kids and a home overrunning with love and chaos, not someone who's going to take off for parts unknown at the drop of a hat without even knowing if he's ever coming back. Get your mind back on business and quit torturing yourself with something you can't have.

Swearing silently, he dropped his arms from her and stepped back, his jaw rigid as he stared past her to the target in the distance. "Squeeze the shot off," he instructed in a voice totally devoid of emotion. "Remember, if you've ever got to use this thing, you'll be in a pressure situation. You've only got one shot. But one will be enough if you don't lose your head."

With agonizing slowness her finger tightened on the trigger. Her arms steady as a rock, she didn't flinch as the bullet exploded from the nickel-plated barrel. With Tucker still standing behind her, she was sure he didn't see her squeeze her eyes shut at the last moment. Sighing in relief, she quickly dropped her arms to her sides, the empty gun now pointed at the ground. "How was that?" she asked, glancing over her shoulder at him.

He lifted a shoulder in a negligent shrug. "Not bad. But if you're going to try to hit someone breaking into your apartment, you're going to have to keep your eyes open."

Her mouth dropped open in surprise before she could stop it. "How did you know?"

"Just a guess," he replied wryly. "With some women it's instinct." He took the gun from her and dropped it into the bag with the spare bullets. "Come on, let's get out of here. I need to take a shower and pack my bags before we go to dinner."

His hand riding at the back of her waist, he urged her toward the car, never giving her the chance to ask if the instinct he referred to was that of a woman closing her eyes in the face of danger or his knowledge of women.

After the tension that had come between them at the shooting range, Lacey should have realized that their night out didn't have a snowball's chance in hell of being a success. From the moment they stepped into her apartment and began to get ready for the evening out, things seemed only to get worse. Tucker showered and left the bathroom steamy with his spicy scent, his cheeks clean shaven, his damp hair curling over the collar of his beige striped shirt. Lacey couldn't help but notice the way his biscuit-colored slacks molded his lean hips and long legs. It was the first time in years she had seen him in anything but jeans, and it was all she could do not to stare at him. No wonder he had women standing in line to catch his eye. He looked good enough to eat.

You never did like standing in line, she reminded herself caustically and retreated to the bathroom for her own bath.

When she emerged thirty minutes later in a red, white and blue scooped-neck sundress, she could have knocked Tucker over with a feather and didn't even know it. Her eyes on her image in her vanity mirror as she caught her hair in a pearl banana clip that allowed her curls to fall freely down her back, she didn't see him stiffen as the scent of her perfume crept into the living room and accosted his senses. It was going to be a long evening, he thought with a soundless groan. And it hadn't even begun.

Without regard to neatness or order, he threw his belongings into his suitcase, cursing himself for not having the sense to catch the first plane out, regardless of where it was going. He could have left by now and spared himself the torment of wanting a woman he had no intention of touching. And he could have gotten a good night's sleep on a decent bed! Instead, he would once again try to scrunch his six-foot-two frame onto a five-foot-two couch. Wonderful!

Leaving out only jeans and a shirt to wear the following morning on the plane, he shut his suitcase with a click. His mood anything but pleasant, he glared into her room, just catching a glimpse of her back as she stood at the mirror. "Aren't you ready yet?" he demanded, then muttered, "What've you been doing for the last half hour—dressing for a ball?"

Even with most of the apartment between them, Lacey heard his impatient grumbling. His temper was stretched to the limit, she thought, then wondered how she could so easily know what he was feeling. Grabbing her purse, she strolled into the living room and said sweetly, "I was wondering the same thing when you took almost forty-five minutes to take a shower. Shall we go?"

His only answer was to narrow his eyes at her and jerk open the door. Biting back a smile, Lacey preceded him down the stairs, hoping that the carnival-like atmosphere and crowds of Bourbon Street would relieve the frustration building between them like a balloon threatening to burst when they least expected it.

Although it was still another hour until dark, the clubs and shops along New Orleans's most famous street had their lights on and doors open for the tourists who were already starting to gather. From the doorways of some of the more risqué bars, scantily clad women danced suggestively in an effort to lure in male customers. And up and down the street, on the thick, humid air, the hot beat of jazz throbbed relentlessly like the pagan beat of drums.

Usually Lacey loved the Quarter when the heat of the day was fading into the sultriness of evening. In the gathering shadows, wrought-iron balconies dripping with hanging baskets of ferns held romantic mysteries, while the air turned soft with the promise of the night to come. But tonight she was distracted, her thoughts on the man beside her rather than her surroundings.

The length of his stride adjusted to hers, he matched her

step for step, his hand inadvertently brushing hers whenever
the throng of people prowling the streets crowded close,
pushing them together. Lacey caught herself before she
could stiffen in reaction as electricity sparked between
them. This had to stop! she silently warned herself. She
couldn't keep acting like a skittish colt every time he came
near her without him eventually noticing. Disgusted with
herself, she unobtrusively edged away from him, needing
some breathing room. But it didn't help. Nothing helped.
She had to endure this torture only for a few more hours,
she thought, then he would be gone. If she ached for him
then, he would never know.

The restaurant they went to was on the edge of Jackson
Square, yet close enough to Bourbon Street for them to hear
the music. From their table on the outdoor flagstone patio,
they could see the riverboats churning down the river, the
carriage stop for the horse-drawn carriages, the paintings
and caricatures done by local artists lining the wide side-
walks. It was bright, festive, colorful.

And too romantic. Wishing their night out didn't feel
quite so much like a date, Lacey waited until after they'd
given the waiter their order before saying, "I didn't think
to ask you if you wanted to have a drink and listen to some
jazz before we ate. We could have gone to one of the
clubs—"

"This is fine," he assured her. "I don't want a drink."
Not now. Any thoughts of having a good, stiff drink had
died a swift death the moment he'd seen her in that sundress. The last thing he needed was liquor clouding his
judgment when it would take all his concentration just to
get through the night without reaching for her.

Silence stretched between them, a silence that pulsated
with jazz, its beat as steady as their hearts. Choosing to
ignore it, Lacey was watching the flickering candle in the
middle of the table when she suddenly felt someone watching them. Glancing around, she frowned at two women on
the far side of the patio who were ogling Tucker and whis-

pering excitedly together. Turning back to Tucker, she lifted an amused brow. "Those women over there look like they're about to swoon over you. They must have seen you on TV after the coup." Expecting him to make a mocking comment, she was surprised when he only glowered at her. "What's the matter? You don't like being the current American hero?"

His jaw clenched. "I'm no hero."

"Maybe not in your eyes, but the embassy personnel you rescued might disagree."

"They don't know all the facts. I was just doing my job."

She wanted to say he'd obviously done a heck of a lot more than that, but from the looks of his closed expression he was in no mood to continue the discussion. She let the subject drop. "So where do you go from Aruba?"

He shrugged. "Who knows? Wherever there's trouble."

"That doesn't bother you? Not knowing from one month to the next where you'll be?"

"It beats being stuck behind a desk somewhere bored out of my mind."

She cocked her head at him, studying his hard face in the candlelight. "I thought it was the fate of all trouble-shooters to eventually end up behind a desk."

"Not this one," he said flatly.

"Dad thinks you'd make a terrific diplomat."

His gaze, as sharp as a lance, pinned her to her chair. Just what had his stepfather told her? "When did you discuss me with Marcus?"

"Oh, I don't know…last month…last year." She dismissed the time period with a wave of her hand. "He brings up your name almost every time we talk."

"Why?"

"I think he has this misguided notion that one of these days we could be friends," she admitted baldly, looking him right in the eyes. "So he tells me all these wonderful stories about you, hoping I'll be impressed."

Imp, he thought, unable to hold back a grin. "And are you?"

She widened her eyes at him, as if surprised that he had to ask. "Not particularly." But laughter flirted around the corners of her mouth.

"I'll never understand why some women don't know a good thing when they see it," he replied teasingly. "Quality isn't easy to come by these days."

"My point exactly," she said with a chuckle, slamming the door on the trap he had very neatly walked into. "You were saying?"

The waiter chose that moment to set their plates of blackened redfish before them. His dark brows drawn together in a fierce frown over twinkling brown eyes, Tucker picked up his fork and pointed it at her plate. "Eat."

After that, the tension between them eased. For a while. They finished their entrées, then lingered over dessert and coffee before once again strolling through the Quarter. As dusk gave way to complete nightfall, the crowds exploring New Orleans's nightlife doubled, along with the sounds of laughter and merriment. Jugglers and tap dancers performed on street corners, while a mime entertained the crowd gathering in front of a magic and voodoo shop. It was a loud, sometimes raucous, sometimes decadent scene.

It didn't become intimate until Tucker took her hand.

Lacey knew why he did it. At one point they became separated by the crowd. At another, a drunk came weaving out of a bar and almost knocked her flat. After that, Tucker twined her fingers through his and pulled her close. The rest of the world seemed to recede, leaving the two of them alone.

Tucker told himself a dozen times it wasn't necessary for him to hold her hand. If the streets were that rowdy, then maybe it was time they went back to her apartment. But there, too, they would be alone, with the bed in the next room and hours left to fill before it was time to go to sleep. No, he decided grimly, the streets were safer. What could happen in this crowd?

They had wandered back to the Moon Walk, a boardwalk along the riverbank, when a riverboat swept past them, churning up muddy water as it headed for the dock downstream. Lacey gazed after it wistfully as the bubbly music of the calliope drifted to them on the breeze. "I haven't been on a riverboat in years."

Hoping the ride would cool his increasingly warm blood, Tucker tightened his grip on her fingers and started off in the direction of the dock. "It's only four blocks," he said, spying a sign on a nearby corner that advertised the rides. "C'mon, let's go."

"No!"

It was the panic in her voice, rather than her negative answer, that stopped Tucker in his tracks. Her face was lit only by the streetlight on the far corner, and he stared down in concern at her unexpectedly pale complexion. Still holding her hand, he stepped closer. "I thought you wanted to go for a ride. What's wrong? Don't you want to walk? It's not that far."

"Yes, I know." It was four blocks lined with dark, abandoned buildings and catacombed with narrow, black alleys. On the very fringes of the French Quarter, yet a world away, it was a derelict area frequented by winos and thieves. Lacey had learned the hard way that it was not a place for the unwary. The armored-car robbery she'd stumbled across had taken place in one of the shadow-filled alleys only two blocks from where they stood.

Resisting the need to cling to his hand, she said evenly, "The armored-car robbery took place there. It's not a safe place to walk at night. We can take a taxi."

"Then why did you walk through there that night?" he demanded. "If you knew it wasn't safe—"

"I didn't know it at the time," she interrupted. "Oh, I knew winos hung out there, but I didn't realize just how deserted and off the beaten path it was until it was too late.''

Until she was face-to-face with a man intent on killing her and there was no one to hear her screams. Fury building in him at the thought of the horror she must have gone through, Tucker tightened his hold on her fingers. Not questioning the protectiveness that surged in him, he turned back toward Jackson Square. ''C'mon, there's bound to be a taxi around here somewhere.''

When the cab pulled up at the dock ten minutes later, most of the other passengers had already boarded the large paddle-wheel boat for its last run of the night. The ticket taker at the gangplank grinned at them as they hurried aboard. ''You almost missed the boat,'' he teased, then laughed aloud at their groans. ''Sorry, I couldn't resist. There's dancing on the main deck with a live band. That's where you'll find most of the younger kids, especially the girls. There's something about a drummer…'' He shook his head as if he couldn't understand it, then continued, ''Personally, I like the top deck. It's got the best view. Look around, find you a spot and enjoy the ride. We'll be casting off any minute.''

They started up the stairs to the next deck. Tucker would have liked nothing better than to keep climbing until they reached the cooling breezes off the top deck. But he couldn't just ignore the dancing when they could both hear the music spilling down the stairs from the deck above. ''Do you want to dance?''

The music was slow and dreamy and incredibly romantic. Lacey hesitated, teasing images playing in her head— lost on a crowded dance floor in Tucker's arms…pressed up against him…unaware of anyone but each other. Tempted, Lacey knew she would have said yes without a qualm if they'd been on a real date. But they were just killing time before he left and she couldn't allow herself to get caught up in a fantasy. Her hand drifted to her thigh and the bruise hidden by her dress. It was healing nicely, but it was the only excuse she could think of. "Maybe I'd better not. Anyway, I'd just as soon sit up on the top deck and watch the city float by."

Relieved, he only nodded. "So would I. Let's go."

They hurried up the steep stairs that led to the next level, then found another flight that led to the deck above that, until they finally stepped onto the top deck just as the stern-wheeler pulled away from the dock. Their hearts pounding and lungs straining from the exercise, they glanced around the open deck and almost groaned. The lights that outlined every deck and gave the boat such a festive air didn't extend to the top deck. It was dark and virtually deserted, the music from below muted. Only one other couple had found their way up, and they stood in each other's arms at the stern, kissing as if there were no tomorrow, totally oblivious to everything but each other.

Common sense urged Lacey to turn around and make a beeline for the dancing downstairs. What did she care if he thought she was afraid to be alone with him in the dark? Despite that, she heard herself say, "It looks like we've got our pick of seats. Where do you want to sit?"

Anywhere but up here, he almost snapped, a muscle ticking along his jaw. So much for cooling his blood! Swearing under his breath, he motioned to the metal chairs set up at the very bow of the boat. "Up front. We might as well see where we're going."

But the seats he led them to were too low, and Lacey couldn't see over the rail. Not that it mattered. She was too aware of the man at her side to sit still. Popping back up to her feet, she gripped the railing with both hands and determinedly kept her eyes fixed on the towering buildings of the city as they slowly passed the downtown area. Normally it was a sight that never failed to move her, but as Tucker rose to stand next to her she stared blindly at the city she loved, all her senses attuned to him.

From the opposite end of the boat, soft, sultry laughter

and whispered murmurs floated on the night air. Although he wasn't touching her in any way, Lacey felt Tucker stiffen. She thought she heard him mutter, "Damn teenagers!" but she couldn't be sure, as the boat pilot chose that moment to blow the boat's whistle.

"They're probably honeymooners," she said when she could be heard again. "The city's a popular honeymoon spot." When he only snorted at that, she frowned. "What's that supposed to mean? Is that your opinion of marriage or what?"

He shrugged, his fists balled in his pockets. "I haven't seen a relationship yet that hasn't been ruined by a wedding. When a man puts a ring on a woman's finger, he's asking for nothing but trouble."

"Oh, really?" she challenged. "And what about our parents? You were there the day my father put a ring on your mother's finger. If they're miserable together, then I should be so lucky. They're two of the happiest people I know."

He couldn't argue with that. "They're the exception, not the rule. The divorce rate gets higher every year. Not everyone lives happily ever after."

Lacey stared at him intently, trying to see past his dark, shadowed eyes. "Not everyone is miserable," she countered. "Sometimes you have to take a chance—"

But he was a man who lived by the odds, and he knew when to respect them. "Not when the odds already stink to begin with."

"But without the risk, without the commitment, what have you got, anyway? Nothing."

As he gazed down at her upturned face, a dozen answers popped into his head, urging him to show her. His common sense tugged away by the wind that played with her hair, he reached out to slide his finger over the magnolia softness of her cheek and promised himself he was just going to touch her one last time. He'd just spent days with her, yet there was so much about her he didn't know…like what made her moan, what made her sigh with pleasure….

"Not necessarily. How about need?" he murmured in a low voice that rasped across her nerve endings like sandpaper. "The kind that burns in your gut until you think you'll die if you can't have just a touch, a taste." His finger slid to her ear and gently delved beneath the tendrils of hair that concealed it. "Or want? The kind that keeps you awake nights, aching in your very bones. Have you ever ached, Lacey?"

She ached so badly then, she didn't know how she found the strength to answer him without swaying into his arms. Her lips dry and parched, she had to run her tongue over them before she could speak. And even then, it was in a voice she would never have recognized as her own. "You're talking about sex."

"No," he argued huskily. "I'm talking about passion. Desire. Let me show you...."

His hand tunneled under her hair to the back of her neck, his fingers settling there with a possessiveness that would have worried him if he'd thought about it. But he'd ceased to think the minute he brought her into his arms with nothing more than a tug. Acting on instinct alone, he leaned down and covered her mouth with his.

She expected passion, the kind that was white-hot and swept you away before your heart had time to beat another beat. He'd just spoken of setting small fires inside her with just words alone. But what she got instead was gentleness, the kind that could bring tears to her eyes. A brush of lips as soft as a whisper, a nibble, the teasing flick of his tongue at the corner of her mouth, gave her just a sample of the heat to come before sliding away and leaving her yearning for...something. Sighing his name, she inched her hands up his chest and around the strong column of his neck.

As if he heard her silent plea for more, he lifted his head only to change the angle of the kiss and let his lips settle more fully on hers. Gentleness slid into hunger and neither noticed the change until their hearts were racing, their hands clutching as the boat seemed to lurch beneath their feet.

Burying his hands in her wild, flowing hair, Tucker groaned as she leaned into him, her response wild and free and hot. How many nights had he lain on her damn couch and dreamed of holding her like this, of giving in to the desire she stirred with nothing more than her presence? God, he had to touch her or he would go mad! Giving in to the need, he found her breast in the darkness. So small. His fingers explored, molded, cherished through the material of her dress. How could he have forgotten how small she was, how delicate?

His thumb moved to her nipple, teasing the peak into a tight nub that sent pure longing rippling through her even as he took the kiss deeper. Lacey heard a moan and was stunned to realize that it came from deep in her own throat. Pressing herself to him, she felt herself losing control, melting bone by bone and going up in smoke in his arms. Delighted, she never thought to fight it, never thought to question where they were as the desire that had been building in her for days came pouring out.

Sometimes you have to take a chance. Not when the odds already stink to begin with. What about need? Or want?

His words echoed in her head, pricking at her, piercing the thick, dark waves of longing dragging her down into passion. With a muffled cry, she jerked her mouth free of his and struggled out of his arms. Breasts heaving, she realized with something close to fury that tears were already filling her eyes. She blinked them back rapidly and knew she was on the verge of making a fool of herself. "Call it what you will," she choked. "You're still talking just sex. That may be enough for some women, but it's not for me. Sorry, guess you'll have to settle for a beach bunny in Aruba." Stepping around him, she hurried toward the stairs without waiting to see if he followed.

When the boat docked forty-five minutes later, she was the first one off the gangplank. Tucker was right behind her, but she didn't even bother to look at him as he hailed a taxi for them. His mouth thinned in a flat line of frustration, he knew it was for the best. He no longer had to worry about how he was going to get through the rest of the night without touching her. If he so much as leaned toward her now, she'd probably scratch his eyes out.

And it was no more than he deserved. He never should have kissed her, never should have let things get out of hand. How the hell had they gotten onto a discussion about marriage, anyway? Lacey Conrad was not the type of woman a man discussed commitment with. He had only to look in her eyes, drag her into his arms, and somehow he found himself changing his mind on convictions he'd thought were carved in stone. It was a damn good thing he was leaving in the morning!

They rode back to her apartment in a silence that was as cold and unforgiving as an arctic front. The minute they stepped into her living room, Lacey went to the closet and pulled out the sheets and bedding he used to make the couch down. After throwing them at him, she set her hands on her hips and glared at him. "Do you need a ride to the airport in the morning?"

He did, but after what had just happened he had no intention of asking her for one. "No. I'll take a taxi."

She nodded stiffly. "Fine." Good manners dictated that she thank him again for his help, but she wasn't able to inject much sincerity into her words. "Thank you for helping me the last couple of days. I hope you enjoy your vacation." And without another word she retreated to her room.

Chapter 6

Resisting the urge to slam her door, she shut it carefully and knew she'd never be able to sleep. But she'd die before she'd give him the satisfaction of knowing he kept her awake nights. Damn him, anyway! The minute they'd stepped onto the top deck, she should have turned around and marched right down the stairs just as fast as her two legs could carry her. Instead, she'd let him give her a lesson in the fine art of kissing that she wasn't likely to forget soon!

"Dumb, Lacey," she muttered, jerking down the zipper of her dress. She snatched up a long, white batiste nightgown that was trimmed in lace and as cool as a summer breeze. "Real dumb. You had to know he was going to kiss you. A man doesn't start talking about sex, then point out the constellations for you. You knew that. But what did you do? You just stood there. Waiting."

She groaned at the memory. She'd have given anything to deny it, but regardless of how it hurt, she didn't lie to herself. Oh, yes, she'd been waiting for him to kiss her, really kiss her, and she hadn't even realized it. No mere brushing of lips would have satisfied her tonight, nor a hard bruising kiss that would have only served to vent the frustration that had been clawing at them both for longer than she cared to remember. No, tonight she'd wanted him to kiss her as though nothing else in the world mattered but those few moments with her, stolen out of time. Only she'd gotten more than she'd bargained for.

Fireworks had exploded into a shower of sparks deep inside her; shooting stars bursting with color had set her aglow. She had, she thought as she pulled back the covers and climbed into bed, come too close to losing herself in the fallout. Even now the aftershocks of unfulfilled desire quaked through her. What an idiot she was to let him hurt her again! Sniffling, she tried to tell herself she was glad he was leaving tomorrow. He'd be gone before she even got up. If hopeless despair settled heavily in her heart at the thought, she refused to acknowledge it. Later, she promised herself, when he was a thousand miles away, she would have to deal with the loss of something precious, something she couldn't even put a name to. But not now.

She punched down her pillow and wadded it under her head as she rolled onto her stomach, determined to pretend to sleep at least. He wouldn't hear her tossing and turning and chasing dreams she couldn't have. Regardless of how miserable she was, she could lie perfectly still and never move a muscle. That was the last thought she had before she fell asleep.

Seconds, maybe hours later, the attack came hurtling right out of one of her nightmares. In the slumbering silence of the night, one of the windows facing the street suddenly shattered. Lacey's eyes flew open, her heart knocking against her ribs before she was even fully awake. Fear, like a dragon in the darkness, grabbed her, terrifying her. Gasping, she bolted out of bed.

At the first sound of breaking glass, Tucker snapped awake. Instantly alert, he knew immediately that the noise had come from Lacey's room. His feet hit the floor running. Without slowing down, he slammed her bedroom door back on its hinges just as a hail of gunfire ripped through the quiet on the street in front of her shop. Annihilated, a plate-glass window exploded downstairs, raining shards as Lacey screamed. Visions of the coup and stray bullets flashing before his eyes, Tucker launched himself at her shadowy figure.

He caught her around the waist, his weight carrying them both to the floor in a tangle of arms and legs on the other side of the bed. Wrapping his arms around her, he rolled her under him in one smooth motion. His heart slammed against hers as he drew back only far enough to see her face in the darkness. "Were you hit?"

"No! What—"

Downstairs, the unseen gun spit out angry bullets. More glass shattered. "Oh, God, my shop!" Lacey cried, unthinkingly pushing at the steely arms that held her down. "Let me up! I've got to—"

"What?" he demanded, pinning her to the floor. "Get yourself killed? Damn it, be still!"

Choking on a sob, she went limp, only to stiffen at the high-pitched squealing of tires burning rubber as a car raced off into the night. In the next instant Tucker jumped up and ran to one of the unbroken windows. But the car was gone, the street as tranquil and deserted as if the attack had never happened. Swearing, he hit the window frame with his clenched fist. "Damn!"

Lacey pushed herself to her feet on legs that were as wobbly as wet noodles, shivering as coldness seeped into her blood. "Did you see anything?"

"No." He sighed in disgust. "We'd better get Ryan down here. This doesn't look good."

The words were hardly out of his mouth when the phone on the nightstand rang shrilly, startling them both. Her eyes wide, Lacey stared at it as if it were a snake with two heads.

A cold feeling of dread dropped into her stomach as she lifted the receiver. "Hel-lo?"

"Tell the police you identified the wrong man," a hoarse voice whispered threateningly in her ear. "You made a mistake, understand? A very big mistake. You'd better correct it or next time more than your shop will be shot up." A heartbeat later, the connection was softly, mockingly broken.

Lacey paled, her fingers shaking so badly it took her two tries before she was able to set the receiver back in its cradle. A nightmare, she thought with a strangled sob. This had to be a nightmare.

Crossing to her side, Tucker flipped on the bedside lamp and watched her struggle for control. Ever since he'd arrived to find her in the hospital, she'd shown him nothing but strength and a dogged determination to go on with her regular routine in spite of the odds against her. What fear she hadn't been able to hide had been only a natural reaction to the memories that still haunted her. But the terror he saw in her ashen face now had nothing to do with memories. She was trembling in reaction, pushed to the edge. He wanted to comfort her, but he was afraid if he touched her now, what control she did have would shatter as easily as her windows had. Balling his hands into fists to keep from reaching for her, he asked quietly, "Who was it?"

Her eyes, dark with fright, lifted to his. "A...man. Th-threatening me. If I don't tell the police I—I identified the wrong man, more than my shop would be shot up." She whirled, uncaring that she was dressed in nothing but a thin gown and Tucker was once again in his underwear. "Oh, God, the St. John antiques!" she cried and ran for the stairs.

Tucker started to run after her, but someone had to call the police. He snatched up the phone, calling after her, "Don't touch anything! I'm calling Ryan."

Lacey hardly heard him. Pausing only to flip on the lights for the shop, she ran headlong down the stairs, her stomach twisting with fear. Everything would be all right, she told herself, clutching at the banister. It had to be. Someone was just trying to scare her, to make her think he'd shot up her shop. This was just someone's idea of a sick joke—

She stopped short at the bottom of the stairs, her horrified gasp reaching the farthest corners of the silent shop. Even as her eyes were registering the devastation before her, her mind was refusing to accept it. Paint. Yellow paint. It was everywhere—dripping from the shattered front windows and the burglar bars that could keep out a man but not bullets, the cash register and almost every piece of furniture in the front half of the shop.

"No!" Her cry of outrage nearly strangling her, she sank down to the bottom step, unable to tear her gaze away from the thousands of dollars of antiques splattered by obscene globs of yellow paint. No! This couldn't be happening! She was having a sale Saturday. There had to be a mistake!

Dressed in the jeans, T-shirt and tennis shoes he'd hurriedly pulled on, Tucker appeared on the stairs behind her with her robe and house shoes in his hand. Not sparing the shop a glance, he draped her robe over her shoulders, then squatted down beside her and slid her feet into the slippers. "Ryan'll be here any minute. They had to get him out of bed."

She nodded, but her eyes were trained on the front of the shop in stunned disbelief. Following her gaze, Tucker jackknifed to his feet in shock. "What the hell!"

Expecting the furniture to be bullet riddled, he strode to the front of the shop, glass crunching under his shoes, his expression thunderous. Stopping at the embroidered fire screen that had been delivered only days ago, he hunkered down to glare at the slash of paint that covered nearly half of the finely worked piece. "How the hell did the bastard do this so fast?" he murmured, stopping just short of touching the screen as he studied it. "The burglar bars were down, but even if they hadn't been, he didn't have time to slip inside and throw paint on everything. Sixty seconds after the first window shattered, he was gone."

"Sixty seconds," Lacey repeated hollowly. Rising to her feet, she slipped her arms into the sleeves of her robe and hugged herself. "How can someone destroy everything I've got in sixty seconds?" Dashing away the tears drowning her eyes, she swore. "Damn the son of a bitch! He isn't going to get away with this!"

Tucker leaned over a secretary and examined it carefully. "Maybe it's not as bad as it looks. I don't see any bullet holes, and the wood itself doesn't appear to be damaged. Paint remover'll strip off the paint fast enough."

"Oh, it can be salvaged," she agreed. Leaving the stairs, she walked toward him, anger battling with sadness as she viewed the once-beautiful pieces. "But the paint remover will remove the wood's patina along with the paint, reducing the value. And it won't work at all on the upholstery, which means all the material on the damaged love seats and sofas will have to be replaced. But the brocades being made today are nothing like the originals."

"So what's the bottom line?" Tucker asked, straightening. "How much are you going to lose?"

She didn't even hesitate. "Possibly thousands. *If* I can manage to salvage all this by the sale on Saturday. If I can't, I might as well close up now. I'll be finished."

Tucker didn't have to see the fury burning in her eyes to know that she would never give up that easily. She was a fighter; she'd never take the easy way out. She'd also never admit defeat to the man who had done this to her. Had it sunk in yet that the nightmare wasn't over? he wondered. In her concern for her shop, had it even hit her that the man she had identified and put in jail had a partner out there somewhere who was after her?

In the distance the sudden wail of a siren snaked through the narrow streets of the Quarter, growing steadily louder. Within seconds a patrol car and a tan sedan pulled up sharply in front of the shop. The minute Lacey hit the switch to lift the burglar bars, then unlocked the front door,

Ryan and two uniformed officers hurried inside, while a fourth man investigated the front of the shop and the street.

Pushing her disheveled hair back over her shoulders, Lacey tried and failed to summon a smile as she greeted the detective. She had no idea how vulnerable she looked, standing there clutching her robe about her, her green eyes dark and troubled, her face too pale. "We never seem to meet under the best of circumstances, Detective. Sorry to have to drag you down here in the middle of the night."

"I do some of my best thinking this time of the morning," he retorted with a grin before his expression turned all business. "What happened?"

She recounted the entire story for him, starting with the shattering of her bedroom window and finishing with the phone call that still had the power to make her shudder. "As soon as I hung up, I ran down here and found—" she gestured helplessly "—this."

Jotting notes on the small notebook he took out of the inside pocket of his slightly rumpled blue suit coat, Jack Ryan nodded toward the stairs and told the officer at his side, "Check it out."

His steel-blue eyes lifted from his notes to Lacey. "Let's go over the phone call again. Was there anything unusual about the man's voice? An accent? Odd phrasing? Any kind of inflection we could use to track him down?"

She shook her head, the threat echoing in her ears like a record stuck in a groove. "No, nothing. He talked in a hoarse whisper, but I doubt that that's his natural way of talking. His voice was deep, though. And cold." Goose bumps slid down her spine. "He meant what he said. I'm sure of it."

"How long after you heard the car drive away before he called?"

The entire nightmare seemed to have lasted aeons to Lacey. She glanced at Tucker. "A minute," he answered for her. "Two at the most."

"Pretty confident, isn't he?" Ryan murmured. "He must have stopped at the first phone booth he came to."

"What I want to know is how he did so much damage in so little time," Tucker growled. "I'd swear he never got out of his car. And he sure as hell didn't have time to throw paint through the burglar bars."

"Paint bullets," said a big, strapping cop as he stepped through the front door. Palm up, he held his opened hand out to the detective to show him the bullet lying on his handkerchief. "Found it out in the street near the curb. Looks like the kind used in survival games."

"Good work," Ryan said. "At least we've got something to work with this time."

The officer he'd sent upstairs came back down holding a plastic sack with a rock in it. "The upstairs window was broken with this," he said. "If we get any prints off it, we'll be damn lucky. Maybe the lab can come up with something."

Ryan doubted it, but at this point he'd take any clues he could get. "After you finish checking out things down here, run it on downtown," he said. "And the paint bullet, too. And on your way, scout out the area for the nearest pay phones. They need to be dusted for prints. It's a long shot but stranger things have turned a case. If you find anything, I want to know immediately."

Leaving the men to finish their scouring of the premises, the detective turned his attention back to Lacey. "We need to talk, and I'd rather do it tonight if you don't mind. Can I beg a cup of coffee off you? This time of night I need something to prop the old eyelids open."

"Oh, of course. I wasn't thinking." She hurried over to the stairs. "I think we could all use something. Come on up."

Instant was all she had, but it was quickly heated in the microwave. Within minutes the three of them were sitting at her kitchen table. The detective waited until Lacey had taken a sip of the bracing liquid before he said, "Martin has been bragging from his jail cell that he'll never be convicted. Up until tonight, we just shrugged it off. But now it's obvious why he was so cocky. The jerk's either got a partner or a friend or family member on the outside working to get him released.''

Tucker set his cup down abruptly. ''Why are you just now getting around to telling us this?''

Considering the circumstances, the detective knew Tucker had every right to complain. ''We hear this type of thing all the time. Everyone we book is innocent, misunderstood or framed. If we listened to everyone we brought in, we'd be out of a job and this town would be in a hell of a mess. And don't say it is already,'' he said quickly, his quick grin diffusing the tenseness. ''We're working on it, believe me.''

Lacey stirred her coffee with a quick, jerky motion that could only be attributed to nerves. ''So Martin is cocky because he knows there's someone on the outside trying to intimidate me,'' she said huskily. ''And if I don't recant my ID of him, then someone's going to shut me up. Permanently.''

Ryan nodded, the crow's-feet at the corners of his eyes deepening. ''I won't lie to you. He may try. You're the only thing we've got against Martin and he knows it. If you say you made a mistake, we don't have a case. If you're not around to testify, we don't have a case. But it's not going to come to that,'' he said fiercely. ''Tell me again what you remember about the robbery.''

It was a story Lacey could tell in her sleep. Wearily, she repeated it. Hoping she might have remembered something new, the detective wasn't really surprised when she didn't. From the first time he'd questioned her, she hadn't wavered in her conviction of what she'd seen. ''So one guard was already dead at the back of the truck when you saw Martin kill the other guard near the front of the truck. And the back door was already open.''

''Then his partner could have been inside the truck,''

Tucker said. "He could have seen Lacey, seen Martin run her down."

Ryan nodded. "It's the only logical explanation. It would also explain why the money didn't turn up in a search of Martin's home. Somewhere in the city he's got a partner holding his share of half a million dollars."

"A partner who somehow knows my name and where I live," Lacey added. "How? Even if he saw me that night, how did he find out who I was? My name was kept out of the papers. Even my closest friends don't know I actually saw one of the robbers."

"The hospital you were taken to was mentioned in the newspaper account of the story," Tucker said. "I read it myself. If someone was enterprising enough, they could track you down through that."

Usually a man with infinite patience, Ryan pushed his empty coffee cup to the middle of the table, then rose to prowl impatiently around the kitchen. "We've known all along that whoever was planning these robberies wasn't an idiot. He's had us working in the dark for months now, but tonight he made his first big mistake. Now that we know for sure that Martin's got a partner, there's got to be a clue out there, something in his background that'll link him to whoever's trying to scare you out of testifying," he told Lacey. "I've just missed it. But I'll find it," he promised her. "If I have to order a background search on everyone he's ever known, ever spoken to, I'll do it. The bastard's not going to walk. Not when we're this close to nailing him."

Tucker watched the detective's eyes harden with resolve and didn't doubt for a minute that Ryan would get his man. But it could take weeks, even months, for him to track him down. "How are you going to protect Lacey while you're out beating the bushes? You heard what that bastard said on the phone. Tonight was just a warning."

"Yeah, I know. And the negotiations to end the strike are going absolutely nowhere. The union wants back pay for overtime instead of comp time, which there never seems to be time for, and the city's digging in its heels." Running his hand through his dark hair, he swore. "While the two sides are arguing over money, every two-bit jerk with a shady past is taking advantage of the shortage of manpower." He frowned at Lacey. "You need to be in a safe house. But that would mean assigning two officers to you for twenty-four-hour protection. We're stretched so thin now, there's no way I can take one man, let alone two, off the streets to hole up with you until this is over."

She set her coffee cup down carefully, but it still rattled when she placed it in the matching saucer. "Are you saying I'm on my own, then?" she asked bluntly.

She hit too close to the truth for comfort. "Not exactly," he hedged. "I'm saying I can't give you the kind of protection I would like to at the cost of hundreds of other citizens. Is there any way you could get out of town for a while? Maybe visit your father?"

Escape. He was offering her an escape from the fear that had been with her ever since she'd awakened to the sound of breaking glass. All she had to do was leave. And abandon her business and the thousands of dollars of paint-splattered antiques that waited for her downstairs. She wouldn't come back, of course. What would be the point? Her reputation as a reliable antique dealer would be in shreds, the losses from this sale only adding to her previous financial problems to push her right into bankruptcy. Everything would be lost, including her family's faith in her.

She shook her head. "I can't. You saw the condition of the furniture downstairs. I've got to salvage it some way in time for the sale I've got advertised for Saturday. Otherwise, I'll lose thousands."

"Damn it, Lace, better that than your life!" Tucker exploded. "Whoever's after you isn't playing games!"

"You don't know that," she argued. "In fact, now that I think of it, maybe that's exactly what he's doing. He's trying to intimidate me. Think about it. If he really wanted to kill me, he wouldn't warn me first. And why didn't he use real bullets instead of paint? He could have got on the roof across the street and taken me out while I slept in my own bed.''

"He could still do that," he retorted. "Have you forgotten that Martin and his partner have already killed six guards? These men are killers and they're not going to let a skinny redhead send them to the electric chair!''

That was a possibility she wasn't foolish enough to dismiss. She glanced at Jack Ryan. "Just how much protection can you give me?''

"After the strike, as much as you want. For now, though, the best I can do is station the one man assigned to the Quarter on the corner half a block away. He'll be within sight of your shop and the alley that runs behind it. Martin's partner may be as bold as brass, but even he's got to think twice about trying to get to you when there's a patrol car parked just down the street from you round the clock.''

"And what about when he gets called away?" Tucker demanded, scowling. "You said yourself every lowlife in the city is coming out of the woodwork to take advantage of the strike. One call for a robbery two blocks away, and Lacey would be a sitting duck. It's not enough," he said flatly.

Jack didn't even try to argue with him. "No, it's not. But under the circumstances, it's the best I can do.''

His jaw hardened. "That's not good enough.''

He was doing it again, Lacey thought. Interfering in her life as if he had every right in the world. Her chair scraping against the floor as she abruptly rose to her feet, she glared at him. "Damn it, Tucker, it's not your place to say whether or not it's good enough. Tomorrow you'll be on a beach in Aruba. This isn't any of your business.''

"The hell it isn't," he snapped, stung. "In case you've forgotten, lady, *trouble* is what I handle for a living. And if you think one cop on a corner half a block away is going to be able to protect you from someone who is set on getting you, you're living in a dream world.'' Shoving his own chair back, he eliminated the distance between them in a single stride. He stood so close she could feel the heat of his anger striking her with every breath he took. ''I've seen foreign leaders surrounded by police *this* close,'' he stressed, leaning down until he was practically in her face, ''assassinated by a nut with a gun who made a mockery of security. If this guy is determined to get you, it wouldn't matter if Ryan assigned a dozen cops to you. He'd find a way to shut you up.''

Every drop of blood drained from Lacey's face, but she faced him unflinchingly. ''If you're trying to scare me, you're doing a damn good job.''

The need to take her in his arms then was stronger than any need he'd ever felt in his life, but he stubbornly kept his hands to himself. ''I'm trying to wake you up,'' he said huskily, then surprised himself by saying, ''If you don't want to go stay with Marcus until this blows over, then come with me to Aruba.''

''No!'' Did he know what he was asking? How could she spend weeks in the tropics with him without going quietly out of her mind? ''No,'' she said again, stepping away from him and the temptation he so easily held out to her. ''I can't leave—''

''Then I'm staying.''

Stunned, Lacey could only stare at him. She knew that set of his jaw, that hard, unrelenting light in his eyes. When he looked like that, he could stand before the devil himself and not bend an inch. ''But you can't!'' she cried. ''You told me your boss practically ordered you to take your vacation in Aruba.''

After what had happened between them on the boat, did she really think he could relax on a beach knowing she could be killed at any minute? ''As long as I'm not working, he won't care if I'm in Aruba or Timbuktu. And he sure as hell wouldn't expect me to go off and leave you when you're in trouble. Especially with my training.''

"Exactly what kind of training are you talking about?" Ryan asked.

"Antiterrorist," he replied promptly. "This guy may not be a terrorist, but he's just as unpredictable as one. He's going to strike when we least expect it, and we can't make the mistake of underestimating him. He already knows he can outfox the New Orleans police—he's done it on three occasions. Even with a cop on the corner, you can bet the half million he stole that he'll do everything he can to get to Lacey. He's going to have to go through me to do it."

It was settled. He was staying until whoever was after her was caught, until he was convinced she was safe. But how could she be safe as long as he was still in her life? After they'd finished their coffee and gone back downstairs, Lacey watched him walk the detective to the front door, and knew that even though he'd been there less than a week he was already beginning to mean too much to her. When he touched her, she forgot the past, forgot that he was a man who shunned ties, forgot that even if he had been the marrying kind he wasn't the kind for her. They were water and oil, night and day, incompatible and unmixable. In her head, those were facts carved in stone. In her heart, though, nothing was impossible.

You keep thinking that way, Lacey, girl, and you're asking for nothing but heartache, she lectured herself. You'd better get your mind off Tucker Stevens and back on the mess you're in. You've got a hell of a lot of work to do if you're going to pull that sale off on Saturday without losing your shirt. Three days. That's all you've got.

Three days! She groaned, her eyes taking in the dozens of pieces of furniture that would have to be stripped, sanded and revarnished. Despair hit her, almost knocking her legs out from under her. How was she going to do it all in three days? She'd have to start now to just make a dent in it.

Even then, after all the work, she'd probably lose thousands.

She stiffened, rejecting the dire prophecy before it could drag her down into despair. She didn't have time to be a crepe hanger. She had too much to do. First she had to get all the damaged pieces back into the storeroom, then decide which ones could be salvaged with the least amount of work. She would redo those first. The more damaged pieces—from what she had seen, there were less than a dozen—would have to be done later. If they weren't ready by Saturday, she could always include them in her next sale. She strode to a small Duncan Phyfe table that had been flawless but now had yellow paint splattered on one of its legs, lifted it easily and turned toward the back of the shop.

She'd taken only two steps when Tucker stepped in front of her, his eyes dark with disapproval. "What do you think you're doing?"

"Putting this and all the other damaged pieces in the back. I'll start refinishing them as soon as the hardware store opens and I get the supplies."

His hands settled on the table next to hers. "Not tonight you're not. I'll put it in the back and you go on upstairs to bed."

"You've got to be kidding! I can't—" She tightened her grip on the table when he tried to take it from her. "Let go! Tucker, this is ridiculous! I'm not going to bed when there's so much work to do!"

But he was stronger than she was, and before the words were even out of her mouth he had taken the table and deliberately set it down, daring her to touch it. "Go to bed," he growled. "A couple of hours aren't going to make any difference, and you need some sleep."

"I already had some sleep—"

His eyes snared hers. "Did you?"

How did he know? she wondered wildly. How did he know she'd stared at the darkness for hours, trying to get him out of her head? Then when she'd finally drifted off to sleep, she'd found him there, in her dreams, waiting for her. Damn him, how could he read her so easily when she couldn't see a single thought that hid behind his dark, enigmatic eyes?

Her nerves were shot, and the frustration, worry and anger she had been so desperately trying to ignore were suddenly too much for her. She lashed out at him because he was the only one there to lash out against. "Damn you, Tucker Stevens, I don't take orders from you or any other man! This is my shop and my home, and I'll do what I damn well please!" she cried, advancing on him until she could pound her words into his chest with her index finger. "And if I want to cuss, I'll cuss! I'll turn the air blue and purple and whatever other color I want to turn it because it's my air! You got that?"

His fingers closed gently around her hand, enclosing it against his chest. "Yes, honey, I got it. The way you're yelling, half the Quarter got it."

She dashed away the tears that flooded her eyes. When had she started to cry? "And don't you dare laugh at me," she ordered thickly, tugging against his hold. "I didn't ask you to come here. I never wanted you to stay. I didn't ask you to kiss me. I don't want you to kiss me—"

"Okay," he said soothingly, stunned by the tenderness that suddenly made him ache to hold her. His arms slipped around her, and his fingers tightened in her hair as she buried her face against his neck. "Next time you kiss me instead. I swear I won't complain. Right now, though, why don't you go ahead and cry and get it over with? You'll feel a lot better."

If he'd argued with her, she could have held her own with him. But he let her rail at him and never said a word in his own defense. With a sob, she collapsed against him, clutching him with both hands.

She didn't know how long she cried. Drained right down to her toes, she felt her sobs turn to shudders, the shudders to an occasional hiccup as she slowly regained control. Mortified by the things she had said to him, she stiffened and started to pull away from him, heat burning her wet cheeks. "I'm sorry," she began huskily. "I shouldn't—"

"Yes, you should," he interrupted, and swung her up in his arms before she could begin to guess his intentions. "Be still. I'm just going to carry you upstairs and put you to bed."

She didn't have the strength to argue. Her arms slipped around his neck as her head dropped to his shoulder. "The shop?"

"Locked up tight," he assured her. "The security bars will keep anyone from breaking in. In the morning's soon enough to start worrying again."

He carried her upstairs as if she weighed no more than a sack of groceries, then gently set her on her feet when they reached the door to her bedroom. "Wait right here until I move the bed."

"Move the bed? But—"

"It's too close to the windows," he explained as he tugged on the frame, gradually working it across the room until it was right in front of the door. "I'm not taking any more chances." With that announcement, he strode over to the dresser and moved it between the bed and the windows as a shield. Only when he was satisfied that she wouldn't be lying in the direct fire of another rock or bullet did he turn to her. "*Now* you can go to bed."

Chapter 7

Sleep eluded her. Restless, Lacy concentrated on just relaxing, on letting her body go boneless. But just as soon as her mind emptied of thoughts, worry rushed in to tug her back to wakefulness. Muttering a curse, she tossed and turned and ended up flat on her back staring at the dark ceiling. An hour before dawn she gave up in disgust. While she was wasting time she didn't have trying to sleep, she could be downstairs starting on the furniture.

Careful not to make a sound that would wake Tucker in the living room, she eased to the side of the bed. She had only to put her feet on the floor to reach her dresser in its new position between the bed and the windows. Holding her breath, she slid the lowest drawer open and rummaged in the dark for the old clothes she used for doing rough work. Only a whisper of sound stirred the silence as she pulled out a pair of ragged jeans and a paint-splattered T-shirt, then headed for the bathroom.

When she stepped into the living room five minutes later it was as dark as a tomb. Her heart thudding, she stood just inside the doorway and waited for her eyes to adjust to the lack of light before cautiously cutting a wide path behind the couch and tiptoeing toward the stairs. Half expecting Tucker to wake at any moment, she didn't see a sign of movement from the concealing shadows where he slept. Relieved, she reached the stairs and quickly but cautiously made her way down.

Her mind already jumping ahead to the work she had to do, she stepped into the shop only to freeze at the sight of the light spilling out of the open doorway of the storage room. She tried to tell herself that Tucker must have left the light on, but then she heard quiet footsteps in the lighted room. Trapped at the bottom of the stairs, she was frantically looking around for a place to hide when Tucker stepped into the open doorway. She wilted like limp lettuce. "Tucker! What are you doing? I thought you were still asleep."

With a flick of his wrist, he turned on the rest of the shop lights and she saw that he, too, was dressed in old work clothes. "I knew you wouldn't stay in bed long, so I figured I'd better get things ready for you."

"Ready? What…" As she glanced past him, her words trailed off in surprise when she spied a damaged table just inside the storeroom. Whirling, she swung her gaze back to the front of the shop. All the paint-splattered furniture had already been moved to the back, the glass from the broken windows swept up. Dazed that he would do such a thing, she turned accusing eyes on him. "You're a fine one to be talking. It must have taken you hours to do this. You didn't go back to sleep at all, did you?"

He lifted one shoulder in unconcern. "I'm used to going without. And I knew you'd try to sneak down here and move everything by yourself if you thought I was asleep. Which is just what you were going to do, wasn't it?" he teased, his dark eyes gleaming with amusement.

There was no use denying it. She was caught red-handed.

"Saturday will be here before I'm ready for it. I've got to get started."

Crossing his arms over his chest, he stood where he was, filling the doorway as she walked toward him. "Before you do, there's a few things we have to get straight."

"Such as?"

"Ground rules," he replied. "Until the nut who's after you is caught, you're going to have to change your routine."

Not liking the sound of that, she felt wariness creep into her eyes. "In what way?"

"First of all, the shop's going to remain closed until the day of the sale."

"Closed! But—"

"You're going to stay inside, away from the windows and out of danger," he continued as if she hadn't spoken. "You can go outside, but only at night, and only on the patio on the roof. I'm not taking any chances on anyone taking potshots at you with real bullets next time."

He wasn't laying down ground rules, he was putting her in prison! "Why don't you just lock me up and throw away the key? That's what you're doing anyway!"

He never batted an eye. "Better than having you end up dead. And that's what you'll be if you don't play it safe." He watched her blanch at the cold announcement, fear once again clouding her eyes. "This isn't a game, Lace," he said gruffly. "Someone is deadly serious. If I'm going to keep you safe, you've got to do things my way. You can't be too cautious."

If she allowed herself to dwell on what could happen when she least expected it, she would go quietly out of her mind. "But the shop," she protested, latching on to another worry thankfully. "I can't afford to lose any more customers."

"Put a sign on the door explaining that you're closed to prepare for the big sale," he suggested. "That'll generate interest, and any customer you lose will be back on Saturday. Anyway, you've only had a dozen or so people in here in the last two days and most of them didn't buy anything. Can you afford to waste time on browsers when you've got so much to do?''

He knew she couldn't. She sighed in defeat. ''All right, we'll do this your way since you're the expert. But if I start climbing the walls from being locked up for the next three days, you've got no one to blame but yourself.''

Chuckling, he predicted, ''You'll be too busy to notice.''

He was right. For the next two and a half days she never noticed the weather, never glanced at the television or newspaper. Ryan called to let them know that the rock that had been hurled through her window was clean of fingerprints and could have come from anywhere. He was still working on the paint bullets, but he wasn't holding out much hope. As for the phone booths in the area, they'd been covered with so many fingerprints it was impossible to link one set to Lacey's caller. If any new developments turned up, he'd keep them posted but for now all they could do was wait.

Thankful for the work she had to distract her, Lacey pushed the investigation to the back of her mind and concentrated on the furniture. She never even looked at a clock except to see how much time she had left. Days shrank into hours and hours minutes, with each tick of the clock becoming more precious than the last. She ate, but she had little appetite.

With a single-minded determination that Tucker couldn't help but admire, she threw herself into the job at hand, pushing herself until she could barely keep her eyes open and didn't have the energy to spit. Even then she didn't quit. She stripped and sanded and varnished every table and chair and chest with a skill and efficiency he hadn't even guessed she had.

The less damaged pieces were done first, her repairs limited only to the areas actually splattered with paint. If the original stain was impossible to match, which it was in most cases, she used a refinishing fluid that melted the old finish so that it could be evenly distributed over the whole. While that was drying, she went on to another piece, then another, never stopping to look back to see what she had accomplished.

It was time-consuming, backbreaking work. Still recovering from her injuries, she had every right to complain, to take any shortcuts she could manage. She did neither. Literally forced to stop at night by Tucker, she allowed herself only a few hours' sleep before she was up again and back at work.

At her side every waking moment, Tucker fought with the ever-growing need to hold her, to take on her burdens just so he could see her smile again. She was exhausting herself, and for what? To prove to her family that they could be proud of her and her business sense? Didn't she know they wouldn't care if she had the business acumen of a turtle? He'd heard them talk about her enough to know that she already was a success in their eyes. She was Lacey, a favorite aunt and sister, the daughter who had unknowingly helped Marcus through his first wife's death. Frustrated, he wanted to tell her she was trying to prove something that didn't need proving, but he knew she'd never believe him. The words she needed couldn't come from him. He could only stand by and watch, helping her as much as he could, and hope she didn't drive herself right into the ground.

Later, Tucker never knew how she accomplished it. By the middle of Friday afternoon she had done everything she could. A few of the more heavily damaged pieces were all that remained in the storeroom. They would be repaired later, when she wasn't under an unyielding deadline. The rest of the valuable collection was already out in the shop and arranged for the sale that would start early the next morning. To the uneducated eye, it looked every bit as good as it had the day it was delivered.

But even then, Lacey couldn't relax. As soon as the last piece was polished and set in place in the shop, she moved to her desk and dragged out the estate inventory list. Alternately frowning and chewing on her pencil, she estimated the price she would have to get on each of the more expensive items just to break even. Everything would be marked above that, of course, but no price was carved in stone and her customers knew it. They would expect her to haggle tomorrow and enjoy it. With so much riding on the sale, not to mention the threat against her life, she already knew she was going to be a nervous wreck.

Putting away the last of the brushes, rags and furniture polish in the storeroom, Tucker heard her weary sigh. Wiping his hands on a clean rag, he stepped to the doorway in time to see her rub the back of her neck. The tired gesture caught at his heart, pulling him to her even as he tried to control the need. They were both exhausted, their defenses down. They'd hardly been out of each other's sight over the past few days. Working side by side in the storeroom, then trudging upstairs together each night when they could both barely manage to put one foot in front of the other, they'd shared a forced intimacy that couldn't long be ignored. If he was smart he'd leave her alone and find himself something to do.

But if he'd learned anything about himself since he'd been in New Orleans, it was that his common sense took a vacation when he was around her. He still wanted her. All the work they'd done and his worries about her safety hadn't changed that. If anything, the need had only intensified. In spite of his best intentions, she'd found a way to get under his skin. If he hadn't wanted her so badly, he'd have been furious with her. And himself. There'd never been a woman he hadn't walked away from easily, and that was more by design than chance. He was not a cruel man. He'd gone out of his way to make sure that he didn't leave any broken hearts behind him when he left. And he always left. The women in his life knew that, accepted it and asked no more of him than he was willing to give.

Lacey would never be that accommodating. She wouldn't be content with an affair, a casual relationship without strings or commitment, with softly whispered words in the night that wouldn't hold up under the light of day. She would demand everything of a man—his heart and soul and eternity—but she'd ask no more than she was willing to give herself.

He told himself that was more, much more, than he wanted to give. If things had worked out the way they should have, he'd be in Aruba now, her scent and her smile only a memory he would, in time, put out of his head. But he wasn't thousands of miles away, and she drew him to her in spite of his best intentions, the remembered feel of her skin under his fingers tempting him past bearing.

Stopping directly behind her, he settled his hands on her shoulders. When she jumped in surprise, his fingers tightened, kneading away the tension that knotted her muscles. "Easy," he said huskily, gentling her. "I'm just giving you a massage."

She swallowed a moan. His hands felt so good on her. Too good. Closing her eyes, she knew she should stop him. Under the best of circumstances, she was too susceptible to his touch. Now, when she was tired and worried and afraid she was on the verge of losing everything she had spent the past seven years working for, she just wanted to turn in his arms and cling to him. Just for a minute, just until some of his strength seeped into her. But if she did, she might not ever be able to let him go.

She stiffened, willing herself to ignore the heat spreading through her from his hands. "I...I need to finish this...."

His fingers moved from her shoulders to slip under her long braid. Without either being aware of it until it was too late, his touch turned to a caress. "What are you doing?"

"Figuring..." Her head dropped forward weakly, allowing him greater access even as she struggled to hang on to the threads of the conversation. "Figuring how fine I can c-cut the sales tomorrow and…and still make a profit." Her breath lodged in her throat as he traced a tendril of hair that had escaped her braid and was curling around her ear. "Tucker…I don't think—"

Her neck looked so tempting he couldn't resist. Knowing he was playing with fire, he leaned down and brushed a kiss just below her ear. "Hmm?"

Beneath his lips, her skin heated. She never expected tenderness from him, never knew how to fight him when he surprised her with gentleness. Her fingers curling into her palms, she knew she only had to turn to be in his arms. But if she did, this time she wouldn't be able to walk away. She would give him her heart, only to have it casually returned to her when he left. At nineteen, she'd crashed and burned over him, and eventually pulled herself out of the devastation that had engulfed her at his rejection. She couldn't go through that again.

She needed distance if she was going to make him understand that he had to stop touching her before they both did something they would regret. Before he could guess her intentions, she pushed to her feet and moved around to the other side of the desk. When she turned to face him, she saw that he hadn't moved, but his dark eyes watched her just as a hawk might before he pounced on his prey. Repressing a shiver, she said tightly, "You established some ground rules the other morning. Now it's my turn."

Impossibly, his gaze narrowed. "What did you have in mind?"

She lifted her chin. "I don't think it's wise to start something neither of us intends to finish. I'd appreciate it if you'd keep your hands to yourself."

He wouldn't have touched her at all if he could have helped himself, but he wisely kept that information to himself. Suddenly it was vitally important to find out just what her objections to him were. "Why?"

A dozen answers ran through her head. She gave him

the most important ones. "Because I don't want to get hurt. And I will if things continue the way they have been. It's inevitable. We have different lives in different parts of the world. Fate has thrown us together for the moment, but eventually you're going to go back to your space and I'm going to stay in mine. I don't want any regrets if we happen to run into each other at our parents' some year for Christmas."

"And you don't think you might regret not seeing where this…attraction…between us is going?" He knew it was the wrong question, one he shouldn't even be thinking, let alone asking. But for reasons he couldn't name, he had to know. "Wouldn't you rather know than find yourself across the table from me at some Christmas dinner ten years down the road and wonder what might have been? By then it might be too late."

"No." She heard the hint of panic in her voice and winced at it. Did he know how he tempted her? "No," she said again, this time more firmly as she stepped back, deliberately putting more distance between them. "Curiosity may be the only reason you need to pursue this… attraction," she said, choosing his term for lack of a better one, "but curiosity also killed the cat. Thanks, but no thanks. I'd rather live with what ifs."

It wasn't curiosity that kept him awake at night, that made him burn in a way he hadn't before. No, this was something that defied logic and reason and all his common sense. Annoyed by her easy rejection, he made no attempt to hide his irritation. "Ignoring it isn't going to make it go away."

"A fire that isn't stoked eventually goes out," she tossed back at him. "Don't touch me and we'll get along just fine." Satisfied that she'd made her point, she disappeared up the stairs with the announcement that she was going to take a bath.

Staring after her, Tucker cursed fluently. Didn't she realize that not touching her only made him want her more?

* * *

She was asking the impossible. As evening approached, Tucker paced the living room like a death-row inmate running out of time. How could he ignore her when even now he could hear her splashing water on herself as she finished her bath? He wasn't made of stone! He wanted her. The day he sprouted wings and a halo he might be able to keep his hands off her, but he wouldn't bet any money on it. Which left him with a hell of a problem, he thought ruefully. They were both already on the edge. If he didn't find a way to diffuse the tension, it was going to blow up in their faces.

Frowning at the shadows that were already starting to gather in the corners of the living room, he switched on a light by the couch, then moved to the floor lamp standing next to an overstuffed chair. He wanted light, lots of light. And the quiet, homemade dinners they'd been sharing ever since he'd arrived in New Orleans had to stop. He'd order pizza, turn on the TV and hope there was a fight on one of the sports channels on cable to keep his thoughts off her. What could possibly be romantic about that?

It should have been the perfect plan. By the time Lacey stepped out of the bathroom in a loose-fitting blue-and-white striped jumper that hid every curve she had, he had everything ready. Using the couch as a backrest, he sprawled on the floor with a beer in one hand and a piece of pizza in the other as he watched a bantamweight fight on television.

When Lacey stopped in surprise and took in the bright lights, blaring TV and his casual position, he motioned to the open carton of pizza on the coffee table before returning his attention to the fight. "Hope you like pepperoni. Wanna beer?"

"Ah…no, thanks," she said, confused. She'd spent the past half hour in the tub trying to decide how she was going to resist him if he tried to change her mind about exploring their attraction for one another. Had she imagined his hands on her downstairs, his kiss burning the back of her neck?

The way he was acting now, she could strip naked before him and still have a tough time dragging his eyes away from the TV. She should have been relieved. Irritated that she wasn't, she said, "I'll have a cola instead. And pepperoni's fine."

Tucker refused to watch her walk to the refrigerator, but he knew the minute she opened the refrigerator, the second she popped the tab on the can and took a long swallow. Staring blindly at the fight on the screen, he didn't see the boxer in the white trunks knock out his opponent. But he knew the exact instant Lacey settled on the couch two feet away from his shoulder. Even if he hadn't heard her, the lemony scent she wore surrounded him, knocking his senses awry. He reached for his beer and gulped down half of it just as she leaned forward to pick up a piece of pizza.

She could have been eating sawdust for all the notice she took of it, but she forced it down, her eyes, like his, deliberately focused on the TV. "The fight's over," she said. "Who won?"

"What?" He blinked. He'd never known a woman who could so easily destroy his concentration! "Oh... the champion." He picked up the remote control. "You want to watch something else?"

She almost said no, but then she thought of the awkward silence that would spring up between them if he turned off the set. "Yes! The...the news. We've been so busy over the last few days, I haven't been able to keep up with what's going on in the world."

Tucker switched to an all-news station and reached for another piece of pizza just as the news anchor announced, "The situation in Costa Oro has stabilized, but the U.S. government is still refusing to accept the dictatorship of Juan Garza. With the backing of Communist forces, he seized power last month in a coup that resulted in widespread bloodshed. Surprised by the midnight attack, the American embassy staff was miraculously—"

Before the anchor could say another word, Tucker jerked

up the remote control and abruptly switched off the set. A hushed stillness fell over the room, disturbed only by the muffled beat of jazz as it drifted through the open windows from Bourbon Street. Lacey hardly heard it as she studied Tucker's set face. "Why'd you cut it off?"

"Because I'm sick to death of hearing what comes next." Taking another long swig of beer, he set the bottle down with a snap and surprised her by saying in a hard voice, "Saving those people was only sheer dumb luck. They could just as easily have died."

"You mean on the way to the airport? Considering the alternative, I'm sure that was a risk they were all willing to take. Otherwise, they would have all died in the embassy when it was bombed."

"If I hadn't misjudged when the coup was coming down, they wouldn't even have been in danger. We could have gotten them out of there weeks before."

So that was what had been haunting him the times she'd caught him staring into space, his face grim with memories. Had he been blaming himself for a mistake anyone could have made? She wanted to reach out to him, to smooth out the deep lines that had suddenly appeared around his mouth, aging him ten years. But she herself had changed the rules, and touching wasn't allowed. She crumpled the napkin she held, denying the need. "What happened?" she asked quietly. ·

"We knew there was going to be a coup, but we were hoping it would be a bloodless one. I rushed down there to meet with Juan Garza and tried to convince him that once President Ochoa realized that he was outgunned and out-manned and had even lost the support of the people, he would step down peacefully." His mouth twisted into a cynical smile. "Garza let me think he was going to be patient. He almost had me believing he was going to wait as long as necessary in order to gain the support of the people. And all the time, he was planning a midnight march on the capital so he could blow it to hell."

"But you still got everyone out," she reminded him. "And with only a few minor injuries."

"Like I said, that was only dumb luck," he retorted bitterly. "The minute I realized it was going down, we fought our way to the airport. While the phone lines were still up, I tried to warn Ochoa, but he and the members of his cabinet refused to believe that Garza would actually fire on the capital. They were all killed."

"But you can't blame yourself for that!" she cried. "You were negotiating with the man. If you warned them of the danger and they ignored it, then you did all you could. Why are you blaming yourself?"

"Because I was too close to the edge," he admitted for the first time. "That's really why I've been ordered to take some time off. My boss is even pushing me to take a desk job. We both know I should have recognized Garza for a lying dog the minute I laid eyes on him."

"So you made a mistake. Is that so terrible?"

"It could have been."

"But it wasn't. If you want to blame yourself for something, then accept the fact that you were taken in by a man who's gotten where he has today by being a smooth talker. But don't you dare blame yourself for the deaths. You did everything you could short of kidnapping Ochoa and his cabinet and dragging them out of the country. And I can just imagine the furor that would have caused. So what were you supposed to do? Stay there and die with them?"

"No, of course not."

"Then what did you do wrong?"

The guilt that had been like an albatross around his neck for almost a month lifted. Kurt, Marcus, his mother, had tried to tell him the same thing. Why did he have to hear it from her before he finally started to believe it? "Obviously not as much as I'd thought," he said, surprised.

You're in trouble, Tuck old boy. Big trouble!

Just that easily, the intimacy was back between them. Unable to tear his gaze away from hers, Tucker knew he was sinking fast, but there didn't seem to be a damn thing he could do about it. He was trapped there, her only protection against the man who was trying to kill her. He couldn't even take a walk around the block to cool off his hot blood. And she didn't want him to touch her.

Great, he thought in disgust as he reached for the half-eaten pizza that lay abandoned on the coffee table. It was turning into a wonderful evening. "If you don't want any more of this, I'll put it in the refrigerator and get me another beer."

She started to rise to her feet. "I'll do it—"

"No!" He needed some breathing room. "Why don't you find us something to do," he suggested, then could have cursed when his thoughts leaped to the wrong conclusion. "A game," he tried again. "Have you got any board games, checkers or chess? Something like that, since there's nothing but reruns on TV?"

"I used to have Scrabble around here somewhere," she said, a frown wrinkling her brow. "I think it's in my bedroom closet."

"Great! While you're getting it, I'll get you another cola. We can play on the coffee table."

Five minutes later they both sat on the floor, the coffee table between them, and started the game. Silence echoed in their ears, but they hardly noticed as they concentrated on their letters. This was, Tucker decided, exactly what he needed—a mind game to distract him from Lacey. Pleased that he'd thought of it, he laid the word _touch_ on the board and quickly figured up his points. So far, they were dead even.

Lacey chewed her bottom lip and stared at the board. Talk about lousy letters! What was she supposed to do with an _l_, _v_, _a_, _e_, _r_, and two _s_'s? Suddenly zeroing in on the word Tucker had just laid down, she grinned. Snatching up all but two of her letters, she laughingly used them with the _c_ in his word to form _caress_. "That's double word, too," she reminded him, chuckling as she added up the points. "Looks like I'm ahead."

"Not for long," he vowed, shifting his long legs under the table to get more comfortable. His foot accidentally brushed her thigh. Did her breath catch in her throat? he wondered, staring unseeingly down at his letters, or was his imagination playing tricks on him? Think! he told himself sternly, and dragged his attention back to the game.

Minutes passed. Slow, silent aeons filled with the sound of the wooden letters being placed on the board, the whisper of their clothes as they each shifted positions in an effort to get comfortable, the sudden sucking in of breath as Tucker stared at the board and realized for the first time just how revealing the words they'd picked were. *Touch. Caress. Love. Kiss. Hold.* His eyes flew to hers. Had she realized yet that they were sending silent messages to each other?

Feeling his eyes on her, Lacey looked up to find him staring at her. She stilled, her throat suddenly going dry as her pulse skipped out of control. Why was he looking at her like that? "What?" she said hoarsely. "What is it?"

His gaze dropped to the words spread out between them before coming back to her. Without saying a word, he told her to read. Puzzled, she, too, stared at the board.

Under his watchful gaze, awareness bloomed in her cheeks like a rose. With shaking fingers, she quickly dropped the letters she held in her hand back to their wooden stand. Tucker would have given just about anything to know what word she had been about to play.

Under the table his leg slid closer to hers until his foot again just brushed her hip. He felt her start of surprise, but he didn't, couldn't stop touching her. "It's your turn," he reminded her in a husky whisper.

She swallowed, but couldn't manage to answer him. With jerky movements she picked up three letters and used the last *s* in *kiss* to spell out a defiant *stop*!

His foot only traced a circle over the full skirt of her

jumper at the top of her thigh. He couldn't stop and they both knew it. His eyes slumberous with need, he dropped a single *n* over the *o* in *stop*.

"Tucker..." She meant to threaten him with dire consequences if he didn't behave himself, but even she could hear the longing in her voice. Cursing herself for a fool, she pushed the table away and scrambled to her feet. "I...I don't want to play anymore."

Her knees trembling, she started past him on the way to her bedroom, but he jumped to his feet, not even sparing the coffee table and game pieces a second glance as he grabbed her arm. "Neither do I," he growled, pulling her against him. "I'm tired of playing games."

"Tucker...please..."

"Look me in the eye and tell me you don't want me to do all those things you just spelled out on that board," he dared her. "I want to hear you say you don't want me to hold you. To kiss you." He drew her closer, his eyes snaring hers as his voice dropped to a deep murmur. "Tell me you haven't thought of making love with me until we're both too weak to move. Go ahead," he urged huskily, leaning down to nibble at her ear. "I dare you."

Somehow she had to find the words, but her mind was blank, empty. With his hot, moist breath teasing her ear, his lips so close she could already taste the promise of his kiss, there was no right or wrong, no yesterday or tomorrow. All she could think of was the need that had been burning in her for longer than she could remember. Only he could put out the fire. For this one night, nothing else mattered. Murmuring his name, she lifted her mouth to his.

Chapter 8

Whenever he'd allowed himself to think of loving her, he'd thought of taking it slow and easy, of drawing out the pleasure with unhurried kisses and lazy explorations that would banish the memories of any other lover right out of her head. But he had ached for her too long, tortured himself too many nights with the image of having her just so, her arms clutching him close, her mouth wild and responsive under his. There was no thought of taking it slow; there was nothing easy about the passion clawing at his insides with sharp talons of need. The minute she melted into him, he stepped into a hurricane. With a groan, what little control he had left shattered.

He wasn't a man to take a woman roughly, but she drove him to a desperation that was new to him, pushing him past reason with nothing more than the taste of her. His blood raging, he pulled her down to the couch with him, his hands already working at the clothes that separated his skin from her. He wanted to touch her, *had* to touch her! Swearing, he tore at buttons and zippers with fingers that were clumsy.

He was trembling! he realized, stunned. He couldn't think of any other woman who had ever reduced him to this! But still, he couldn't stop, couldn't take the few deep breaths he needed to regain a measure of restraint. Muttering a curse, he whipped off his shirt, then grabbed the hem of her jumper and snatched it over her head. Tossing it aside, he reached for the clasp of her bra before her dress had even floated to the floor.

With a startled cry of delight, Lacey arched against the hand that closed around her bare breast, heat flushing her skin and turning her bones fluid. He was moving too fast, sweeping her down into a red-hot, swirling eddy of desire, but she couldn't protest, couldn't do anything but move with him and let her emotions fly. Passion. She had never tasted passion like this, dark and dangerous and urgent. It enveloped her, consumed her, took her beyond herself to a world that began and ended with the man who held her as if he would draw her into his very soul.

The hated couch was as soft as a piece of plywood as he pulled her down to it, but she didn't notice. His hands rushed over her, touching, caressing, claiming every inch of her. She only had time to realize that his fingers played at her breast, teasing and tormenting the rosy crests into hard buds before he lowered his head and took her into his mouth, sucking greedily. Need tugged at her, dragging a gasp of surprise from her. "Tucker...please..."

He only turned his attention to her other breast, driving her to the very edge of reason with nothing more than his teeth and tongue. Under his mouth he could feel the wild pounding of her heart, the short, shallow pants of her breath, her soft whimpers. In an abrupt move he lifted his head, his mouth, hot and seeking, closing over hers as his hands moved between them to unfasten his jeans. Never taking his lips from hers, he kicked them away and gathered her to him. Hot skin glided against hot skin. His searching fingers skimmed her bare stomach, the curve of her hip, traveling steadily downward until they closed over the thin swatch of lace and silk that concealed the heart of her desire.

The world, the apartment, could have gone up in flames around them and they never would have noticed. His breath, torn from his lungs, rasped against her ear. Her sighs, like moist darts against his face and neck and chest, drove him on. He wanted to savor her, to linger until every curve, every shudder, every cry of need that escaped from her parted lips was committed to memory. But her hips were moving against him in a silent plea that made him throb. His body hard and tight and ready to explode, he swept away the last of their clothes and parted her thighs.

From the first day they had met all those long years ago, they had been moving to this moment. He knew it as he slid into her with one sure thrust and heard her sob with pleasure. She knew it as she closed around him and found a completeness she had never known. But neither could have guessed it would be like this. Sweet, rough yet tender, incredible. Brown eyes locked with green; there was no breath left to speak. He moved, she lifted to him, catching his rhythm as easily as if they'd made love countless times. Thoughts clouded, senses blurred, sighs mingled. In the time it took their hearts to beat in unison, they were lost.

He was a man she could love…might already love.

The thought was there, waiting for Lacey the minute she floated back down to earth. Flat on her back, blanketed by Tucker's satisfyingly heavy weight as she held him against her, she stared at the ceiling and let the knowledge ripple through her. Love. How had she let herself get even close to that dangerous emotion? Eight years ago she'd been a foolish teenager dealing with an attraction she hadn't had the experience to handle. She'd been determined not to make the same mistake twice. She'd thought she'd succeeded. Until tonight.

Squeezing her eyes closed, she tightened her arms around him, unable, even now, to deny herself these few precious moments. In a matter of days, possibly weeks, he would be leaving, eventually returning to a world she wanted no part of. And she would be alone. She'd known that from the beginning, accepted it because things could be no other way. Now she would have to watch him leave with the memory of their lovemaking playing in her head, tearing her apart. Dear God, what had she done?

Catching back a sob between her teeth, she tried to stop the hurt, but it was far more painful than anything she'd felt at nineteen. This devastated her very soul, and lying in his arms was only going to make it worse. Forcing back the tears that burned her eyes, she wiggled out from under him.

Sated, too relaxed to move, Tucker could have spent the rest of the night just holding her. Pushing up on an elbow, he reached for her. "Hey, where're you going," he growled huskily. "Come back here."

"No." Evading his hand, Lacey stumbled over the Scrabble pieces on the floor as she pushed her tousled hair out of her eyes. Her vision blurred, she snatched up the first piece of clothing she saw. It was his shirt. His scent surrounding her, she pulled it on, her fingers shaking as she struggled with the buttons.

Tucker's eyes narrowed as he watched her jerky movements with the buttons. Her eyes were downcast, her face totally devoid of color but for the patches of blush on her cheeks. Uneasiness stirred in him. She hardly looked like a woman who had just enjoyed a bout of wild lovemaking. "What's wrong?" he demanded quietly. "Did I hurt you? I know I was rough. I'm sorry—"

"No!" Her sharp cry cut through his words before he could finish them. Dear God, she didn't think she could handle an apology now. "You weren't too…rough." No, he'd been wonderful, but she couldn't allow herself to think of that now or she'd dissolve in tears at his feet. Lifting her eyes to him, she felt heat steal up her body from her toes as she took in his nakedness. But she didn't flinch as she said flatly, "This was a mistake. It can't happen again."

Pain sliced through him like a knife between the ribs, stunning him. When had he given her or any other woman the power to hurt him? Pushing to his feet, he reached for his jeans and tugged them on. The sound of the zipper was like a scream in the tense quiet that enveloped them. Resisting the urge to let loose a string of curses, he clamped his jaw and stared at her. His shirt swallowed her and fell to the middle of her thighs. Just that quickly he wanted her again.

He bit out an oath while his eyes shot accusations at her. "It takes two to make love, and you were with me every step of the way."

She didn't deny it. How could she? They both knew she'd come apart in his arms. Wishing the floor would just open up and swallow her, she looked him squarely in the eye. "We were both caught up in the moment. But it was still a mistake."

Furious, he fought back the need to cross the room and shake her. But if he touched her now, they'd end up right back on that couch whether she wanted it or not. "You think you're just going to forget this and act like it never happened?" he demanded harshly. "Is it that easy for you?"

She would have laughed if she hadn't been afraid it would come out as a sob. *Easy!* How could he think it was easy when her heart was in shreds? "Easy or not, it's what I'm going to do," she retorted. "I suggest you do the same thing." Her eyes settled on the rest of her clothes scattered on the floor, and suddenly she knew she couldn't take any more. She snatched them up, hugging them to her chest. "I'm going to bed," she muttered, pivoting toward her bedroom. "Tomorrow's going to be a long day, and it'll start early."

It took all her control not to slam her bedroom door and shut out all the memories that were already plaguing her.

After closing it quietly, she moved toward her dresser for her nightgown. She would not sleep in his shirt! But she'd taken only two steps when the door crashed back on its hinges. Her heart in her throat, she whirled to find Tucker standing in the open doorway, his rugged face set in harsh lines as he glared at her. "Leave it open," he ordered coldly. "Regardless of what just happened, you're still in danger, and it's my job to keep you safe. I can't do that through a closed door."

Unable to offer a single word of protest, she nodded mutely.

Clamping his teeth on a curse, Tucker stormed back into the living room. Stepping on one of the Scrabble pieces, he gave serious consideration to burning the whole game in the fireplace. Instead, he squatted down to pick up the pieces. But the memories of Lacey were too fresh, the taste of her still on his tongue. With every letter he dropped into the box, he was reminded of her and the way he had stripped her of her clothes and filled his hands with her. A muscle ticking along his jaw, he shoved the game into the closet, then switched off the lights one by one until the apartment was pitch-black. But that only intensified the images that teased him. From her room, he heard the mattress give as Lacey settled onto her bed and pulled the sheet over her. After that there was only silence, as if she knew he was listening. Swearing, he jerked his eyes away from her bedroom door and stared at the dark shadow that was the couch. There was no way he was going to be able to sleep there tonight.

He needed a drink, he thought in disgust as he moved to the window to stare unseeingly out at the night. A good, stiff drink. Hell, he could drink the whole damn bottle, but it wasn't going to do any good. He wasn't going to be able to forget.

A mistake, he brooded, his thoughts churning. How could she call what had just happened between them a mistake, for God's sake? She'd turned him inside out and now she wanted to claim it was all a mistake that wouldn't happen again? he thought incredulously. Like hell! She might try to lie to herself, but he was the one who'd held her, who'd felt her turn to flames in his arms. She'd been just as eager as he had, just as caught up in a magic unlike anything he'd ever known before. If she thought he was going to let her walk away from that—

His thoughts ended abruptly as a sudden, stealthy movement in the darkness caught his eye. He froze, the sixth sense that always warned him of trouble clanging in his head. On the roof of the building next door, a figure dressed all in black separated itself from the shadows. Swift and sinister, the intruder started down the angled roof that butted into Lacey's rooftop patio. Even in the darkness Tucker could sense his deadly intent. And the only entrance to the apartment from the patio was the French doors in Lacey's bedroom. Springing into action, he stepped into her room on silent feet.

Wide awake, her body still pulsing with the ecstasy of his lovemaking, Lacey heard him the minute he crossed the threshold. Her heart tripping over itself, she bolted up and clutched the sheet to her breasts as if he could see her in the darkness. Grabbing at an anger that was her only defense, she exploded. "Damn it, Tucker, what do you think you're doing? I told you—"

"Call Ryan," he interrupted in a hard, no-nonsense voice she'd never heard before. "There's someone on the roof."

"*What!* Where?" she cried, but he was already slipping soundlessly out the French doors to stalk the man. Alarmed, she jumped up to race after him, only to stop. The police. She had to call the police. She swung back to the bed, almost tripping over the long folds of her white nightgown in her haste. Afraid to turn on the light and alert the intruder that they were on to him, she fumbled for the phone on the nightstand, her fingers searching for the correct numbers in the dark.

Muttering a curse, she heaved a sigh of relief as the 911 operator came on the line. Shaking with nerves, she quickly gave her name and address, then explained the situation. The operator assured her Detective Ryan would be notified and help was on the way. But when she hung up, she found little comfort in that.

Racing to the double doors that opened onto the patio, she stood well back in the shadows so she wouldn't be seen, and gazed anxiously out into the night. Tucker had already crossed the patio and was halfway up the angled roof of the building next door. Even as she watched, the darkness swallowed him whole.

Suddenly chilled, she shivered, though the air was muggy and still. Unchecked, fear surged into panic as she searched the shadows for some sign of Tucker and the intruder he had seen. The night, however, was empty. Overhead, the moon played hide-and-seek in the clouds, and in the distance Bourbon Street still hummed with life. Everything was terrifyingly normal. Lacey felt sweat break out on her brow. Who was Tucker stalking? A burglar who had decided to take advantage of the police strike and had, just by chance, chosen to hit her shop and apartment tonight? Or was it the man who had threatened her? If so, he would have come prepared to kill her.

Her heart stopped dead at the thought. Tucker had run out in nothing but his bare feet and jeans. If the moon came out from behind the clouds and the man he chased was armed... Before the image could play itself out, she spun away from the window, rushed to her nightstand and jerked open the top drawer. The pearl-handled derringer winked up at her in the darkness. She snatched it up and ran for the patio doors, Tucker's safety the only thought in her head.

It was not his night, Tucker decided as the moon swept out from behind the clouds when he was just halfway across the patio. His jeans were dark, but his bare shoulders and chest gleamed in the moonlight like a neon sign. The intruder, halfway down the sloping roof, spied him instantly. Spitting out a curse, he whirled and scrambled back up the way he had come. In the blink of an eye, Tucker took off after him.

Crossing the patio at a dead run, he jumped up on the angled roof and grabbed for purchase as his bare feet threatened to slip out from under him. Ahead of him he heard the labored breathing of the intruder and the thud of his feet as the roof leveled off, giving him the advantage. The moon increased that advantage when it slipped back behind the clouds. His face grim, Tucker never slowed his pace. Closing his fingers around a nearby exhaust pipe, he hauled himself up and renewed the chase.

The world shrank to the dark rooftops of the French Quarter. Darting around pipes and antennas, jumping over walls that separated buildings, dodging chimneys, Tucker closed the distance between him and the man in black. Fifty yards. Only fifty yards and he could get his hands around his throat.

Without warning, the moon avoided the clouds to pick him out of the darkness like a spotlight. A fraction of a second later a bullet came whizzing at him, the hot lead coming so close he felt the heat of it warm his shoulder. Muttering a coarse oath, he dove for cover behind a chimney before a second bullet could part his hair. His heart slamming against his ribs, he flattened himself against the old bricks, listening. Was the bastard hiding behind the dormer roof just up ahead or had he taken off again? Tucker hit his clenched fist against the bricks. Why hadn't he thought to grab Lacey's gun? he thought in disgust. Now he didn't have any choice but to turn back or get picked off the roof like a sitting duck.

He wasn't, however, going anywhere until the moon went back behind the clouds. Resting against the chimney, he waited impatiently, his ears cocked to catch the slightest sound from the man who shared the roof with him. Nothing moved. Seconds slipped into an eternity as tension scraped his nerves raw. Overhead, the moon flirted with a cloud before finally giving up the game and slipping behind it. Tucker knew better than to wait for a second chance that might never come.

Crouched low, he darted to a low wall twenty feet away and vaulted over it, half expecting a bullet to come chasing him. Only silence followed him. The nerves knotted in his gut eased, but only a little. Only a fool relaxed his guard before he was sure the danger had passed. For all he knew, the bastard could be waiting out there for him to lift his head so he could do some target practice in the dark. He was going to have a hell of a long wait.

Following the wall, Tucker bent low and soundlessly jumped over it. The second his feet touched the neighboring roof, he was off and running. A slanted skylight fifteen feet away offered the closest protection. He headed straight for it, then threw himself behind it, the thudding of his heart echoing in his ears as he took a moment to catch his breath. In the apartment below him a dog suddenly barked in alarm, giving away his position. Swearing, he silently bolted to the next chimney.

The dog quieted; a hush settled over the night. Almost within sight of Lacey's apartment, Tucker started to heave a sigh of relief when he suddenly caught the furtive sound of someone moving on the roof just ahead of him in the darkness. He stiffened, his sharp eyes searching the shadows. But the moon was still behind the clouds, concealing him as well as the man he shared the roof with. Had the bastard slipped around behind him to catch him by surprise? His jaw hardened with anticipation at the thought. They would see who was surprised. Quickly darting around to the opposite side of the chimney, he tensed, ready to spring.

Lacey moved cautiously over the roof, the gun clutched nervously in her damp palm, her heart beating in her chest like a war drum. Half afraid to breathe and miss the sound of Tucker moving somewhere in the darkness ahead of her, she glared up at the clouds that concealed the moon before quickly dragging her gaze back to the shadows before her. Danger. She could almost smell it on the night air as the fine hairs at the nape of her neck tingled a warning. She wanted to run then, straight back to her apartment to wait for the police. But if the intruder had a gun, Tucker could be dead by then. Straightening her shoulders, she started around the chimney that suddenly emerged out of the blackness in front of her.

In the next instant she was grabbed from behind and slammed up against the bricks. Startled, she opened her mouth to scream as a hard, male body pressed up against her, threatening to flatten her.

At the touch of her soft, unbound breasts against his chest, Tucker swore and jerked back as if he were jumping back from a hot flame. "Damn it to hell, what are you doing out here?" he stormed in a fierce whisper as his fingers bit into her bare shoulders. The moon, choosing that moment to come out of hiding, slid out from behind the cloud to reveal the white batiste nightgown that covered her slender body so alluringly. His body, with a will of its own, heated in response, infuriating him. "Do you realize you're nearly naked? What are you trying to do, get yourself raped? Or killed? In case you've forgotten, there's someone out here who would like nothing better than to see you dead!"

And to think that she'd actually been worried about him! "I haven't forgotten anything!" she snapped. Shrugging off his hold, she jabbed her hand against his shoulder and pushed him back, glaring up at him like David taking on Goliath. "I was the one who was run over, remember? I was also the one who already witnessed one murder. Whoever's out there," she said coldly, motioning abruptly to the dark rooftops surrounding them, "wants to shut me up. That means he'll try just about anything to do it, including taking you out of the picture if he has to. I was stupid enough to be worried about you." Grabbing his hand, she shoved the small derringer into it, forcing him to take it. "I thought you might need this." Without another word, she turned and stalked off to her apartment.

Dumfounded, Tucker stared after her. She'd risked her life because she'd thought he was in danger. Had anyone, man or woman, ever done that for him before? Stunned, he started after her. "Damn it, Lacey, wait a minute!" She didn't even slow down, let alone stop. Increasing his pace, he caught up with her in three long strides. He would have taken her arm then, but one look at her set jaw warned him to back off. He couldn't really blame her. "I'm sorry I jumped down your throat," he said quietly, "but I don't want you taking any chances. Especially for me. I had the situation under control."

"Don't worry, it won't happen again," she assured him stiffly, staring straight ahead. "It was my mistake." Pain clutched at her, squeezing her heart. No, she silently corrected herself. Mistake was too mild a word to describe what she'd done. She'd fallen in love with him. Again.

Blinking back stupid tears, she called herself seven kinds of a fool. Even now she wanted to deny it, but she couldn't forget the way she'd felt when she'd realized that he was the one who'd grabbed her and pushed her up against that chimney. She loved him. Completely and irrevocably.

Dear God, how had it happened? For eight long years she'd told herself she never wanted to lay eyes on him again. Had she been aching for the sight of him, the feel of his arms around her, even then? Waiting for him to one day show up on her doorstep admitting that he'd made a mistake by ever letting her get away from him?

Fat chance, she thought with a silent sniff. Even if he'd made that admission, what did it change? Nothing! They were two ships passing in the night. She winced at the corny description, but there was no avoiding it. They weren't heading in the same direction and they never would be. She might as well accept it now. She would love him until the day she died, but she couldn't have him.

"Lace...honey," he tried again when she didn't respond. "It isn't a mistake to be concerned about someone—"

The wail of sirens cut him off just as they reached her patio. Lacey sighed in relief. The last thing she wanted to do was get into a discussion about her feelings for him. "It sounds like Detective Ryan brought half the force with him. Will you go down and let them in? I need to put on a robe."

Since he didn't want her greeting Ryan and his men like that, he didn't have much choice in the matter. Promising himself they would finish the conversation at a later date, he hurried inside to let the police in before they decided to break down the door.

Ryan and his men took over the apartment and the rooftops of the French Quarter. The minute Tucker opened the door, they charged inside and up the stairs, pausing only long enough to learn that the man they were after was armed before they drew their weapons and spread out onto the patio and neighboring roofs. After listening to Tucker's account of what happened, Ryan called in a helicopter to aid in the search. Soon the steady whir of helicopter blades beat at the night air. The pilot, armed with a powerful light, aimed it at every nook and cranny of the uneven rooftops. If even a rat moved, he would see it.

In her apartment, Lacey clutched her robe closed and restlessly paced the length of the living room, her nerves stretched as tight as catgut on a tennis racket. Downstairs, the harsh crackle of the police radios bounced off the walls of the surrounding buildings, while the revolving red and blue lights of the patrol cars' light bars soundlessly turned like stuck records. She should have welcomed the noise, the lights, the reassuring presence of the police, but she'd have given just about anything then just to have five minutes to herself. Maybe then she would have been able to deal with a world that had managed to turn upside down in the span of an evening.

But she didn't get five minutes. She didn't even get five seconds. One of the cops who had stormed through her bedroom just seconds after she had belted her robe stepped into the living room to update Detective Ryan on the search going on outside. "Nothing," he said flatly. "We haven't turned up hide or hair of him. He either found a hole to crawl into or he got away."

"What about the two bullets he fired?" Jack Ryan demanded. "Any sign of them?"

The officer shook his head. "Not so far. We're still searching, but we'll probably have to wait for sunup. Even with the moon, we could pass within six inches of them and never see them."

Ryan nodded. "Do whatever it takes. We need all the clues we can get."

Lacey watched the detective rake his fingers through his hair and prayed, just for a moment, that they were all jumping to the wrong conclusion. "I don't suppose there's any chance that this could have been nothing more than a bungled burglary, is there?"

A lie would have reassured her, but it wasn't going to keep her safe, and that was his main priority. "You said yourself you're only robbed when you're not at home," he reminded her. "Martin's partner, whoever the hell he is, is getting desperate. Threats haven't worked, and he's running out of time. The longer he waits to shut you up, the more time we have to discover his identity."

Tucker propped a shoulder against the doorjamb of the bedroom. "So he decided to slip in here and shoot us both before that happened." He aimed a hard look at the detective. "Where was the man you assigned to the corner? He should have been here less than two minutes after Lacey called for help."

Ryan's mouth thinned in disgust. "He was following up

a call we got about a suspected burglary by the market,"
he replied. "It turned out to be a false alarm."

"Probably called in by our uninvited guest," Lacey
guessed bitterly. Needing to throw something, she snatched
Tucker's pillow up off the couch and hurled it across the
room, where it fell harmlessly to the floor. "God, I hate
this! When is it all going to end?"

The older man rose to his feet. "Maybe sooner than you
think," he informed her. "The union agreed tonight to the
new contract proposed by the city. The vote will be taken
tomorrow, but it's got a ninety-nine percent chance of passing since the union is behind it."

She stopped her pacing to turn to him in surprise. "So
the day after tomorrow you'll have more men to put on the
case?"

"No, we won't have to wait that long. Some of the night
shift came in tonight. More will be in tomorrow," he assured her. "Which means I can put you in a safe house and
have the men to protect you."

Tucker straightened away from the doorjamb. "When?"

"Right now," he replied. "The sooner the better."

Two days ago Lacey would have been thrilled by his
announcement. Now it couldn't have come at a worse time.
After the close call Tucker had just had, she had no intention of refusing the safe house, but her sale started in only
a matter of hours. Her eyes drifted to the stairs. "Now?"

Tucker hadn't forgotten the sale or the long hours of
exhausting work she had had preparing for it. "I'll stay and
run the sale for you, okay? You just get out of here and go
someplace where it's safe."

"But you don't know anything about antiques," she argued. "I have to be here. I'm the only one who knows
which pieces I can cut the prices on and which ones I
can't." She turned to the detective. "If you have enough
men to protect me, can't you post them around the shop
until after the sale? No one's going to try anything in a

shop full of customers, anyway. And the shop will be full. I guarantee it.''

His dark brows knit into a straight line, Ryan rubbed his jaw consideringly. ''The chances of you having any more trouble tonight are slim,'' he finally admitted. ''We came in with a show of force, and everyone in the Quarter knows we're here. The perp will probably retreat to a hole somewhere and rethink his strategy.'' He gave her a fierce look that dared her to argue. ''By the time he comes up with another plan, you're going to be safely tucked away out of reach.''

''I'll go to the safe house without a word of protest,'' she promised. ''Just as soon as my sale is over.''

He nodded. ''All right. You'll have two men here undercover during the sale. Until then, one of them will be in the shop and the other one on the roof. I'll also put someone back on the corner, but this time his only assignment is to watch the shop and the entrance to the alley. After the sale, I'll arrange to have you taken to the safe house.'' He glanced at Tucker. ''Are you going with her or are you going to let us take it from here? I'll warn you right now, it could be a while.''

Tucker's eyes locked with Lacey's. He could think of a dozen reasons why he should take the easy way out. He was getting in too deep. She already had him tied in knots. She regretted making love with him. That should have been enough to send him packing to Aruba. But whether she wanted it or not, they were already involved. He didn't know where the hell it would lead, but he did know he couldn't walk away. Not now.

''I'm staying,'' he told her softly. ''To the end.''

Chapter 9

Detective Ryan left soon after that, leaving the two undercover cops as promised. But with one of them downstairs and the other out on the patio, Lacey was once again alone with Tucker. *To the end. To the end.* The words throbbed in the silence that engulfed them as soon as the last patrol car sped away, a threat and a promise at one and the same time. What did he mean, to the end? she wondered wildly, a frown etching her brow as she watched him lounge on the couch as if he hadn't a care in the world. To the end of what? The trial? Their affair? Eternity?

The tauntings of her own mind brought her up off the chair she had sunk into. No! she silently cried. She would *not* torment herself this way. Dreams of happily-ever-after and wishful thinking would only make her miserable. If he chose to stay until the trial, it was only because he was concerned about her safety, nothing more. And making love with him one time hardly constituted an affair. As for eternity, it might take her that long to forget him, but that was the only future they had together.

Agitated, her eyes burning with the tears already clogging her throat, she turned toward her room. "I might as well get ready," she said thickly. "The first customers will be arriving soon."

Tucker glanced at the clock and arched a brow. "I thought the sale didn't start until eight? You've got hours yet."

"It doesn't. But the fire marshall only allows a certain number of people in the shop at one time," she explained. "To make sure those who get here first get in first, I leave a legal pad by the front door for them to sign. Some people get here at six, sign their names on the list, go have breakfast and then make it back in time to get into the shop with the first group at eight."

"Good Lord, why? I can't imagine being anywhere but in bed at six o'clock on a Saturday morning."

Against her will, Lacey's eyes strayed to the couch. Hot memories singed her cheeks until they were as bright as the red highlights in her hair. She squared her shoulders, only pride keeping her hands from flying to her face to hide the blush. "Other dealers and collectors want first shot at the rare pieces that don't usually come up for sale." Heading for the door, she threw over her shoulder, "Since we'll be leaving directly after the sale, you'd better pack now. You probably won't have time later."

Her emotions rigidly held in check, she knew he was watching her through the open door as she moved from her dresser to her closet, gathering clothes to take with her. Determinedly, she kept her eyes on her task, never once looking in the direction of the living room. But the minute she stepped into the bathroom for a shower, the strain of pretending nothing had changed caught up with her. Turning the water on full force, she lifted her face to the hot spray. Tears filled her eyes and spilled over her lashes, mingling with the water running in rivulets down her cheeks. She made no attempt to stop them. There was no one there to see.

Half an hour later, however, there were no signs of her tears as she stepped out of the bathroom. Dressed in mint-green slacks and a peach silk blouse, her hair neatly braided down her back, she was all business. She absolutely refused to wear her heart on her sleeve for Tucker Stevens more than once in a lifetime!

While he took a shower, she cooked breakfast. If she was aware of him when he stepped out of the bathroom in tan slacks and a white long-sleeved shirt, the fresh, spicy scent of him teasing her nostrils, she gave no sign of it. Quickly transferring the food to two plates, she joined him at the table and immediately brought up the sale. "We'll start by opening the doors to the first thirty customers," she said as she poured syrup over her pancakes. "The fire marshall allows more, but I've found if I let in too many, people can't browse the way they would like and the sales suffer. I'll handle the cash register and any haggling on prices, but I'd appreciate it if you'd take charge of the front door. Is that okay with you?"

He took a bite of bacon. He'd rather glue himself to her side to make sure she was safe, but considering how determined she was to keep things strictly business between them, he didn't think she'd stand for that. He wouldn't push the issue. For now. But once the sale started, a fly wouldn't get near her without him being there to swat it away. "Sure." He shrugged, reaching for his coffee. "What do I do?"

"After the first thirty, let five more people in every time five leave until the crowd thins. Business usually slacks off by the middle of the afternoon, so the customers can just walk in as they arrive."

He nodded. "Sounds fine to me. I'd planned on being near the door, anyway. I want to keep a close eye on who's coming and going."

"You may have your hands full," she predicted. "I advertised all over the South. I'm expecting a big turnout."

"I can handle it," he assured her. "It'll be a piece of cake."

Three hours later Lacey and Tucker stood at the front door waiting for one of the numerous mantel clocks in the shop to chime the hour of eight. Outside, a swarm of people waited expectantly in a line that circled down the block and around the corner. "I never would have believed it if I hadn't seen it," Tucker muttered, staring out the window that had been repaired the day after the attack. "There must be four hundred people out there."

Almost beside herself with excitement, Lacey stared out at the gathering throng, her green eyes fairly dancing. "I can't believe it! I knew this sale would draw a crowd, but I never expected anything like this."

Behind them, the clock merrily struck the hour. Tucker grinned. "You wanted customers, you got 'em. Stand back so you don't get trampled in the rush."

At Lacey's nod, he opened the door with a flourish, the legal pad he held almost filled with names. One by one he admitted the first thirty to the shop, among them the two undercover cops who would be staying for the duration of the sale. Not a flicker of recognition showed in his sharp eyes as he examined the two men and every other customer who stepped over the threshold. There wasn't a suspicious face in the bunch. For all he knew, the man intent on killing Lacey could look as innocent as the proverbial boy next door. It was going to be a long day.

Throwing herself into the sale, Lacey greeted old customers as if they were long-lost friends, and was soon up to her ears in price dickering. She hardly had time to complete one sale before she was called away for another. Two hours passed before she even had a chance to catch her breath and she loved every minute of it.

Juggling figures in her head, she was edging her way through the press of furniture and customers to answer a question about a fainting couch when Mary Blackstone stopped her by simply catching her arm. "I want that fire screen," she announced in a haughty tone that refused to be denied as she nodded at the delicate piece. "But you're asking an outrageous price for it."

Lacey held a grin. The older woman was the first customer she'd had when she'd opened her shop seven years ago. That day she'd bought a pine sideboard, but only after arguing over the price for thirty minutes. New to New Orleans then, it had taken Lacey three weeks to discover that Mary Blackstone was one of the wealthiest women in the city. She also came from a long line of horse traders, and trading was in her blood. There was nothing she enjoyed quite so much as bargain hunting.

Leaning back against the counter that held the cash register, Lacey arched a brow at her, her green eyes sparkling. "Now, Mary, you know that screen's a steal at that price. Why, I bet I could sell it for twice that much to any number of people outside waiting to get in."

The older woman only snorted at that, enjoying the game as she struggled to hold back a smile. "I doubt that. Why, anyone can see that it's been refinished."

Lacey didn't attempt to deny. She nodded, smiling. "That's why the price is so low. It's quite a bargain, isn't it?"

It was and they both knew it. Deciding she had to have it, Mary retorted, "Take fifty dollars off the price and I'll buy it."

"I'd keep it myself for that price." She chuckled. "I was thinking more along the lines of ten."

"Make it thirty-five and you've got a deal."

"Thirteen-fifty," Lacey suggested.

The older woman drew herself up to her full height of five foot seven as if she'd just been insulted. "Twenty dollars off and not a penny less."

Lacey might have fallen for the act if she hadn't seen her lips twitch. "I can put a Sold sign on it for fifteen," she replied, her smile stretching into a grin. "I should warn you that Mr. Thompson was just asking me about it—"

"I'll take it," Mary said quickly, her frown fierce. "Don't you dare let anyone buy that out from under me!"

"I wouldn't dream of it," Lacey said with a laugh, and stepped across to the screen to place a red Sold sticker on it. She'd made almost twenty dollars more than she'd dared to hope for on it! "Would you like to look around some more or pay for it now?"

"I'll look around," she retorted, eyeing a Louis XIV armchair across the room. "I'll be lucky to get out of here with a penny left to my name."

Regally making her way through the crowd, she left Lacey standing by the fire screen, flushed with success. Now if the rest of the damaged pieces could sell as easily! Unable to stop the smile that seemed to be permanently etched in her face, she turned to survey the rest of her customers, but her eyes landed on Tucker instead. He still stood at the door like a guard dog, his narrowed eyes inspecting everyone in the shop as if he expected them to turn into ax murderers at any moment.

Stepping around a woman looking at the jewelry locked in the glass display case, she hurried to Tucker's side. "What are you doing?" she demanded in a low voice, glancing quickly around to make sure no one had noticed his harsh stare.

He spared her only a quick look before turning his attention back to the people browsing through the shop. "What do you mean, what am I doing? What does it look like I'm doing?"

"Scaring my customers," she retorted through her teeth as she smiled at an older man standing nearby. "Lighten up! Nothing's going to happen with so many people around."

"Don't be too sure of that. I've told you before, if this nut really wants to get to you, he can." His gaze lingered on a tall, thin man dressed in a light gray summer suit examining a table near the door to the storeroom. "See that man over there," he said, nodding slightly in the man's direction. "For all we know, he could have plastic explosive concealed inside his suit coat and is looking for a place to hide it. All he'd have to do is walk out of here, set if off, and no one would ever connect him with the crime. It's that easy."

Lacey paled. "No! He couldn't! It's not possible—"

"It is," he said quietly. He watched the pleasure she'd found in the sale pushed aside by fear, and cursed himself. But she had to realize that as long as someone was out there trying to kill her, there was danger even in a crowd. He reached out, needing to comfort her. "Honey, I'm sorry, but that's the way it is."

At the touch of his fingers on her arm, his strength flowed into her. Before she'd even recognized the need, he was there for her to lean on. But for how long? she thought, and pulled back while she still could. "I'd better get back to work," she said abruptly and forced herself to move away from him.

After that, the sale dragged for her. By two o'clock, when the crowd finally began to thin, she'd already topped her projected sales figure, but she could find little joy in the knowledge. Now as suspicious as Tucker, she found herself watching everyone, searching for some sign of deviousness in the faces of friends and strangers alike. When she didn't find a single thing to be alarmed about, her anxiety only doubled. Had she already missed the man who stalked her? Had he slipped inside with a handful of others, possibly even spoken to her, then lost himself in the crowd to conceal a deadly calling card? Did she even now have only seconds to live?

"I don't have to ask how you're doing," a deep, slightly mocking voice suddenly said behind her. "The word is all over the Quarter that you're having the sale of the year. Congratulations."

The forced smile she'd been wearing ever since she'd

talked to Tucker froze in place and brought a chilly look to her eyes. John Solomon. She'd know his smooth voice in the pits of hell. Slapping a firm hold on the dislike that surged inside her, she slowly turned to face him, her face expressionless. "Hello, John. What are you doing here, checking out the competition? I'm afraid you're too late. Most of the good pieces are already gone."

"So I see," he said easily, taking a quick, knowledge-able survey of the merchandise she had left. The last time he'd visited the shop it had been overflowing with pieces he would have given his eyeteeth to have. Now all of the rarer treasures were gone, already shipped off to their new owners. "I would have been here this morning, but I couldn't get through the mob. Did you know there was even a TV crew outside earlier? You've made quite a splash."

She hadn't known, but she wasn't surprised. Before he'd left that morning, Detective Ryan had warned her he planned to release her name and the circumstances concerning the attack on her shop to the media. Since the man who was after her already knew her identity, there was no longer any need to keep it a secret. The press coverage and the curiosity seekers who would turn up because of it were just one more factor that would help keep her safe.

"Anyone would have made a splash with this estate," she replied easily. "I was lucky to get it."

He shook his head, giving credit where it was due. "You did your homework and beat me to the punch. Next time I won't make it so easy for you."

"Good," she countered. If he thought to intimidate her, the half smile she gave him as she met his gaze unflinch-ingly told him that he had failed. "I don't like being taken lightly."

"Considering the turnout you've had today, only a fool would do that. I knew there wasn't any truth to the rumor on the streets that you were about to go under."

The curl of her mouth turned mocking at that, her green

eyes dangerous. If there were any rumors circulating about her, she wouldn't be a bit surprised if he wasn't the one who had started them. She intended to end them right now! "It'll take more than a few robberies and some stiff competition from you to do that," she said sweetly. "So if anyone else says anything, you can assure them I'm here to stay." She knew from the glint in his eyes that it was a point well taken.

Hovering protectively in the background, Tucker heard the entire conversation. As soon as the older man left, he moved to Lacey's side. "That was real classy, lady," he said in approval. "You just spit in that old devil's eye and smiled while you did it! He was probably chewing nails when he walked out of here."

She grinned. "How does that TV commercial go? Never let 'em see you sweat?"

"There wasn't much chance of that." He chuckled. "You were as cool as a cucumber. I didn't know you had it in you."

"When I'm pushed to the wall, I've got a backbone of steel," she replied, her smile fading as she realized her words held a warning he would do well to heed. As far as he was concerned, her back was to the wall. For her own self-preservation, she couldn't let him get too close again.

Dragging her eyes away from his, she said huskily, "Someone wants to look at the jewelry. Excuse me."

She hurried away before he could stop her, vowing to avoid him the rest of the afternoon. But she couldn't avoid his eyes. She told herself she wasn't looking for him, but every time she chanced to glance up, every time she turned away from a customer, his gaze seemed to lock with hers. And the message she read there was always the same. She could run, but she couldn't hide. Not from him and not from her own emotions.

She could feel the panic start to take hold, and it scared her to death. Suddenly she was struggling against something that defied reason and common sense, that defied her very will, and there didn't seem to be anything she could do about it. Caught in a quicksand of longing, she only sank deeper when she struggled. In growing desperation she told herself *she* was in charge of her own heart, her own destiny. Tucker Stevens could wait from now to judgment day, but it wouldn't do him any good. Then her eyes locked with his, her pulse skidded, and without saying a single word he made a mockery of her resolves.

Just as quickly as the sale had started, it ended. From her position by the cash register, Lacey sagged against the counter, totally drained, as Tucker closed the door behind the last customer. She'd done it! She'd sold almost every piece of furniture and jewelry that belonged to the St. John estate and her shop was nearly empty. Another time, under different circumstances, she would have been exhilarated. The profits she'd earned would get her through the next two months and put her business back in the black. For now, though, all she could think of was the night to come and the safe house she and Tucker would share.

Lost in thought, she didn't even hear Jim, one of the undercover cops who had covered the sale, approach until he was standing right next to her. "We've got the trip to the safe house all set up, Ms. Conrad. Tina and Dave, two other officers, will arrive any minute. Tina will change into some of your clothes while I disguise myself as Mr. Stevens. Once we're ready, the two of us will hurry to the patrol car waiting out front, and Andy here," he continued, nodding to the other undercover cop standing next to Tucker at the front door, "will drive us away. While we're posing as a decoy, Dave will have a car waiting in the alley. He'll get you out of here without anyone being the wiser, okay?"

The need for such an elaborate scheme chilled her blood. "Is all that really necessary? Surely no one could follow us in broad daylight without you seeing them?"

"It doesn't hurt to be too careful, ma'am," he said simply.

In other words, Lacey thought, better safe than sorry. Her throat dry, she swallowed. "I'll find Tina something to wear. Tucker, have you got a shirt—"

"Right here." From one of the suitcases he'd brought down a few minutes earlier, he pulled a T-shirt with Land Shark emblazoned across the front of it and tossed it to the younger cop. "With the jeans you've already got on, that should do."

Five minutes later, Tina arrived. Shorter than Lacey and at least five pounds heavier, the policewoman could never have been mistaken for her. Her blond hair was as short as Lacey's was long, her face rounder. But when she changed from her uniform into one of Lacey's summer jumpers, then donned a reddish-brown wig, she could easily have passed for her from a distance.

Lifting Lacey's suitcase, she explained, "Jim and I will take your suitcases with us so it will look like you're really leaving. They'll be brought to you later at the safe house."

Jim, in jeans and Tucker's T-shirt, checked to make sure they were all in their places, grabbed his suitcase, then pushed on dark sunglasses, as did Tina. "Okay, everybody, let's do it."

At the front of the shop Andy opened the door, made a quick survey of the street to make sure it was empty, then quickly motioned for Jim and Tina to hurry to the patrol car. Lacey didn't have time to see more. Dave, the huge bear of a man who had accompanied Tina to the shop, locked the front door and ran to the back. A quick surveillance of the alley assured him it was empty but for the plain brown sedan parked directly in front of Lacey's delivery entrance. Jerking open the back door to the sedan, he said, "It's clear. Let's go!"

Her heart thundering, her head down, Lacey ran to the car and ducked inside. Tucker, so close she could feel his breath on her neck, was only half a second behind. The minute he slammed the car door, Dave jumped into the driver's seat and started the motor. Before Lacey could reach for her seat belt, he was pulling out of the alley.

Lacey expected him to race through the Quarter and quickly leave it behind. Instead, he moved through the narrow streets at a sedate speed that wouldn't draw attention to them, making unexpected turns without using his signal, one eye trained on the rearview mirror, the other on the road in front of them. With every turn, they left her apartment farther and farther behind.

With very little effort they could easily have pretended they were out for a chauffeured drive around town. The sun hadn't set yet, but it was low in the sky, casting long shadows. Shops that didn't cater to the nightlife of the area were already starting to close, while others were just starting to open. On Bourbon Street, tourists began to gather. Five blocks away, a church had cordoned off the surrounding streets for a block party that was crowded and well under way.

Not expecting the roadblock, Dave had to make a quick turn into one of the deserted streets at the west end of the Quarter. Picking up the transmitter of his radio, he called in his position to Detective Ryan at the station. "All clear here," he assured him. "I had to make a detour at St. Mark's Church because of a block party, but I'll be back on route any minute n—"

He never finished the last word. From out of a side street a black car suddenly ran a Stop sign and plowed into them at thirty miles an hour. Her seat belt holding her in place, Lacey gasped as the sudden impact sent her recently injured shoulder slamming against Tucker, who whacked his head against the window. Biting out an oath, he slipped his arm around her, steadying her. Before their car even jarred to a stop, the black vehicle backed up. Its front end bashed in and steam pouring from the radiator, it burned rubber as it raced away from the accident site.

"What the hell!" Tucker snarled. Throwing open his

door, he jumped out to get a license number. But the black car was unlicensed, its darkly tinted windows concealing the driver as he sped away. "Damn it! Do you see that? That bastard just drove off!" Turning back to her abruptly, he demanded, "Are you all right? Dave—"

But Dave was unconscious in the front seat. He'd taken the brunt of the hit and was now slumped sideways at an awkward angle. Blood trickled down the side of his ashen face.

Gasping in horror, Lacey unhooked her seat belt with unsteady fingers and leaned forward to check the pulse in his throat. It beat steadily but far too faintly. "He's alive, but he needs an ambulance!"

Only just now hearing the static-garbled, frantic words of Detective Ryan, Tucker jerked open the front passenger door and reached for the radio transmitter. "Damn it, answer me! What happened?" Ryan was saying.

"A hit-and-run," Tucker growled into the transmitter. "We need an ambulance for Dave. He's unconscious and bleeding from the temple."

"It's on the way," Ryan replied. "Give me a description of the car. Did you get the license number?"

"There wasn't one," Tucker said as he handed his handkerchief to Lacey to press to the injured officer's head, then gave Ryan a quick, detailed description of the car.

Her eyes on Dave's pale face, Lacey whispered hoarsely, "It was the same car that was used in the robbery."

Tucker shot her a sharp look. "Are you sure?"

She nodded, suddenly cold. "I've seen it too many times in my dreams not to know it when I see it."

He spit out a terse curse. "The bastard already left one accident scene and lived to regret it. I don't think he'll make the same mistake again. We've got to get out of here before he comes back."

Ryan heard the entire exchange and growled, "Where the hell do you think you're going? You sit still until I can get some men there to protect you."

"We already tried that," Tucker argued, "and came damn close to getting killed in police custody. Face it, Ryan, you can't protect her. Now we're going to do things my way."

"And what way is that?"

"We're going to disappear. New Orleans is a big city with lots of dark corners where no one cares who you are or where you've been as long as you mind your own business. We'll find a hole somewhere to crawl into and lie low."

On the other end of the radio, silence was his only answer. Tucker scowled, reading the older man's mind. There would be no cops, no guns, no protection. To Jack Ryan, that could add up to nothing but lousy odds. But the odds didn't mean crap when you ran out of options.

"All right," Ryan said heavily. "I don't like it, but it beats anything I've been able to come up with. Find yourself somewhere to stay off the beaten path, then let me know where you are. And use an alias! I'll contact you when it's safe to come out."

"We'll be waiting," Tucker promised and lifted his eyes to Lacey. "Get your purse and let's get out of here while we still can."

She looked down in dismay at Dave, who was still unconscious, though the bleeding at his temple had finally stopped. "We can't just leave him," she protested.

Abandoning the injured man didn't sit any better with him than it did with her, but they were in too much danger where they were. Even now, the driver of the black car could be ditching the car and doubling back with a rifle to finish his handiwork. "There's the ambulance now," he said as the wail of a siren suddenly reverberated through the narrow streets. "It'll be here any second. Let's go."

Lacey didn't need a second urging. Grabbing her purse, she stumbled out of the car on legs that were still shaky. When his hand closed around hers, her fingers gratefully gripped his. "Which way?"

"There," he said, and pointed to the spire of the church in the distance. It was the same one holding the block party.

Darting around the corner, they ran as if the black car that had hit them was at their heels, bearing down on them with deadly intent. Lacey felt fear drop into her stomach like a chunk of ice as she fought the need to glance over her shoulder. *Run!* The word pounded in her head to the beat of their feet on the pavement. She tried not to think of what had happened the last time she'd tried to run from that same black car, but she couldn't run far and fast enough from the memory. Huffing, she focused her gaze on the church. Twenty steps and you'll be safe, she promised herself, her lungs straining. Ten. Only ten more. Then the music from the band on the church steps was surrounding them, and the sea of faces that parted to allow them entrance to the crowd closed around them again, hiding them.

But the same crowd that unknowingly offered them concealment could do the same for the man who had just tried to kill them. He could easily be tracking them, watching their every move, waiting for the chance to get them alone.

His arm tense around Lacey's shoulder, Tucker urged her through the milling throng at a slow pace. To all appearances, they had all the time in the world. Her nerves shot, Lacey slipped her arm around his waist and clutched at him as she tried to match her pace to his. But all her instincts pushed her to run until she couldn't run another step. Her fingers curled into the material of his shirt at his side. "Tucker—"

"Mabel, sweetheart, you know the name's Harry," he drawled, his brown eyes almost black as they flashed her a warning. Hooking his arm around her neck, he pulled her closer. A quick glance behind them showed that no one was paying them any undue attention. "Smile, honey," he whispered in her ear. "You look terrified."

"That's because I am," she said between clenched teeth,

giving him a grimace of a smile. "What if he comes after us?"

"He'll have a hard time finding us in this crowd," he assured her. "But just in case..." Suddenly pulling her to a stop in front of a vendor selling bright, colorful tinsel wigs, he bought a red one and plopped it on her head, then got a rainbow-colored one for himself. Giving her a crooked grin, he said with a chuckle, "It's you," and draped his arm across her shoulders again as if they were lovers out on a date.

She couldn't have denied herself his touch at that moment if she'd tried. Laughing in spite of herself at the ridiculous wig, she said, "You're not supposed to be enjoying this, *Harry*. We're running for our lives, remember?"

He only grinned and reached up to playfully tug at the wig tilted haphazardly on her head. "We only go around once, *Mabel*. You might as well grab for the gusto when you can."

Was that what she was to him? Gusto? Someone to be enjoyed to the fullest until circumstances tugged him to another part of the world? Her eyes locked with his, searching, as the carnival atmosphere surrounding them receded to the farthest edges of their consciousness. Did he know how she longed, just for this moment, to be the type of woman who could ask for nothing more than the moment? Maybe then, being this close to him, knowing that this was all she would ever have of him, wouldn't tear her apart so.

Wanting to drown in the emerald depths of her eyes, Tucker had to tear his gaze away before he jerked her against him and forgot about everything but the ache that she could bring to him even when all his concentration should be focused on protecting her. The woman could distract the devil himself! His face set in grim lines, he searched the crowd for the least sign of danger without ever appearing to take his attention from Lacey.

At the back of the cordoned-off area, a driver returned to his bread truck after delivering hamburger buns to a food booth. He loaded the empty racks, slammed the back door shut, then started around to the driver's side. Tucker didn't wait to see more. He dropped his arm from around Lacey's shoulder and grabbed her hand. "C'mon. There's our ride out of here!"

164   *Jennifer and Lacey*

hood. He looked up quipp . . . . back door
and, then, started toward . . . the . . . . . . truck a ride. Tucker didn't
wait to see more. He dropped his arm from around Lacey's
shoulder and grabbed her hand. "C'mon. There's our ride
out of here."

Chapter 10

The driver, a short, redheaded youth who couldn't have
been a day over nineteen, looked at Tucker as if he had
lost his mind. "You want a ride? In a bread truck? Why?"

Tucker slipped his arm around Lacey's waist and nodded
back to the crowded block party behind them as if they had
friends watching. "Mabel and me made a bet with Betty
and Joe that we could talk you into giving us a ride. They
said you wouldn't do it 'cause it was against company pol-
icy."

The driver nodded, his eyes lingering in obvious fasci-
nation on Lacey and the festive wig she wore. Suddenly
realizing he was staring, he blushed furiously and snapped
his eyes back to Tucker. "Uh...yeah, it is. Sorry."

Just his luck, Tucker thought with a groan, he had to
pick someone who played by the rules. Summoning up a
conspiratorial smile, he tried again. "Look, we've got fifty
dollars riding on this. You give us a ride and we'll split it
with you fifty-fifty. What d'ya say? Have we got a deal?"

He hesitated, but it wasn't the money that attracted him.

It was Lacey. He couldn't seem to keep his eyes off her. He stepped back as if he were backing away from temptation, his Adam's apple bobbing jerkily as he swallowed. "I don't think so...."

Lacey would have had to have been blind to miss his enthrallment with her. Realizing that Tucker was getting nowhere fast, she stepped forward and gave the boy a smile that should have melted his knees. "No one will know," she promised. "If we set in the back on the floor, you won't even know we're there. C'mon, what's it going to hurt?"

His Adam's apple bobbed again. "We-ell..." He winced painfully as his voice cracked, his cheeks now fiery. "I— I guess it w-would be okay...."

"You won't regret it, I promise!" Pleased, Lacey turned to Tucker and shot him a triumphant grin. "Give him his twenty-five dollars now, Harry, so he'll know we weren't making this all up. He can take his girlfriend out when he gets off work."

Without a word, Tucker pulled out his wallet. But his rueful eyes spoke volumes.

The youth took the money reluctantly and warned them, "I can't bring you back here. I've got another delivery on the west side of town."

Tucker waved off the warning and quickly pulled Lacey with him into the truck before the kid had a chance to change his mind. "No problem. We'll call a taxi from there and catch a ride back. Thanks!"

Five minutes later the bread truck raced out of the French Quarter as if it were going to a fire, flying around first one corner then another. Sitting out of sight on the floor, Tucker swore under his breath and made a quick grab for Lacey before they were both flung all over the back. Laughing, she collapsed against him and pushed the lopsided wig out of her eyes. "Did we make him late for his next delivery or what?" she whispered, chuckling. "Something sure lit a fire under him."

"Not something, *someone*," he muttered. "You've got

the poor kid so shook up he doesn't know if he's coming or going.''

''Me? What did I do?''

''Don't give me the Miss Innocent act,'' he chided, grinning. ''You knocked him out of his shoes and you know it. *C'mon, what's it going to hurt?*'' he mimicked. ''That smile you gave him must have raised his temperature twenty degrees.''

Lacey felt the heat climb into her own cheeks. ''I had to do something. He was going to turn you down flat.''

''I guess I could have batted my eyes at him the way you did, but somehow I don't think it would have had the same effect,'' he teased.

''I didn't—'' she began.

''Oh, yes, you did. You turned those big green eyes on him, and the kid melted like cheese on a burger. He never stood a chance.''

''Is that what you do when I look at you?'' she dared softly, surprising both of them. ''Melt?''

She didn't see him draw closer, but suddenly he was only inches away, his breath a hot caress on her cheeks as he challenged, ''What do you think?''

Her eyes dropped to the sensuous lines of his mouth. Just that easily she ached for a kiss. Nothing more. Just the hungry pressure of his lips on hers, his tongue dancing with hers in the dark, secret recesses of her mouth. Liquid heat stole through her. She only had to lift her chin a scant inch and lean toward him—

The wordless invitation was almost completed when she froze. What was she doing? After what had happened last night, neither of them would be satisfied with just a kiss. Heat fanning her cheeks, she drew back abruptly, her eyes flying to the front of the truck. Although the redheaded driver kept his gaze studiously fixed on the road, he only had to lift his eyes to the mirror to see their every move. ''I think we need to remember where we are,'' she said with a calmness that she had to struggle to find. "Exactly *where* are we?"

Tucker's fingers curled into his palms to keep from grabbing her chin and turning her mouth back up to his. This wasn't going to work, damn it! He couldn't be this close to her and not burn to pull her into his arms and love her. She had to feel it, too. He could see it in her eyes—the need, the yearning, the longing that refused to be denied. She could turn her back on him, act as if he'd never dragged her down to the couch and lost himself in her, but this…craving…they had for each other wasn't going to go away. Somehow he had to find a way to make her admit that. But she was right. The back of a bread truck wasn't the time or the place.

Following her gaze, he stared out the windshield at the passing scenery. The wide thoroughfare they had turned onto had all the earmarks of what had once been a major artery into town before the building of the interstate. The rerouting of traffic had obviously depressed the area. Fast-food restaurants and half-occupied shopping strips gave way to old motels, poorly kept travel courts and dilapidated buildings with For Sale signs out front.

It was, Tucker decided as the bread truck came to a stop behind a hamburger restaurant, the kind of area tourists avoided and locals turned a blind eye to because there didn't seem to be a cure for the decay. It was the last place Lacey's attacker would probably expect her to stay. And even if he did, he'd know better than to start nosing around. People here would be suspicious of strangers asking too many questions.

Tucker jumped out of the truck as soon as the back doors were open, then took Lacey's hand and helped her out. "There's a phone out front," the youth said, frowning worriedly as he realized he was dumping them off in an area he wouldn't walk through at night alone. "I hope you'll be able to get a taxi way out here. I didn't stop to think—"

"We'll be fine," Tucker assured him with a smile, his

hand at Lacey's elbow to nudge her toward the restaurant. "Don't give us a second thought. You've done enough just by giving us the ride."

He looked as if he were ready to argue further, but Tucker didn't give him a chance. With a final nod of thanks, he hurried Lacey around the side of the building. The minute they were out of his sight, he snatched the tinsel wigs off both their heads and stuffed them in the nearest garbage can. "The last thing we want to do now is draw attention to ourselves," he said quietly, and pulled her to a stop as they reached the front of the restaurant. With the ease of long practice, he surveyed the street with sharp eyes and still managed to look as if he were waiting for a bus.

Lacey told herself they were perfectly safe. But her imagination had kicked into high gear the minute they'd left the bread truck, and she could almost feel imaginary eyes on them. Repressing a shiver, she edged closer to Tucker. "Do you think we were followed?"

He shook his head, his gaze still on the street, constantly moving, assessing. "Not in that black tank that hit us. It was losing water fast. And the driver would have had to have been damn fast on his feet to catch up with us at the church, then find new wheels in time to track us out here. He may be good, but he's not that good."

Reassured, she still found herself surveying the street, unable to relax. It had little to recommend it. "Now what? Where do we go from here?"

"There." He pointed to a neon sign in the shape of a palm tree two blocks away. The paint was peeling, the name barely readable. Palm Courts.

The old-fashioned travel court was nearly as unkempt as the old sign out front. Well back from the road, a series of small, individual cabins lined the long, oval drive that ran at a right angle from the highway. In the center of the mall formed by the drive was a cracked and empty swimming pool surrounded by the palms that had obviously given the place its name.

It wasn't the pool that drew Lacey's eye, but the cabins themselves. Seedy. It was the first word that sprang to mind and the only description Lacey could think of. They hadn't seen a paintbrush—or soap and water, for that matter—in years. The windows were grimy, the porches and carports sagged, and the little bit of green paint that still clung to the trim was dingy and closer to gray than green. She didn't want to think what it looked like on the inside.

Unable to stop herself from dragging her feet, she protested, "Maybe we could find something better somewhere down the street. Or we could always try back the other way...."

"No, this is perfect," he insisted. "No one would expect you to stay in a place like this. And the cabins are back from the road and spaced far enough apart that we don't have to worry about nosy neighbors."

Lacey wasn't convinced, but he was already tugging her after him into the office and greeting the thin, haggard woman sitting behind the counter puffing a cigarette. "We need a room," he said easily. "How about the one farthest from the road? We don't want to be disturbed by the traffic."

Lacey cringed at that. She could almost read the woman's thoughts as her knowing eyes looked them up and down. Her fears were verified when the woman pushed a registration card across the counter at them and let out a stream of smoke. "You want it just for a couple of hours or all night?" she drawled.

Tucker's jaw clenched. "Several nights," he retorted coldly as he began to fill out the card. "Is that a problem?"

She lifted a bony shoulder. "Not for me, but it might be for you. I can't hold nothing for nobody if I don't have the money up front. You want the room for three days, you pay now."

The world wasn't exactly beating a path to her door for a cabin, but Tucker didn't even blink an eye at her demand. "How much?"

Once again her eyes went over them, this time measuring the quality of their clothes. "Thirty a night."

He almost laughed at that. Maybe in her dreams! Pulling out his wallet, he slapped down two twenties on the counter. "Take it or leave it. We won't need maid service—if you've got it—we'll clean it ourselves. And we might stay a week or longer *if* the conditions are right."

It was the best offer she'd had in three months and she wasn't foolish enough to turn it down. Snatching up the money, she took the registration card and gave it a quick glance. "Enjoy your stay, Mr. and Mrs. Smith."

Lacey wanted to sink through the floor, but Tucker only grinned and reached for the key she handed him. "We intend to."

"I can't believe you did that!" Lacey seethed as she waited for him to unlock the door. "*Smith*, for God's sake! Couldn't you have used something a little more original? There's no telling what that woman thought."

"And here I thought you were going to be upset because I claimed we were married." He laughed. "It wouldn't have mattered what name I gave her—no one gives his real name in a place like this. And it's perfectly obvious what she thought," he said as he pushed open the door and gestured for her to precede him. "She thinks we're having an affair."

She withered him with a look that could have melted chocolate at fifty paces. "It's nice to know one of us is finding this amusing." She stepped past him as he hit the light switch by the door. "I—"

Hot, stale air hit her in the face, stopping her in her tracks. The rest of her sentence dwindled into stunned silence as, eyes wide, she got her first good look at the cabin. "Well," she said finally, "we knew it wouldn't have a four-star rating. Do you suppose the roof leaks?"

Right behind her, Tucker bumped into her, his hands automatically dropping to her shoulders. Over her head he cast a critical eye over the two small rooms and bathroom and had to wince. She had good reason to ask.

The ceiling was water stained; the bare bulbs that hung from the ceilings in each of the bedrooms were swinging in the breeze that rushed in through the open door. The cheap paneling that covered the walls had holes as big as a man's fist, and the doorway that separated the two small bedrooms was missing a door. He didn't even want to speculate on what had caused the brown stains on the carpet.

"Maybe it's not as bad as it looks," he suggested hopefully, crossing to the air conditioner. He turned it on and was met with nothing but silence. He swore under his breath. "Looks like we'll have to open the windows."

While he struggled with the horizontal windows that were set high in the walls, Lacey inspected the rest of the cabin. The bathroom fixtures were old but in working order if you didn't mind a little mold. As for the television sitting on a scarred dresser, it had good sound but the picture never stopped rolling. Feeling like a drunken sailor, Lacey turned it off and moved to the bed in the smaller of the two rooms. Half afraid of what she would find when she turned back the faded orange bedspread, she sighed in relief at the sight of the clean, fresh-smelling sheets.

After finally getting the windows in the front room open, Tucker appeared in the doorway. "Well?"

She straightened to find him watching her as if he expected her to turn up her nose and walk out any minute. She grinned. "The bathroom needs a good scrubbing, the TV needs a good repairman, but we don't have to sit up all night. The beds will do."

Every other woman he knew would have been raking him over the coals for daring to drag her into such a dump. But Lacey never had been and never would be like any other woman. Why had it taken him so long to see that?

"There's a store down the street," he said, resisting the sudden need to pull her down to the bed. "I'll go buy something to clean the bathroom with and get us some clothes, since Ryan has our suitcases. With a little work, we should be able to tolerate the place for the next couple of days.''

She was already heading for the door. "Let's go."

"Oh, no, you don't!" he said, his hand whipping out to catch her wrist and pull her back in front of him. "You'll stay here with the door locked. The less people who see you the better. You can call Ryan while I'm gone and let him know where we are. He's probably beginning to worry."

Her eyes flashed at the order. "You said just less than fifteen minutes ago that you didn't think there was any way we could have been followed," she reminded him. "Give me one good reason why I have to stay here by myself."

"Because I've been known to be wrong."

With just a handful of words, he took the wind out of her sails. "That was hardly the same situation, and you weren't wrong. You just miscalculated."

He had to smile at her quick, fierce defense of him. "All right, I miscalculated. I'd bet a year's salary I haven't this time, but don't forget we're trying to second-guess a criminal who's outsmarted the police for over six months." He cupped her face with his hands, turning her eyes up to his. "I won't take any more chances with you, honey," he said huskily. "You're staying here."

Why? she wanted to cry. Because you care? Or because you don't want any more near disasters on your conscience? Afraid of the answer she might get if she voiced the question, she whispered instead, "Be careful."

"I'll be back as soon as I can. I don't expect any problems, but don't answer the door to anyone but me."

She forced a wobbly smile. "I'm sure I'll be fine."

He was sure, too, or he never would have left her alone. But he still hesitated at the door of the cabin, reluctant to leave her. Staring down into her upturned face, he suddenly pulled her to him for a quick, hard kiss. "Lock the door," he ordered thickly and stepped outside.

The door shut quietly behind him, the click of the lock loud in the silence. Leaning her head against the warped wood, her mouth tingling from his kiss, Lacey listened to his footsteps as he walked away from her. It was a sound she was going to have to get used to, she thought as she swallowed a sob.

When Tucker returned to the cabin nearly an hour later, Lacey was pacing the floor anxiously. She'd called Detective Ryan, then found herself listening for Tucker's return. Instead, she'd heard every truck that passed on the highway, every rustle of the palms as the wind whispered through their fronds. Just when she'd started to think she had the travel court completely to herself, a radio blared on in the cabin next door, scaring her to death. Unable to sit still, she prowled up and down across the worn carpet like a tiger looking for a way out. And in her head an invisible clock silently kept count of the minutes Tucker had been gone. Where was he? And what was taking so long? Had he run into trouble?

His soft knock on the door caught her by surprise. She froze, her thundering heart in her throat. "Who is it?" she called shakily.

"Me," he answered in a low voice. "Open up."

With trembling fingers, she threw the lock and jerked open the door. "Where have you been? I've been worried sick!"

Loaded down with a shopping bag, he held up a smaller sack from one of the nearby fast-food restaurants. "I got us something to eat, too. You hardly ate anything during the sale."

She looked past him into the darkness that had fallen since they'd arrived at the cabin, and doubted that she'd be able to eat anything now, either. Quickly shutting the door after he was inside, she bolted it and turned to face him. "Did you see anyone suspicious while you were gone?"

"The place is empty except for the two winos next door,

and all they're interested in is their bottles." He handed her a hamburger and a milkshake. "Did you get in touch with Ryan?"

She nodded, sipping on the milkshake. "They found the black car near the river. It had a police radio."

"So the minute Dave radioed in about the block party, he gave away our position," he said in disgust. "Did Ryan have any idea who owns the car?"

"Not yet. He's having it checked for fingerprints and running down the motor number since it didn't have any plates."

"It's probably stolen."

"He may not need it, anyway. The second background search he ordered on Robert Martin has turned up another suspect. He expects to make another arrest soon, and—"

"Until then, we stay put," he finished for her.

She watched his narrowed eyes make a sweeping tour of the two bedrooms, the missing door between them, the two beds that had only a thin wall between them. In a cabin that was less than half the size of her living room, intimacy took on a whole new meaning. How was she going to deny her need for him when every time she turned around he was in her path?

What little appetite she had deserted her. Abruptly setting down the remains of her meal, she said, "I'm not really hungry. I think I'll clean the bathroom."

She escaped into the bathroom with the cleaners and bleach he had bought, and quietly closed the door, shutting him out. With a muttered curse, Tucker set down his own food. It was going to be a long night.

An hour later, the lack of sleep the previous night, the stress of the sale and everything that had happened since caught up with Lacey. Bone tired, she helped Tucker move the dresser in front of the cabin door to block it just in case they had any unwelcome visitors, then announced wearily, "I'm going to bed."

He nodded, his face expressionless. "I bought you a nightgown and some other things I thought you might need. It's in the sack by your bed. I had to guess at your size."

Tension coiled in her stomach at the thought of him picking out lingerie for her. "I'm sure it'll be fine," she said huskily, moving toward her room. "Thank you." She didn't have to turn around to know that his eyes followed her every step of the way.

The gown he'd bought her was of a soft, yellow, crinkly cotton that was as thin as mist. Crushing it in her hands, Lacey felt her blood warm. It was perfect, as were the panties and bra that were also in the sack. She shouldn't have been surprised. He was a man who survived by paying attention to details.

In the front room he turned out the lights. Silence dropped like a bomb in the ensuing darkness. Lacey placed the nightgown on the bed, then reached for the zipper tab of her slacks. Her ears suddenly as finely tuned as radar, she heard Tucker shed his jeans and the whisper the material made as it slid over his legs. Cursing her too-sensitive ears, she quickly threw off her own clothes and reached for the nightgown. The springs groaned underneath her as she crawled into bed. From the front room she heard Tucker's bed creak in protest, too. Her heart thudded dully.

The air was still and heavy; there wasn't so much as a breeze to stir the darkness. Thunderstorms were predicted for sometime between midnight and dawn, but they were still miles away, only a faint rumble in the distance. Kicking off the sheet that seemed to cling to her, Lacey ignored the sultry heat and willed her mind to empty. On the highway in front of the courts, a trucker changed gears as he headed out of town. It was the last thing she heard before sleep overtook her.

The thunderstorm arrived with a vengeance at two in the morning. It wasn't the lightning that flashed across the sky or the crack of thunder that followed it that woke her, but the rain that blew in through the open window above her bed. Jerking upright, she stared in confusion at the dark, unfamiliar surroundings. Another bolt of lightning ripped through the night, stripping away the sleepy haze that blocked her memory. She was at a travel court. With Tucker.

Scrambling up on the bed to reach the window, she scowled at the rain that hit her in the face before she finally managed to get it closed. Wind whipped around the corners of the cabin, moaning as it searched for a way to get in. It was an eerie, keening sound that sent chills racing over her damp skin. Shivering, she wiped the moisture from her face and turned to frown at the dark doorway to Tucker's room. She hadn't heard him move so much as a muscle. And his window faced the same direction hers did.

She hesitated, hoping he would wake up. But he didn't, and the rain continued to tap against her window with increasing force. The carpet under the window in the front room was probably already soaked, and Tucker showed no signs of waking. Sighing, she got out of bed and padded quietly into his room.

Lightning flared again just as she drew even with the bed. Sprawled on his stomach, the sheet kicked free of his bare legs and trailing the floor, she could see, just for an instant, the broad expanse of his back, the lean hips covered only by his underwear. Her heart tripped, skipping a beat. Tearing her eyes away, she hurried over to the window.

Sometime during the past thirty years someone had done a poor job of painting the window frame and sill. Unable to get any leverage because it was over her head, Lacey tugged, muttering a curse as the window resisted all her efforts to close it. And all the while, rain poured in on her in waves, drenching her to the skin.

Suddenly Tucker appeared behind her, his voice rough with sleep as he reached above her and said, "Here, I'll get it. Why didn't you wake me?"

"I thought I could do it." With a groan of protest, the

window slammed shut. "Thank God!" Pushing her wet hair out of her face, she gave him a rueful smile. "Well, I guess this answers my question about the roof leaking. It seems to be holding up so far."

Somewhere nearby, lightning slammed into the ground and was immediately followed by a loud boom of thunder. But that was nothing compared to the storm that suddenly raged in Tucker's blood as he saw that her nightgown was plastered to her, revealing her sweetly beaded nipples. His dark eyes hungry, he watched her shiver and wrap her arms around herself. The need to bring her close and warm her with his body was almost more than he could stand. "Go to bed, Lace," he rasped. "Now."

Startled, her eyes widened with awareness. The air, suddenly thick between them, seemed to lodge in her throat. If she didn't return to her room immediately, he was going to make love with her. She knew that as surely as she knew she loved him. As surely as she knew he was not the man for her. But she couldn't step away from him. She'd been a fool to think his leaving would hurt less if she didn't let him touch her again. The only thing he could give her was memories. How could she deny herself another night in his arms?

She stepped toward him, stopping only when her breasts were just a heartbeat away from his chest. "No."

His eyes narrowed in the darkness. "I thought you didn't want me to touch you."

"No," she said softly. "I always wanted you to touch me. I just didn't want to want you to touch me."

Her words slid over him like a caress, but still he didn't reach for her. "What made you change your mind?"

She shrugged, the movement graceful and sensuous as her eyes locked with his. "I thought the need would go away if I denied it," she said simply. "But it won't."

Her honesty was his undoing. He wanted to tell her to be sure. If he got her in his bed and his arms again, he wouldn't be able to let her go. But his fingers were already sliding up her arms to her shoulders, pulling her to him. Folding her close, he brought his mouth to hers.

Thunder boomed overhead, but he didn't hear it. All he could hear was the wild beating of his heart and the soft sigh that escaped from her throat as she leaned into him, trusting him to hold her. His senses swam; his only thought was to make the night last forever. There would be no quick loving now, no mindless, hurried groping in the dark. Time. He had aeons of it, an eternity to show her all the unfamiliar tenderness she brought out in him, the gentleness he'd never felt the need to give to anyone else. When dawn came he would know that he had given her a night like none she had ever had before.

He knew how to touch her until she was steeped in pleasure, until she cried out for release and begged him to take her. But for all that knowledge, his fingers still trembled as they slid to the small, pearl buttons of her gown that trailed down between her breasts to a point just above her navel. All thumbs, he fumbled with the first one, as shaky as a green boy with his first girl. He thought he heard her laugh softly against his mouth, but then the button slipped free and he moved unhurriedly on to the next. Lifting his lips from hers, he took a slow, thorough tour of her face, drinking the moisture from her skin, content for now with filling himself with nothing more than the sweet taste of her.

And all the while, his fingers trailed lower, seeking another button. Dipping his head, he nuzzled the material until it parted, then touched the sensitive skin between her unbound breasts with just the tip of his tongue.

Drifting on a sea of delight, Lacey felt the air sizzle between them. But before she could clutch him and bring his mouth to the aching crest of her breast, he moved lower, his hands soothing her, arousing, slowly heating. Restless, she shook her head, murmuring a protest.

He pressed a kiss to the soft, silken skin just below her breasts. "I know, honey. But first we've got to get you undressed. You're all wet."

His words hardly registered. Her body was already starting to throb, and her fingers tightened in his hair. "Please..."

"Yes," he growled, releasing the final button and planting a hot kiss just above the top of her thighs. "I'm going to please you even if it takes me all night."

"I'll be dead by then," she moaned, her knees starting to buckle. "Hold me."

In one swift movement he was on his feet and gathering her into his arms, his chest caressing her breasts as he laughed low in his throat. "I've never heard of anyone dying from pleasure. C'mon, let's go to bed."

Picking her up, he carried her the short distance to the bed, chuckling as the mattress sank in the middle. Stripping away the last bit of material they each wore, he lay down next to her, his laughter turning to a groan as the mattress rolled them together. Hunger threatening his control, he covered her mouth with his, slowly increasing the pressure with each kiss until the storm that raged outside was matched by the tempest within them and the thunder echoed in the roar of their pounding hearts.

After that, there was no time for talking, no time for anything but soft whispered sighs, gasps of need and breaths that tangled between parted mouths. With devastating thoroughness he learned every inch of her body with his hands, then his mouth and tongue. Lacey, still shaking from the shattering experience, returned the favor and drove him half out of his mind with her hesitant explorations. Then, when she thought they were both too weak from pleasure to move, he showed her that she'd known nothing of loving before he came to her bed. He parted her thighs and plunged into her. Before she'd even caught her breath, she was racing for the first peak. In a heartbeat he sent her tumbling over it, then rushing for the next one. Gasping, clinging to each other, they were suddenly flying in a world of comets and rockets and she never even knew when they left the ground.

* * *

The storm was long gone when Lacey awoke, dawn just breaking. Lying on her side, her body deliciously languid and at peace, she opened her eyes to find Tucker sitting on the side of the bed, his back to her as he punched out a number on the bedside phone. He was dressed in nothing but his slacks. Lacking the energy to get up, she lazily reached out to trace the edge of his waistband with her index finger.

At her first touch, he shifted sideways on the mattress. His brown eyes, nearly black with a passion that hadn't abated during the night, ran over her possessively. Her hair was wild about her bare shoulders, her mouth slightly swollen from his kisses. His fingers twined with hers as he spoke into the phone. "Detective Ryan, please."

Lacey pulled his hand to her mouth and planted a kiss on his palm. "Good morning," she murmured huskily as he waited for the call to be put through. "How'd you sleep?"

"With you in my arms," he answered gruffly, leaning down to give her a slow, leisurely kiss. Before he could deepen it, however, a voice in his ear pulled his attention back to the phone. Dragging his mouth from Lacey's, he greeted the detective, then asked, "Any news?"

Before her eyes, Lacey watched shutters drop over his expression. Apprehension shivered through her. Pushing herself erect, she hugged the sheet to her breasts. "What is it?" she whispered.

Tucker only shook his head and said into the phone, "When?"

Something in the curt question turned her apprehension to alarm. Her eyes wide, she moved closer to him. "What's wrong?"

He only motioned for her to wait, then spoke into the phone again. "Are you sure?" Whatever reassurances he received did nothing to lighten his mood. It wasn't until he hung up that she found out why. "They picked up Martin's partner at three o'clock this morning," he told her grimly. "You can go home now. It's all over."

Chapter 11

Less than thirty minutes later they were on their way back to her apartment in a taxi. To look at them, you couldn't tell the night they'd spent in each other's arms had ever happened. Dressed in the clothes they'd worn to the sale, they sat over two feet apart, not touching, while the silence grew. Their driver, casting quick glances at them through the rearview mirror, frowned and reached over to turn the radio on before returning his attention to the road. The soft, mellow tones of jazz filled the car.

Lacey stiffened, her fingers tightening around the strap of her purse. Would she ever be able to listen to jazz again without thinking of Tucker and the game of Scrabble they'd played while music drifted in through the open window? Or hear the lonely strains of a horn and not find herself back in his arms on her couch? Oh, God, it was over, she thought with a sob, and he would be leaving soon. How could she have known it would hurt this much?

Unable to listen to another beat of the music without breaking into tears, she broke the silence. "Did Detective

Ryan say how they tracked down Martin's partner? Who is he?''

Tucker turned from the window he had been staring out of unseeingly. ''His name's Raymond Finch. His name turned up when Ryan ordered a more extensive background search on Martin. Last year the two of them were cellmates when Martin served time for a DWI.''

She frowned. ''But how does that link him to the armored-car robberies? If Martin has a long rap sheet, he's probably served time with a lot of people.''

''True, but Finch is the only one who wasn't able to account for his whereabouts during the robberies and the night your shop was attacked. That's just circumstantial, of course, but a search of his home turned up a basement full of cash. There's still a couple of hundred thousand dollars missing, but Ryan's pretty confident he's got enough for an open-and-shut case.''

The tension that had been with her ever since she'd stepped into that alley all those nights ago and had seen a man shot down before her eyes eased. But the relief was nothing compared to the misery that swept through her like a black cloud. Summoning up a smile that almost cracked her face, she said brightly, ''Thanks to Ryan wrapping this up so quickly, you'll be able to get out of here quicker than you'd planned. Are you going to go scuba diving while you're in Aruba? I've heard the water is beautiful.''

His mouth flattened into a thin line. ''No, I don't imagine I'll do much of anything.'' Except think of her. Damn it, he couldn't leave her! Not for a vacation. Not for his job. He didn't even know how it had happened. He'd always sworn that no woman would twist him up in knots and carve a place for herself in his thoughts. When a man in his position made that mistake, he was useless in the field. When he needed his wits about him the most, he couldn't afford to be worrying about what his lover was doing back home all alone. He'd be better off taking a desk job and making sure he was with her every night.

A desk job.

The words teased him, taunting him, tempting him. How long had he been considering the advantages of it without even realizing it? he wondered in stunned surprise. When Kurt had dangled it in front of him, then sweetened the pot by trying to entice him with the hint of an ambassadorship, he'd all but thrown the offer back in his face. He'd wanted no part of rules and regulations and *routine*. What had happened to change his mind?

Lacey.

The answer came so easily he never had a chance to deny it. Faced with the choice of working within the system in order to have her at his side or turning his back on her and walking away, he realized there was no longer a choice to be made. That decision had been made the first night he'd kissed her in her apartment. He'd been fighting so hard against it, he just hadn't realized it.

And so had she. Oh, she didn't fool him by acting as if she expected him to just walk out on her at the first opportunity. Even now, the memory of the slow smile she'd given him when she'd awakened to find him sitting on the side of the bed warmed him, the kiss she'd pressed into his palm moving him in ways he'd never expected. No, regardless of her apparent nonchalance, she wasn't a woman to share intimacy lightly. She could never have given herself to him the way she had unless she had felt much more than desire. Now all he had to do was get her to admit it.

They would talk, he promised himself. Just as soon as they got back to the apartment.

But the phone was practically ringing off the hook when they stepped into her living room. Hurrying over to the phone, Lacey snatched it up. "Hello?"

"Is Tucker Stevens there?" a voice barked in her ear. "This is his boss, Kurt Donovon. I need to speak to him immediately."

Lifting a brow in surprise, she told him, "Just a moment," and held the receiver out to Tucker. "It's your boss. It sounds urgent."

Scowling, he took the phone. Kurt wouldn't have gone to the trouble to track him down unless there was a problem. And that was something he didn't need right now. "I thought I was supposed to be on vacation," he said as a greeting. "If this is about work, find someone else."

"The hell I will!" he growled. "We've got a potential disaster on our hands and you're the only one who can handle it. Where the hell have you been? Haven't you seen the news? I've been trying to locate you all night! What are you doing in New Orleans?"

"It's a long story," he said, shrugging off an answer. "What's the problem?"

"Pedro Ramirez."

Every muscle in Tucker's body seemed to freeze. The head of a rebel group in the small island country of Santa Maria, Pedro Ramirez was a dangerous man who enjoyed the limelight. Tucker had butted heads with him on more than one occasion and had little liking for the man. Unfortunately, Ramirez had taken his dislike as a compliment and enjoyed matching wits with him.

He braced himself, instinctively knowing he wasn't going to like what came next. "What's he done now?"

"Taken three American missionaries hostage during an independence celebration."

"What! When?"

"Last night. He claims the missionaries are spies planted by the dictator to ferret out the rebels."

Swearing, Tucker grabbed the phone base in his free hand and paced back and forth across the living room, dragging the cord after him. "Who have you got working on it? Have they made any headway?"

"Do you think I'd have tracked you down if they had?" he muttered. "I've thrown everyone but the president at him, but he refuses to talk to anyone but you. You're going to have to go down there."

"No." The word was out before he could stop it, his eyes flying to Lacey. She stood at the window, half turned away from him as if she was already starting to shut him out of her life. He couldn't leave her now. There was too much between them that needed to be settled, too many words that still needed to be said.

"What do you mean, *no*?" Kurt demanded incredulously. "Damn it, Tucker, I know you're on vacation but—"

"Forget the vacation," he cut in. "This has nothing to do with that. I just think I may be able to handle this on the phone. Who have you been able to get into Santa Maria?" he asked, motioning to Lacey for a pen and paper. "Give me the information you've got and I'll see what I can do from here."

Donovon wasn't pleased with his decision, but he'd learned a long time ago that Tucker worked best when he was left to his own devices. Quickly giving him a concise report on the negotiations that had failed so far, he said, "Keep me posted. I'll be at the office until I hear that this has been resolved."

"It could be a long day," Tucker warned him and hung up. The instant he got a dial tone, he dialed one of the numbers Kurt had given him.

"What's the problem?" Lacey asked as he waited for the call to go through.

"Three missionaries taken hostage in Santa Maria. Hopefully, I'll be able to straighten it out without going down there. The department will reimburse you for the calls." A voice spoke in his ear, dragging his attention back to the crisis. In the blink of an eye he switched to fluent Spanish.

Not understanding a single word he said, Lacey watched him try to reason with whoever he was able to get on the line. When that didn't work, he switched to a firmness that was clearly understood in any language. But it didn't work.

Slamming down the phone, he spit out a colorful curse and dialed another number.

The second call led to another, then another, until he could no longer contain his impatience. He obviously wasn't making much progress, and Lacey knew it was only a matter of time before he admitted it. He was leaving. Deep in her heart she had hoped he would spend the rest of his vacation with her, but she wasn't foolish enough to think that she could distract him from his work. Tucker was a lifer. She'd known that from the beginning.

Unable to stand there and watch him make plans to leave her, she grabbed her purse and headed for the door. "I'll be back in a minute," she told him when he paused in his conversation to listen to the caller on the other end.

Frowning, he quickly covered the mouthpiece with his hand. "Where are you going?"

"Around the corner to the drugstore to get you something to read on the plane."

"I'm not going anywhere until we have a chance to talk," he retorted. Before he could say another word, the voice in his ear had him swearing again and turning back to the phone.

Soundlessly, Lacey slipped out of the apartment and let herself out through the front entrance of the shop. Last night's storm had washed the sky a cloudless blue and lowered the humidity dramatically. It was a beautiful Sunday morning, the shops were still closed and those tourists who were out at such an early hour were blocks away at the French Market enjoying *beignets* and café au lait. Caught up in her troubling thoughts, Lacey hardly noticed she had the streets to herself as she hurried around the corner and headed for the drugstore three blocks away.

So he wanted to talk, she thought, feeling as if a fist had closed around her heart and was squeezing the life out of her. She could just imagine about what. Tucker was a man who always tied up loose ends. He would want to part friends. He would have to do it delicately, of course, so as not to cause a major rift in the family, but he was an expert at delicate negotiations. Swallowing a sob, she increased her pace. The sooner she got back, the sooner he could have his little discussion, the sooner he could be blithely on his way. And the sooner she could start getting over him. Again.

Caught up in a misery unlike anything she had ever known before, she never heard the stealthy movements of the man who crept up behind her on rubber-soled shoes. Without warning, pain flashed in her head as she was struck from behind. She didn't even have time to cry out before she crumbled like a rag doll into strong, ruthless arms.

"Well?" Donovon demanded. "What have you got?"

"Nothing but a headache," Tucker snapped. "Ramirez is playing coy. He refuses to take my call. Claims the only way he'll talk to me is face-to-face."

"Then get your butt on a plane," his boss ordered. "We can't afford to sit on our hands on this, Tucker. I've already got five senators breathing down my neck and an army of reporters camped outside my door. They want some answers, damn it, and I haven't got them!"

"All right, all right, I'm working on it. I've got a few more tricks up my sleeve. Let me make a couple more calls—"

"Eighty-six the calls!" he retorted sharply. "We can't afford to waste any more time."

Tucker scowled at the phone. Damn Ramirez, why did he have to pick now to pull one of his stunts! "One hour," he replied. "If I don't have this cleared up in an hour, I'll be on the next plane out. Think of the money it'll save the taxpayers—"

From downstairs, someone pounded on the front door of the shop so hard the sound carried easily up the stairs to him. He frowned. Was that Ryan calling Lacey's name? "One hour," he repeated. "I'll be in touch." Hanging up before the other man could protest, he hurried downstairs.

"Thank God!" Ryan exclaimed when he finally opened the door. "I've been trying to call you for the last fifteen minutes!"

"I've had the phone tied up with State Department business...." The explanation died on his tongue as he noted the grimness of the detective's face. He hardly looked like a man who had just cracked a baffling case. Suddenly uneasy without knowing why, he demanded, "What's wrong?"

There was no easy way to admit to a major blunder, so Jack Ryan didn't even try. "We arrested the wrong suspect," he said bluntly.

He had expected fury, possibly even contempt for a mistake that could only be described as inexcusable. What he had not expected was the sudden alarm that filled Tucker Stevens's eyes. His gaze flew past him to the stairs that led to Lacey's apartment. "Where's Lacey? Upstairs?"

"She went around the corner to the drugstore." Tucker could feel the panic rising in him, threatening to choke him. How long had she been gone? He hadn't even noticed the time when she'd left! Struggling for control, he stared down at his watch and frantically tried to think. "Thirty or forty minutes ago, I think." His gaze snapped back to the detective's. "She should have been back by now."

Ryan didn't wait to hear more. "I've got a squad car right outside. Let's go."

They raced outside and jumped into the car, the siren wailing as they pulled away from the curb. His nerves drawn tight as piano wire and his eyes moving constantly, Tucker searched the sidewalk for any sign of Lacey. But she was nowhere in sight. His stomach knotted as fury began to boil deep inside him. If something had happened to her...

Swearing, he stifled the thought before it could take root in his mind. "She knew I was going to be tied up on the phone for a while. She may have decided to go for a walk."

Ryan nodded, his eyes, too, on the street. "We'll find her. Wherever she is."

Tucker's fingers curled into fists. "How the hell did this happen? What kind of department are you running if you can't even arrest the right suspect?"

Ryan had been asking himself the same questions for the past half hour. "I'm not making any excuses, but there's been a lot of pressure to tie this thing up. Finch looked like the perfect suspect. Everything linked him to Martin, even the money. He didn't have an alibi and he wasn't talking. We thought we had him cold."

"What makes you think you don't?"

"His girlfriend came waltzing in nearly an hour ago claiming he was with her at the time of the robberies and every time Lacey was threatened."

"What about the money? How did she explain that he just happened to have a couple of hundred thousand dollars lying around the house?"

"It's drug money. He's a coke dealer." When Tucker shot him a disbelieving look, he said, "We checked out her story. That's why it took me so long to get to you. She's telling the truth. She took one of my men to a warehouse by the river. It was full of the stuff."

Tucker felt his control slip another notch and could do nothing to stop it. Right this very minute Lacey could be in the hands of the man who was trying to kill her.

Two blocks from the apartment, the detective turned another corner and muttered a curse at the sight of the patrol car drawn up to the curb. The lights on its light bar were still spinning as a crowd started to gather on the sidewalk. He pulled over, braked sharply and threw the gearshift into Park. Tucker was already jumping out and striding quickly to the crowd before he'd even turned off the ignition.

"I saw the whole thing from my bedroom window," a short, elderly woman told the tall, burly officer who stood before her taking notes. She pointed to a spot on the sidewalk near the curb. "It happened right there. That poor girl never knew what hit her. One minute she was walking along and the next, boom, she was out like a light.''

''What girl?'' Tucker cut in harshly. ''What did she look like?''

The officer in charge scowled at him and started to object, but the detective joined Tucker at that moment and lifted a hand, stopping him. ''What did the girl look like, ma'am?'' he asked quietly, repeating Tucker's question. ''And what else did you see?''

Thrilled to be the center of attention, she preened. ''I'm not a busybody, you understand. I was just looking out the window and marveling at how beautiful the morning was after all that rain last night. I never would have noticed the girl except that there was this man sneaking up behind her. For a minute I thought he was maybe a friend of hers, sneaking up on her to scare her. But then he hit her with a billy club!'' Clicking her tongue, she shook her head in dismay. ''I tell you, I never saw anything like it in my life! He just scooped her up and tossed her in the back of a white van like she was a sack of potatoes, then drove off. For all I know, he could have killed the poor girl. She never made a sound.''

Tucker didn't have to hear a description of her to know it was Lacey. In his gut he already knew she was in deep trouble. But still he had to ask. ''You never said what she looked like.''

A frown wrinkling her already wrinkled brow, the woman closed her eyes, trying to bring her image to mind. ''Well, let's see. She was about five foot six or seven, but very skinny. We would have called her willowy in my day. I didn't pay much attention to her face, but she had beautiful reddish-brown hair that fell almost to her waist.''

Beside him, Ryan could feel Tucker stiffen as his worst fears were confirmed. ''And the man who attacked her?'' he asked quickly. ''Did you get a good look at him?''

She shook her head regretfully. ''Not really. He wore a hat and kept his head down, so I couldn't see his face. But he was tall, at least a foot taller than she was, and dressed all in black.''

''And the license plate of the van? Did you happen to get it?''

''Of course,'' she retorted indignantly, and rattled it off without the least hesitation.

Ryan sighed in relief. A break. It was the only one they were likely to get. He just hoped it wasn't too late. Turning quickly to the uniformed officer who had arrived first on the scene, he said, ''Get a full statement, then check every apartment and shop on the block to see if anyone else saw anything. If you get anything else, I want to know immediately. I'll be at the station.''

Within seconds they were racing out of the Quarter. Sitting impatiently in the passenger seat, Tucker listened to Ryan issue an APB on the van, then a check on the license number. Every law officer in the state would be on the lookout for the van, but Tucker knew it wasn't enough. Her abductor was through playing games. There would be no more attempts to scare her into not testifying. He was going to kill her. If he hadn't already.

Terror battled with rage at the thought, each struggling for control. But it was the rage he concentrated on, the rage he fed. If he gave in to the terror, he'd never be able to function. And that was something he couldn't allow to happen. She was out there somewhere, hurt. He wouldn't even consider the possibility that he wouldn't get to her in time. He would find her even if he had to tear the town apart with his bare hands.

Letting someone else take control had never been his strong suit. At the station he restlessly prowled the floor as Ryan ordered every available officer out on the streets. Martin was hauled from his cell to the interrogation room and threatened with dire circumstances if he didn't talk. But he was almost gleeful in his satisfaction, taunting the detective with the reminder that he'd already warned him that the case would never go to trial. The state couldn't convict him without evidence, and their only witness had just disappeared off the face of the earth. Wasn't that too bad? Tucker, sitting in on the questioning, sprang at him then, his only thought to get his fingers around his throat. It took two quick-moving officers to stop him.

Knowing he'd have done the same thing if he'd been in Tucker's position, Ryan nodded at the uncooperative prisoner. "Get him out of here."

Shaking off the hands that held him, Tucker headed for the door. "Where are you going?" the detective called after him.

"To look for her myself," he retorted without slowing his pace. "I can't just sit here and do nothing."

But just as he reached the threshold, a fresh-faced officer stepped around him and said excitedly, "Detective Ryan, we just got a call in on the APB. An unmarked car spotted the van on 51 heading for the west side of the lake."

"Radio back and tell him to keep it in sight and keep us apprised of its position. I'll need three backups." And with Tucker right on his heels, they ran for his car.

Pain. It beat at the back of her head as if it were a hammer striking red-hot iron on an anvil, dragging her back to a consciousness in which even the ends of her hair hurt. Her eyes squeezed tightly shut, Lacey lay unmoving, waiting for the agony to level off, her thoughts coming in and out of focus with the waves of pain that rolled over her. What had happened? The drugstore. She'd been on her way to the drugstore. Then…nothing. Only a flash of pain and darkness. What—

A sudden jolt had her eyes flying open. A van, she thought dazedly, staring blankly at the back doors of the vehicle. She was in the back of a van and being driven over a very bumpy road.

The fear started then, a cold, insidious terror that crept soundlessly through her body, chilling her to the bone. Someone must have knocked her out, then dumped her in the van. Why? The silent cry reverberated in her dazed head. Why would anyone want to kidnap her? She had no enemies except for the two armored-car robbers. And they were both in jail. Or were they?

Her heart stumbled to a stop, terror clawing at her. How was it possible? Martin had been denied bail, Finch couldn't even have been arraigned yet. So who was the man driving the van? A third partner? Or had Ryan made a mistake and arrested the wrong man? Either way, the result was the same. She was now in the hands of a man who had every intention of killing her. And Tucker didn't even know she was in danger.

She was on her own.

Think! she told herself furiously, fighting the urge to throw herself at the back doors and beat her way free. Acting like a hysterical female was only going to get her killed. She had to see what she was up against before she could even begin to act.

Soundlessly drawing in a bracing breath, she willed herself to calmness. Pain hammered at her head, but she ignored it, focusing all her attention on her thinly stretched control. In her ears, the reassuring words Tucker had whispered to her during target practice echoed softly. *Easy. Don't panic. You only have one shot so you can't afford to miss.* Slowly, the tension knotting her muscles relaxed its grip.

Outside, branches slapped at the sides of the van as it slowed to a crawl on a gravel road that was as corrugated as a washboard. All five of Lacey's senses sprang to alertness. She sat up, straining to see where she was. But the van was full of boxes piled to the ceiling and all she could see was a thin pathway that allowed a narrow view of the console between two bucket seats and a small part of the windshield. Past the short hood of the van, there was nothing but thick trees and brush and a nearly invisible track that led deeper into the undergrowth.

Fear backed up in her throat as she saw a large, masculine hand move to the gearshift to downshift. Thick wristed, with long, thin fingers, it was the only part of her kidnapper she could see. It was enough. If the size of his hand was any indication, he was as big as a house. She wouldn't have a chance in hell of overpowering him.

So you'll just have to outwit him, a voice in her head retorted. He didn't take the time to bind you, and he doesn't know you've regained consciousness. You'll have the advantage of surprise.

Yeah, right, she thought mockingly. But after the surprise wore off, then what?

He braked suddenly, bringing the van to an abrupt stop and cutting the engine. Lacey froze, her one and only chance to come up with a plan vanishing. Afraid to blink so much as an eyelash and have him hear her, she lay unmoving on the hard metal floor, listening, her heart lurching sickeningly. But instead of stepping over the console and coming after her as she'd expected, he opened the driver's door and stepped outside. In the echoing silence, she could hear the crunch of his footsteps as he started around to the back of the van.

She had only seconds to do something. Frantic, she looked wildly around for something to defend herself with. But there was nothing in the back but cardboard boxes and she couldn't see anything in front but...*the keys!* Stunned, she stared at them hanging just above the gearshift in the ignition, unable to believe her eyes.

She didn't stop to think; she didn't have time. Jumping up, she battled her way to the front through the boxes. Just as she slid into the driver's seat, she heard the back doors open. No! Her hand flew to the key and gave it a sharp turn. The motor roared to life, drowning out the angry bellow that came from the back as her kidnapper realized she was slipping through his fingers. Her jaw clenched, she shifted into first gear and stomped on the accelerator. The van shot forward, dirt and rocks flying out from behind the back wheels.

Trees and underbrush flew by, slapping at the van as it fishtailed down the track. Her heart in her throat and her palms damp, Lacey clamped her fingers onto the wheel and struggled to stay between the trees. Her arms started to shake. She'd done it! she thought with a laugh that held traces of hysteria. She'd escaped!

She never heard the bullet that was fired after her. But suddenly, without warning, it streaked through the open back doors and shattered the windshield. She gasped and sank low in the seat as shards of glass rained down on her, but her foot only pressed harder on the accelerator.

A split second later a second bullet hit a tire, destroying it. The van swerved out of control. Crying out in alarm, Lacey fought the steering wheel that tried to jerk out of her hands, but she was fighting a losing battle. The trees hovering threateningly by the side of the path seemed to close in on her. She jerked the wheel, trying to avoid them, and suddenly found herself face-to-face with an oak that looked as though it had been there since the beginning of time. Before she could even brace herself for the impact, she plowed into it.

She would have gone flying out through the shattered windshield if she hadn't had the presence of mind to tighten her grip on the wheel at the last second. Instead, she was thrown against the steering column, striking her head with a resounding bang. Dark spots flew before her eyes. Groaning, her breath tearing through her lungs, she was too stunned to move. The van, with a tired groan of its own, gave up with a soft hissing of steam from the radiator.

She needed to move. The thought nagged at her, prodding her out of the stupor that had shrouded her brain at the moment of impact. Suddenly remembering she was still in danger, she shook her head to clear it, reaching for her door handle. She had to hide!

But before she could push the door open it was suddenly

wrenched out of her hands. Her startled gaze flew to the man who stood towering over her with murder in his eyes and a .38 Magnum in his hand. Every drop of blood drained from her face as she recognized him. "Oh, God, no!"

Chapter 12

John Solomon's fingers wrapped around her arm, digging into the flesh as he gave her a cruel, mocking smile and dragged her from the van. "Oh, yes, Lacey, it's me. Surprised?"

Stunned, she could only stare at him, her mind reeling. This couldn't be happening, she thought dazedly, stifling a cry of pain as his grip on her arm turned viselike. She'd always known he was a greedy, single-minded businessman who would barter his own mother to beat a competitor out of a sale. But an armored-car robber? A murderer? Was he capable of that?

She stared up into his face searchingly and found herself trapped in the black, bottomless depths of his eyes. The sadistic pleasure she saw there touched her soul like a cold north wind. She shivered, fear pooling in her throat, threatening to cut off her air. This man was a stranger to her, the pretense of friendship he usually showed her stripped away like a mask he no longer needed, to reveal the monster underneath. Instinctively she knew that no amount of pleading or reasoning would gain her the slightest mercy from him.

"Why?" she choked, stumbling after him as he jerked her back to the spot where he had originally parked the van. "You've stolen business from every dealer in town. Wasn't that enough for you?"

His thin lips curled contemptuously. "Only a fool would be satisfied with that. Oh, it was gratifying watching all of you struggle to keep your heads above water and still match my prices. But why should I have to constantly hustle just to earn a decent living when there were poorly guarded shops and armored cars right on my doorstep waiting to be picked off?"

"Poorly guarded shops!" she sputtered, anger sparking in her eyes as realization suddenly slapped her in the face. "Are you saying *you* are responsible for the increased robberies in the Quarter lately?"

Her fury rolled off him like rain off a slicker. Releasing his hold on her, he pointed the gun straight at her heart. "I can't take the blame for all of them, but I did all right. And why shouldn't I have?" he demanded without the least remorse. "You and the other shopkeepers left yourselves wide open to a robbery. You were begging for it! Every time you went out of town on a buying trip, you broadcast it by locking everything up tight and not finding someone to cover for you while you were gone. All I had to do was walk in at night, take what I wanted and fence it on a buying trip. It was almost too easy."

"How boring for you," she retorted scathingly. "Is that why you started hitting the armored cars? Because you needed something more challenging? Somehow I don't think a jury is going to accept that as a legitimate reason."

Smug and arrogant, he only laughed. "Oh, there'll be no jury, no trial. Haven't you realized it yet, Lacey? I pulled off the perfect crime. *Twice!*"

She wanted to throw his self-satisfied words back in his face, but she had to keep him talking, had to distract him long enough for her to figure out a way to escape. "How?" she demanded, her mind working furiously as she glanced out of the corner of her eye at the surrounding trees. "The police had already figured out when you were going to hit. They even had the armored-car company change its routes. How did you know they were going to use the southeast end of the Quarter that night?"

"That, my dear Lacey, was the easiest part of all. I was a customer," he reminded her mockingly. "Part of the money they were in danger of losing was mine. I had the right to know where it was being taken and how. All I had to do was put a little pressure on the company for their carelessness during the first two holdups, threaten to talk all my neighbors into taking their business elsewhere, and they were only too eager to spill their guts."

The smile fell from his face, turning his dark features dangerous as he scowled down at her. "Fat lot of good it did me. Everything was going just fine, then you came along and tried to ruin everything. You didn't see me, but I saw you from inside the armored car and recognized you immediately. Robert should have killed you when he had the chance. I thought he had. When I heard a witness was in the hospital, I knew I'd have to take care of you myself. You can't expect me to just stand by and let you send my brother to jail."

"Your brother!" she echoed incredulously. "The police did a thorough background check on Robert Martin. He's a Cuban immigrant. There was no mention of a brother."

"Of course not. We were partners in Cuba. Do you think that we would take a chance on anyone tracking down our records and linking us together? We changed our names and made sure we were never seen together. It was safer that way."

He was so sure that he had thought it all out and put himself beyond the reach of the law. She was his one mistake, and unless she could keep him talking until Tucker discovered she was missing, he and Martin would both go free to commit other murders and robberies. "You won't get away with it," she said desperately, her eyes searching the heavily wooded track for a way out. If she could just distract him, then lose him among the trees...

Reading her thoughts, he suddenly grabbed her wrist and jerked her around in front of him, giving her arm a vicious push halfway up her back. At her cry of pain, he jabbed the gun under her chin and hissed in her ear, "Yesterday I would have agreed with you. When I lost you at that church, I thought it was all over. Then this morning I heard on the radio that the police had arrested another suspect. Fools! I knew you'd come home then. All I had to do was wait. Wasn't I lucky that you walked right into my arms?" Still holding her arm up her back, he pushed her before him through the trees. "You take one step I don't tell you to, and you won't take another one. Now walk."

Ten minutes behind them and two hundred yards away, Tucker, Ryan and the backup units that had accompanied them were just getting out of their cars to track the van on foot when they heard shots fired and then a crash. Tucker's heart stopped dead. *"No!"* he cried hoarsely, breaking into a run.

But he'd taken only three steps when Ryan and another officer tackled him. "You want to get her killed?" Ryan growled angrily when Tucker began to fight. "Stop and think, man! If he hasn't put a bullet in her head already, he will if you go charging in there like a mad bull without knowing what you're up against. Now you either calm down and do this my way or I'll cuff you and put you in the car. You got that?"

Fury flamed in Tucker's brown eyes, burning them as black as cinders. But he only nodded, a muscle ticking ominously along the side of his jaw. "I want a gun," he said flatly.

"No way," the detective retorted. "You just worry about Lacey—she's going to need you when this is all over with. We'll take care of the law enforcement." Knowing Tucker had little choice but to agree with him, he turned to his men. "We'll spread out and make our way through the trees. Watch where you're walking. I don't want anyone stepping on a branch and giving us away. I don't think we've been spotted, so we've got surprise on our side. Take advantage of it, but watch out for the girl. We're here to rescue her, not get her shot." With one more pointed look at Tucker, he motioned for the officers to spread out among the trees. "Let's go."

With agonizing slowness and guns drawn, they picked their way through the woods and underbrush toward where they had heard the sound of the crash. Clamping a tight lid on his impatience, Tucker told himself that Lacey hadn't necessarily been shot just because her kidnapper had fired a gun. They would reach her in time. They had to! And when he got her back, he was never letting her out of his sight again!

Through the trees he caught a glimpse of the van smashed against a gnarled oak. But it wasn't that that stopped him and the police in their tracks. It was the sight of Lacey being dragged to a stop in front of an open grave, the fresh dirt piled high beside it indicating that it was no shallow ditch that had just been dug. But it was Lacey, not the grave, that Tucker devoured with his eyes. Her face was pale and drawn, etched with a grimace of pain, but she appeared unhurt. Relief washed over him, almost weakening his knees. Only then did he allow himself to look at her abductor.

He recognized the tall, black-haired man immediately. John Solomon! "Son of a bitch!" he murmured furiously.

Ryan shot him a warning glance before quickly turning his attention back to the drama unfolding before them. The way the antique dealer held Lacey before him, there was no way they could take a shot at him without endangering her. Swearing under his breath, he had no choice but to signal his men to wait until they had a clear shot.

Solomon, unaware of anything but the woman who had

been more trouble to him than she was worth, came to an abrupt stop and gave her a vicious push toward the grave. "Take a good look at that, my dear. That's where you're going to be spending eternity."

Caught off guard, Lacey stumbled and almost fell head-long into the dark pit before she could stop herself. Her eyes widened in horror, she jerked to a stop just in time. Cornered like a hunted animal, she whirled to confront him, her breath tearing through her lungs at the sight of the gun pointed at her heart. "Don't do this, Solomon. You're only going to make things worse for you and your brother, and it won't solve anything. Even if you kill me, the police won't stop looking for you. Is that what you want? To be tracked like a rabid dog until they find you? You'll never have a moment's peace, never be able to relax without having to look over your shoulder—"

"Oh, please," he drawled, rolling his eyes, "save it. By the time the cops even begin to suspect me, Robert and I will be long gone, living like kings on our own tropical island." Lifting the gun until it was pointed directly be-tween her eyes, he mocked, "So long, Lacey, it was nice knowing you—"

Her heart jerked in her breast as a shot rang out. Instinct screamed at her to run, but her feet slipped on the loose dirt underfoot. Crying out in terror as she lost her balance, she tumbled backward into the yawning cavity of the open grave.

Every muscle in Tucker's body froze as he watched her cry out and disappear into the grave. Ryan, who had shot the gun out of Solomon's hand, was already advancing on the wounded man and motioning his men to close in, but Tucker didn't notice. Running to the grave, he dropped down to his knees and half threw himself over the edge.

Expecting Solomon to be standing over her with the gun, she stared up in amazement at the man she loved. "Tucker!"

"Were you hit?" he demanded.

"No...I don't think so...." Confused by the sudden turn of events, she glanced down at herself as if the body she inhabited were someone else's, the terror that had held her captive ever since she'd regained consciousness in the back of the van suddenly setting her limbs shaking in reaction. Wrapping her arms around her middle, she squeezed her eyes shut, struggling to pull her shattered control back together. "I...I—I don't kn-know wh-what's wrong with m-me."

Tucker jumped down beside her and quickly hauled her into his arms. "You're in shock," he said huskily against her hair, pulling her closer until he could feel every inch of her from breast to knee. "After what you've been through, you're entitled." Warming her with his stroking hands, he murmured to her over and over again, needing to touch her as desperately as she needed to be held. "It's okay, honey. It's all over. You're safe. Nothing's ever going to hurt you again."

Later, Lacey didn't remember much about the ride back to New Orleans except that Tucker held her close the entire time. Too exhausted to move, she only wanted to go home and forget everything that had happened since she'd walked out of her apartment. But the police needed her statement, so she and Tucker accompanied Ryan to the station. While she wearily told the story of her kidnapping and everything that Solomon had told her, the antique dealer was booked and two officers dispatched to search his home and shop. No one was really surprised when the stolen money was discovered there, as well as some of the paint bullets he'd stolen from a nearby survival camp to shoot up Lacey's shop. Also in his safe were two pieces of jewelry that had been stolen from her months ago.

Robert Martin, realizing he hadn't a prayer now of beating the murder and robbery charges against him, cooperated with the police in order to save his own skin. He wanted guarantees that his sentence would be reduced. Ryan, however, was quick to let him know he was holding all the cards. He made no promises, but Martin was desperate. He told how he and Solomon had sat at his kitchen table on New Year's Eve and decided they were never going to get rich just robbing the shops in the Quarter. If they were going to take the risk, it might as well be for something worth risking everything for. They planned their first armored-car robbery that night. The third one was to have been their last one. Instead, it had turned out to be their undoing.

With the money recovered and the police in possession of enough evidence to put the two brothers away for a very long time, Tucker took Lacey home, satisfied that there would be no more surprises, no more unknown partners to appear out of nowhere to threaten her. Oh, there was still the trial to come, but the danger was past and she could get on with the rest of her life. And he had every intention of being part of that future.

As soon as they stepped into her apartment, he took one look at her pale face and knew this was not the time for a serious discussion. The hell she'd been through had etched tense lines around her mouth and turned her green eyes murky with a fear that hadn't yet retreated. But he'd almost lost her without having once told her how much he loved her, and he needed the reassurance of knowing that she was his.

Placing both hands on her shoulders to gently ease her down to the couch, he ordered huskily, "Sit. We need to talk. Would you like a drink first?"

"No. Nothing." Her heart suddenly racing almost as madly as it had when she'd looked up to find John Solomon pointing a gun at her, she popped up from the couch like a jack-in-the-box. If he was going to talk about leaving now, she just couldn't stand it! Agitated, she glanced toward the kitchen. "I changed my mind. I think I will have something—"

"In a minute." He captured her before him by simply

returning his hands to her shoulders. "Look, honey, I know this isn't the time—"

"If you're trying to tell me you're leaving, you don't have to beat around the bush," she said stiffly. "I'm a big girl now. Just tell me straight out and get it over with. After all, we both knew you were only staying until I was safe, so what more is there to talk about?"

Such pride. Torn between the need to shake her or kiss her senseless, Tucker drew her closer, wanting to wrap her in gentleness. "Oh, I can think of several things," he replied, his brown eyes tender with amusement. "Do you really think after all we've shared that I'm just going to turn my back on you and walk away?"

Hadn't she known from the very beginning that he had an overdeveloped sense of family responsibility? Hot tears suddenly stinging the back of her eyes, she pulled free of his touch. "You don't owe me anything," she retorted thickly, turning blindly toward the windows before he could see her tears. "You never have. I tried to tell you that when you turned up at the hospital, but you wouldn't listen. There's only the thinnest family connection between us, and that's through the marriage license of our parents, not blood."

"Thank God for that," he said with a chuckle. Grinning at her ramrod-straight back, he crossed to her and wrapped his arms about her waist to pull her back against him. "Proposing to you would be impossible if we really were related."

Lacey couldn't have been more stunned if he'd told her his mother was an alien from Mars. Standing perfectly still in his arms, she whispered, "What did you say?"

Turning her to face him, he looked down into her wide green eyes and found himself saying words that he had never expected to say to any woman. "Marry me," he said huskily as he captured her face in his palms and tilted her head back so he could see every expression that darkened her eyes. "I don't want just a few weeks with you. I want forever."

If she hadn't been clinging to his wrists, Lacey was sure the world would have spun away beneath her feet. Joy exploded in her like a Roman candle on the Fourth of July, but in its shadow was a pain that twisted her heart. She wanted to back away from it, from him and the temptation he held out to her, but she could only stand there and shake her head as tears spilled over her lashes and slid down her pale cheeks. "I can't," she rasped.

Whatever he had been expecting, it wasn't that. A quick scowl furrowed his brow. "What do you mean, you can't. I love you! And I know you love me. If it's the job you're worried about, then don't be. I'm not going to go back into the field and take any chances on making you a widow. I've decided to take the desk job."

"Don't make that decision because of me. It won't make any difference."

She was serious! he realized, hurt. Dropping his hands from her, he couldn't believe what he was hearing. "Are you saying you don't love me?"

Denying it might have made things simpler, but she couldn't lie to him. Lifting her chin, she said, "I've been fighting it for years, but I've loved you since I was nineteen years old. But I can't marry you."

"Why the hell not?" he thundered, frustrated. "Do you think what we've found together is something that grows on trees? When Solomon had you, I was terrified of losing you before I could tell you how I feel. Damn it, Lacey, we've got something special here and I'm not going to let you throw it away!"

Just as frustrated and hurt as he was, she wiped the tears from her face and cried, "Can't you see it's because I do love you so much that I can't marry you? I grew up in the diplomatic corps, Tucker. You've heard stories about what a trial I was to my father. Sure, I've grown up, but that doesn't change the fact that I can't live that way anymore.

I would make a lousy diplomat's wife. And that's what you are. A diplomat. Oh, I know you've always considered yourself a troubleshooter, but one of these days you're going to make a hell of an ambassador. You need a wife who will be an asset to you, not a liability.''

"I need a wife who loves me as much as I love her," he argued. "The rest is just bull—''

The ringing of the telephone cut through his curse like a knife. Crossing to the phone before she could, he jerked it up, intending to get rid of whoever was calling as quickly as possible so he could talk some sense into her. "Hello!"

His angry greeting was met with another one from his boss. "Would you like to tell me what the hell you're doing?" Donovon demanded. "I expected you to be close to solving this mess by now, and instead, I learn from our embassy in Santa Maria that no one's heard from you in over two hours! What's going on, Tucker? And you better make it damn good because Ramirez is getting impatient. He's threatening to take drastic measures if he doesn't meet face-to-face with you sometime today.''

Tucker swore. "What kind of drastic measures?''

"He's leaving it to our imaginations, and frankly, I don't like what I'm imagining. We're not going to push him on this, Tucker," he warned him. "There are too many lives at stake. I've already got a plane waiting for you. It's cleared to take off just as soon as you arrive.''

Torn, Tucker knew he had little choice but to comply with the order. His personal life would have to wait until after the crisis was over. "I'm on my way," he said grimly. "I'll report in just as soon as I've got some news.''

Hanging up, he turned to Lacey, black clouds of frustration churning in his brown eyes. "I've got to go. Will you drive me to the airport?''

She wanted to say no. She couldn't stand and watch him leave. But how could she deny herself these last few precious moments with him? She nodded, the hot tears welling in her throat making her voice thick. "Of course. Let's go."

They hurried down to her car without another word and headed for the airport. Tension throbbed between them in a silence that remained unbroken. Cursing the fates that had given him time to tell her how much he loved her before jerking him away from her, Tucker struggled to find the words that would convince her they belonged together. But there was too little time.

Before either of them was ready to say goodbye, Lacey was braking to a stop outside the terminal. Leaving the motor running, she turned to him. "I won't go inside with you," she said quietly. "I hate goodbyes."

Nodding, he grabbed the suitcase he'd retrieved from the police station after Solomon was arrested. He pushed open his door, but he didn't get out. "This isn't goodbye, Lace," he promised her, his dark eyes trapping hers. "I'm only leaving now because I have to. But you can bet your shop that I'll be back. Our discussion isn't over. *You are going to marry me.*."

"No, I'm—"

He cut off the rest of her denial by leaning over and giving her a hard, quick kiss that was over far too quickly. "Yes, you are," he said against her mouth before releasing her. "So you'd better get used to the idea while I'm gone. I'll try to call you tonight." Just that quickly he was gone. After slamming the passenger door, he walked into the terminal and never looked back.

The minute she stepped into her apartment, Lacey knew she couldn't stay there. Everywhere she turned, she found herself confronted with a memory of Tucker that refused to leave her in peace. The apartment had become more their apartment than hers alone. Roaming the empty rooms, she felt as if she were just waiting. Waiting for him to return. And he would return; there wasn't a doubt of that in her mind. He'd be gone just long enough to make her ache with missing him, then waltz back into her life as if there weren't a doubt in his mind that she'd welcome him with open arms. And she would, God help her. She loved him so much, he had only to kiss her senseless and she'd agree to whatever he wanted, including marriage.

A sob caught in her throat, breaking the empty silence that engulfed her. She couldn't let him do that to her, to them. She could never be what he needed in a wife and he would only end up resenting her. Why did he find that so difficult to understand? She knew he'd heard the stories of how her father had bailed her out of one childhood mess after another....

Her father! she thought, realization dawning. Of course, why hadn't she thought of him earlier? He knew her better than anyone, and he and Tucker had been good friends long before they became stepfather and son. He would be able to make Tucker understand that marriage to her could only lead to disaster.

Hurrying to the phone, she quickly dialed the airport and booked the first available flight. New Orleans to New York to London. There would be a more direct route available tomorrow, but she didn't want to wait. Her father was the most rational man she had ever known, and suddenly she desperately needed to hear him say she was doing the right thing. Maybe then she'd be able to believe it herself.

Late the next morning she arrived on Marcus Conrad's doorstep in a state of exhaustion, looking as if she were a cake that had been taken out of the oven half-baked. She hadn't slept the entire trip, and her eyes were red rimmed and hot with fatigue, her cheeks devoid of color. Tucker's mother, Elizabeth, took one look at her and immediately pulled her inside. "Lacey! What a wonderful surprise! You should have let us know you were coming—we'd have been at the airport to meet you. Here, come in. You look exhausted! Have you slept?" She scowled at the stupidity of her own question and shook her head in self-directed annoyance. "No, of course you haven't. Who can sleep in an airplane? Let's get you upstairs and into bed. We'll talk later."

A small, petite woman whose hair had turned white overnight after Tucker's father had died at the age of thirty-two, she was like a whirlwind that just swept Lacey's tired body along in her wake. Within minutes of her arrival Lacey found herself in bed, the shades drawn to block out the beautiful summer day and sleep overtaking her before she could even begin to offer an explanation for her unexpected arrival.

When she awoke hours later, the shades were no longer needed to block out the sun. It was pitch-dark outside. Stunned that she'd slept so long, she scrambled out of bed and quickly pulled on jeans and a loose-fitting green-and-white-striped T-shirt. She had just finished braiding her hair when there was a soft, familiar double tap at the bedroom door. Grinning, she opened it and threw herself into her father's arms. "Dad!"

Marcus Conrad squeezed her tight. Ever since Elizabeth had called him at the embassy to tell him Lacey had arrived in a state of near collapse, he'd been worried sick. Easing back, he studied her, relieved to see that the sleep had done her good. She looked merely tired now, not exhausted. But there was a pain clouding her eyes he hadn't seen before.

"Okay, are you going to tell me what's wrong or do I have to guess? And don't tell me nothing's wrong," he continued before she could say a word. "I know you too well, young lady. The environmental summit wraps up tomorrow, and you wouldn't be within a thousand miles of all the hullabaloo around here unless something was wrong. What is it? The trial? The last time you called, you said the police had arrested another suspect."

"It turned out to be the wrong one." Downplaying the danger she had been in, she told him the whole story. "I've still got the trial to get through, but with Solomon and his brother both in jail and most of the money recovered, it seems to be a pretty airtight case. I'm sure I'll get through it just fine."

"Then if it's not that, what is it? Tucker?" At her look of surprise, he chuckled. "I might have been distracted with my marriage to Elizabeth when you and Tucker met for the first time, but I wasn't blind. I saw the way the sparks flew between you. I also know you've spent the last eight years avoiding him. Would you like to tell me what's going on this time? Since I couldn't come to check on you myself, I was hoping that the two of you would be able to put the past behind you and iron out your differences if you spent some time together. Obviously I was wrong. What happened?"

"He asked me to marry him."

Delight flared in Marcus Conrad's eyes before he quickly hid it. "What was your answer?"

"No, of course!" Without waiting for her father's reaction, she turned to restlessly pace the elegantly furnished guest room, her arms wrapping around herself to try to cut off the flow of tears that her admission had released. But the battle was lost before it had even begun. "I tried to tell him what a lousy diplomat's wife I would make," she sniffed, "but he refuses to even listen to me. Oh, Dad, what am I going to do?"

Marcus leaned a shoulder against the doorjamb and watched her with a frown. "Do you love him?"

"Well, of course I do! Do you think I would be this upset if I didn't?"

Struggling to hold back a smile, he said, "No, I guess not. So what's this nonsense about you making a lousy diplomat's wife? Where'd you get that idea?"

She was stunned that he even had to ask. "Have you forgotten the time I nearly created an international incident when I pushed an Italian diplomat's son into a fountain when I was sixteen? Or how I nearly gagged on octopus at an embassy function in Japan and ended up on the front page of the paper?"

"No, but I also haven't forgotten how you made friends with an old antique dealer in Paris whose business was on the verge of going under. You got all the diplomats' wives to visit his shop and soon he couldn't keep up with the demand. You were fifteen, and he's still in business today. You made the papers that time, too, and did wonders for Franco-American relations."

"What does that have to do with anything?"

"Everything," he retorted, pushing himself away from the door and crossing to her to slip his arm around her shoulders. "Sweetheart, you've come to the wrong man if you want me to talk you out of marrying Tucker. I've always thought you two were perfect for each other. And you'd be a wonderful asset to his career! You're just like your mother." At her look of disbelief, he grinned. "It's true. And she was just as reluctant to marry me as you are to marry Tucker. She was sure she would wreck my career. She was too free spirited, too spontaneous, totally unsuitable for the role she would have to play as my wife. But I knew she was going to be a breath of fresh air at stale diplomatic functions, and she proved me right. She made friends wherever we went, not just with the heads of state, but with the people themselves. Don't you remember?"

Her mother had died when she was seven. She had only vague memories of her, but somewhere in a hidden corner of her heart she was warmed by the recollection of a smiling, laughing woman who had always seemed to enjoy life with a passion. Brushing away tears, Lacey leaned her head against her father's shoulder. "I don't remember much," she said huskily. "Am I really like her? I know I favor her in looks, but everyone always said how she was the perfect diplomat's wife. I just assumed that we were nothing alike. How come you never told me?"

He stared off into space, remembering the woman who had made the years of his youth so special. "Because I missed her for years after she died, and I couldn't talk about her. Every time I looked at you, I saw her. I thought you knew.''

Lacey shook her head, swamped with emotions. ''I never even suspected.''

''Well, now that you do, don't sell yourself short, honey,'' he replied, patting her shoulder reassuringly. ''Don't deny yourself a shot at happiness because you're afraid you may not measure up. Why, you've got potential you haven't even tapped yet. Once you let go of the fear, you'll be surprised how easy everything falls into place. Think about it,'' he advised. ''If you love Tucker and he loves you, isn't that all that matters? The rest will take care of itself.''

Two days later Lacey sat in her father's library and tried to distract herself with a book, but her mind was still reeling with everything she'd learned about her mother and herself. For years she'd thought of herself as something of a misfit in her family, the rebel who could never quite conform as easily as her sisters. She'd grown up thinking she had something to prove, when all the time she hadn't needed to defend being her mother's daughter. Wanting to laugh and cry at the same time, she felt as if someone had opened the door and let the sunlight into her heart, freeing her to be the woman she was always meant to be.

And with that realization came another. Her father was right. She couldn't deny herself a chance at happiness with Tucker. If she hadn't known she loved him before, the past two days would have proven it to her. She was miserable without him, every waking and sleeping moment filled with thoughts of him. How could she have ever imagined she could live without him? It had been only three days since he'd given her that quick, hard kiss at the airport, then walked away, but it seemed like forever.

She'd learned through her father and news reports that he had somehow managed to obtain the release of the missionaries. But where he was now she hadn't a clue. Was he safe? After being in the field again, had he changed his mind about taking a desk job?

Just the thought of him in danger was enough to pull her from the overstuffed chair she'd curled up in to read. Turning to pace, she stopped in her tracks at the sight of the tired, angry man standing in the open doorway of the library. Her hand flew to her throat and the pulse that suddenly thundered there. "Tucker!" He was dressed in jeans and a wrinkled white shirt that looked as if it had been slept in. His hard jaw was darkened with several days' growth of beard, his dark blond hair attractively disheveled, his brown eyes black with emotion as they trapped her before him.

Joy shot through her, but before she could do anything but whisper his name he had slammed the library door behind him and was striding toward her. "What the hell are you doing here? When I told you I'd be back to finish our conversation, I didn't know I'd have to chase you halfway around the world to do it. Did you think I would let you run away so easily?"

Her back straightened at that. "I wasn't running—"

"No?" he growled, reaching for her. "It sure looked that way when I came back to New Orleans and found your apartment deserted. I had to call Marcus to find out where you were. Come here."

The last two words were muttered against her mouth as he hauled her close for a long, hungry kiss. Surprised, Lacey had no time to think, only to feel. Need, hot and sweet, poured through her as he gathered her against him, desperation in his every touch. In growing wonder she laid her hand against the tense line of cheek and jaw, feeling the undercurrents seething within him. Had he really thought she could turn her back on him and the love they had for each other so easily?

Dragging her mouth from his, she pressed a kiss along his jaw, then moved to tenderly explore his neck. "I was coming back," she murmured, loving the raspy feel of his beard under her lips. "I needed to talk to Dad."

"So he'd take your side?" he countered, turning her mouth back up to his. "He won't do it, you know. We were made for each other, and he knows it." He kissed her again as if he were starving for the taste of her, only letting her up for air when they were both weak with need. He rested his forehead against hers, his breath a hot, moist caress against her throbbing lips. "It's true, honey. Can't you see it? I don't like protocol and rules any more than you do—why did you think I avoided a desk job all these years? But my boss was right. There's a time to get out of the field. I just never had a reason before. Until now. Until you. None of it means anything without you."

She opened her mouth to tell him about the conversation she'd had with her father, but he stopped her before she could say a word. "I'm not asking you to give up your business," he said quickly. "I know how much it means to you. You can hire an assistant to run it and fly back to New Orleans whenever you need to. Just because we're getting married doesn't mean we have to be joined at the hip."

Noting how he had assumed that the matter of their marriage was settled, Lacey couldn't help but smile. "Oh, I don't know," she said softly, melting against him, "I sort of like the idea of being joined at the hip. It might be better to sell it now that I have nothing left to prove."

Expecting the same argument she'd given him before, he drew back only far enough to get a good look at her face. "Did I miss something?" he asked suspiciously. "It sounded like you just agreed to marry me in the same breath you suggested selling your shop. The last time we talked, you—"

"I wasn't thinking too clearly," she agreed, grinning. "The last thing I expected from a confirmed bachelor was a proposal. I also hadn't talked to my father." Pulling him down to the couch with her, she slipped into his arms again and told him everything she had learned about her mother. "I was so afraid I would ruin your career," she finished. "It never entered my head that my mother might have had the same fears when she married Dad. But she adjusted and became one of his biggest assets, and I know I can do the same for you. I'm not sixteen anymore. I do have some self-discipline."

"Not much, I hope." He chuckled, kissing her. "I'm not marrying an asset, I'm marrying the woman I love. I'm counting on you to drive me crazy for the next sixty or seventy years."

Toying with the buttons of his shirt, she sent him a teasing glance. "What happened to the man who said putting a ring on a woman's finger was asking for nothing but trouble?"

Flashing her a grin, he growled, "Haven't you heard? Trouble is what I handle best," and covered her mouth with his.

* * * * *

Silhouette

SPECIAL EDITION

TM

SPECIAL EDITION

Stories of love and life, these powerful
novels are tales that you can identify with—
romances with "something special" added
in!

Fall in love with the stories of authors such
as **Nora Roberts, Diana Palmer, Ginna Gray**
and many more of your special favorites—as
well as wonderful new voices!

Special Edition brings you
entertainment for the heart!

SILHOUETTE® Desire®

Do you want...

Dangerously handsome heroes

Evocative, everlasting love stories

Sizzling and tantalizing sensuality

Incredibly sexy miniseries like **MAN OF THE MONTH**

Red-hot romance

Enticing entertainment that can't be beat!

You'll find all of this, and much *more* each and every month in **SILHOUETTE DESIRE**. Don't miss these unforgettable love stories by some of romance's hottest authors. Silhouette Desire—where your fantasies will always come true....

DES-GEN

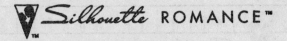

What's a single dad to do when he needs a wife by next Thursday?

Who's a confirmed bachelor to call when he finds a baby on his doorstep?

How does a plain Jane in love with her gorgeous boss get him to notice her?

From classic love stories to romantic comedies to emotional heart tuggers, **Silhouette Romance** offers six irresistible novels every month by some of your favorite authors! Such as…beloved bestsellers **Diana Palmer, Annette Broadrick, Suzanne Carey, Elizabeth August** and **Marie Ferrarella**, to name just a few—and some sure to become favorites!

Fabulous Fathers…Bundles of Joy…Miniseries… Months of blushing brides and convenient weddings… Holiday celebrations… You'll find all this and much more in **Silhouette Romance**—always emotional, always enjoyable, always about love!